Mi
(Oppos   ., ᴅᴏᴏᴋ 1)

By Melinda Di Lorenzo
Copyright 2015, Melinda Di Lorenzo

Cover Image courtesy of Viorel Sima | Dreamstime.com

Other books by Melinda Di Lorenzo

Snapshots By Laura

Long Way From Home

Tattoos and Tangles

Bad Reputation

Pinups and Possibilities

Deceptions and Desires

Trusting A Stranger

MILE HIGH WEEKEND

Friday
One

Ginnie Silver sat at the airport bar, staring forlornly into her half full gin and tonic.

"Half empty," she muttered at the drink, annoyed that her positive brain managed to somehow override the irrefutable negativity of her situation.

Because there sure as hell wasn't *any*thing good about being glued to a stool inside the first class lounge when you were actually supposed to be glued to your hot-doctor-husband on your way to Vegas for a what-happens-there, stays-there long weekend.

Ginnie twirled the swizzle stick in her drink, stabbing at the lemon slice, wondering how the hell she'd let her best friend – who was also her adoptive brother – talk her into taking the trip anyway. The seat beside her was notably empty, just as the seat on the plane would be. The hotel reservation included a bottle of champagne and *two* glasses.

I can't do this.

Ginnie lifted her drink to her lips, determined to finish it and be on her way. But the second she slammed the empty glass down on the counter, her phone lit up with the embarrassingly loud, embarrassingly techno-fied version of the theme song from some now defunct hospital-themed TV drama.

Lawrence's ringtone.

Given how bad he left things – how bad he left *her* – Ginnie would like to have let it just go to voicemail. Should have let, in fact. Except she couldn't, and not just because ten pairs of fellow airport bar-hopping eyes were already turned her way in response to the noise. She had dedicated all four of her college years to Lawrence. Held his hand when his first patient died on the operating table. Let him teach her everything she knew about what it meant to be a woman. She'd waited for him – the perfect man – her whole life. So no matter how much she currently loathed him, she couldn't shake the faint, vain hope that he was calling to tell her it was all a big misunderstanding. That the humiliation hadn't been real.

Weak.

Ginnie slid the phone on, wondering if she should be more concerned about love than embarrassment, and issued her greeting with what she wished wasn't quite so much quiet desperation. "Lawrence."

The responding groan on the other end didn't belong to her ex at all. "Jesus, G-dog. Could you sound more pathetic?"

Ginnie's face screwed up, midway between tears and fury. "You are the *worst* brother in the world, Jase."

"I'm just a fake brother. And the worst? That's debatable. There has to be *someone* out there who's worse."

Ginnie rolled her eyes. But she was also smiling, which was probably Jase's goal. He had been friend and confidant since, at twelve years old, the two of them were taken in by – and later adopted by – the Silver family.

"What do you want, Jase? I mean, besides to torment me."

"I want to know why you didn't delete the douchebag's ringtone the second he stomped on your heart."

Ginnie gritted her teeth. "It was on my to-do list. Right after telling mom where you keep your dirty magazines."

"Haha."

"Why do you have Lawrence's phone, anyway?"

Her brother sighed. "I don't, Ginnie. I just reprogrammed all your ringtones so mine would come up as the stupid song."

"What? Why?"

"To prove a point."

"That it's easy to become a spectacle in an airport bar?"

"No. That you need to get to Vegas and get that asshole out of your system for good."

"Jase…"

He sighed again, louder and even more emphatically. "Did you even *look* when the phone rang? Or did you just grab it, hoping it was him, thinking that just maybe he was going to give you one more chance to prove you weren't like a…what did he call you? Right. Like a repeat virgin in bed, with a hymen that magically regrew each night."

Jase's words stung, and Ginnie wished – not for the first time – that she hadn't got drunk and revealed every detail of her and Lawrence's breakup to him.

Their closeness, with none of the boundaries of flesh-and-blood siblings, was the epitome of what it meant for something to be both a blessing and a curse. She shared everything with him, even when she didn't want to.

"Do you know how gross it is to hear you say the word *hymen*?" Ginnie asked.

"Do you know how gross it is to know that you had one?" her brother countered.

The bartender set down another gin and tonic and walked away before Ginnie could even manage a headshake. She'd had enough. More than enough, probably. She wasn't really much of a drinker. Not before meeting Lawrence, or during the time she was married to him. Though she was making a damned good show of making up for it now.

"Let me ask you something, Ginnie," Jase said.

"Hang on." She grabbed the second, unwanted drink, and gulped half of it down, then spoke again. "Okay. Go."

"What were you about to do, right before I called? And don't lie. I'll know."

Ginnie wished her brother's statement wasn't true, but she knew it was, and there wasn't much point in being dishonest anyway.

"I was about to leave the airport."

"Which is exactly what you promised you wouldn't do."

"Which is exactly what you knew I *would* do."

"Ginnie…"

"Ja-ay-se," she said back mockingly.

"Do something for me," he replied.

"Do what?" Ginnie knew the suspicion in her voice was well-warranted.

More often than not, every time Jase asked her to "do something" for him, it involved illegal activity. Or covering up illegal activity. After this many years, Ginnie knew she just had to brace herself and hope it was something that wouldn't get her arrested.

But what came out of his mouth was much, much worse.

"I want you to look around the bar and find a guy to sleep with."

Ginnie's face went red, and she buried it in her drink, sure that someone must've heard the inappropriate suggestion.

"Ginnie?"

"Dammit, Jase."

"I didn't mean that literally."

"Somehow, that doesn't help."

Her brother chuckled. "I want you to look at all the men in the bar, and pick one who you wouldn't hate to jump."

"Why?"

"Because Lawrence made you think of yourself as an asexual being. I want you to feel like you can get some action."

Ginnie gulped down her gin and tonic, then lied, "I've had *plenty* of action."

"You can't do it, can you?"

"Of course I can!"

"You can look around the bar and completely objectify each and every man in there? You can reduce him to the sum his physical parts and imagine him naked?"

"I *can*. I just *won't*."

But it was too late. Jase had planted the seed in her head, and now Ginnie's alcohol-infused gaze was roaming the room, resting briefly on each man seated throughout the bar, taking stock.

Ten years too old.

The right age, but dressed *ten years too old.*

Too intellectual.

Too pretty.

And then.

Uh oh.

Ginnie's eyes landed on him just as he swung open the frosted-glass door. And she couldn't look away.

He was tall enough to attract notice in any crowd, and his shoulders were wider than a linebacker's. Even if those two physical attributes hadn't made him stand out, the rest of him was equally attention-grabbing. Especially inside the otherwise conservative bar.

Him, she thought. *That's a guy I wouldn't mind jumping.*

His jeans were faded and well-worn, and not in an artful way. They hugged his thighs, but rode loose across his hips, and when he lifted a hand to stop the door from swinging back, Ginnie caught a breathtaking glimpse of his perfectly sculpted abs and the sexy 'V' that dipped under his belt.

As his off-white, short-sleeved dress shirt slid back down, Ginnie dragged her eyes up to his chest. Its breadth was as impressive as the rest of him, and through the shirt, she could make out the taut lines of his pectoral muscles. He'd left the top two buttons of his shirt undone, exposing a tattoo that crept from his collarbone to his throat then wrapped around to a spot right between his hairline and his earlobe.

Unconsciously, Ginnie leaned forward, trying to get a better view of the ink. Was it something tribal? Something Celtic? Or maybe a completely unique piece of art. He looked like the kind of guy who'd have something specially designed.

And his *lips.* They were full and even, just a tad less ruddy than his strong jaw, and a glittering ring looped through on the left side of the bottom one. When he flicked out his tongue to tap the piercing in an absent, habitual way, Ginnie's mouth watered. She could practically feel the cool metal against her own mouth.

Dear god.

She was so engrossed in her own perusal of the man's finer assets that she almost didn't notice his gaze had found her as well.

Busted.

Embarrassed, Ginnie cast her eyes down into her drink. But she was too flustered to make a full recovery, and as she tried to keep her senses in order, she fumbled with her phone, dropping it to the bar-top counter with a clatter. She looked back up, hoping desperately that he hadn't seen her clumsy mistake. No such luck.

From where she sat, she could see the deep caramel color of his irises. Framed by dark, make-a-supermodel-jealous lashes, they rested on her for a long moment, making her heart beat at triple time and sending her imagination into overdrive.

Boxers or briefs? Or better yet…Commando? How far down did that tattoo go? Did he have more?

And then he looked away, glanced down at his phone, and moved across the bar.

Ginnie's whole body sagged as she exhaled a breath she didn't even know she'd been holding.

What the hell are you thinking? she asked herself. *That guy is* nothing *like what you need. Bones jumping or otherwise.*

He wasn't even the kind of guy she'd normally bother checking out. Too broke-the-mold-and-I'm-proud-of-it. Too rebellious.

Too dirty-hot.

Abruptly, she became aware that her brother's irritated voice was still carrying through the line.

"Hey!" he was yelling. "You there, or what?"

Ginnie snatched the phone back up and pressed it into her ear. "Yeah, Jase. Just taking your advice."

"You mentally undressed a guy?"

He sounded like he didn't believe her, and Ginnie narrowed her eyes.

"I didn't just mentally undress him," she retorted, determined to shock him. "I stripped him down, spanked him, and put my lips on his – "

Jase let out a strangled cry. "Stop!"

Ginnie grinned, pleased with herself. "Your idea."

"You've been drinking, haven't you?" her brother accused.

"For the love of God! You're the one who *told* me to let loose – "

He cut her off again, this time gleefully. "Aha!"

"What?"

"You *can* take orders," Jase stated. "So hang up the phone, stick it in whatever drink you're not finishing right this second, get on the goddamned plane, and pretend you're anyone other than Ginnie Silver, former wife of Dr. Lawrence Michaels. Or so help me, I will find every nude, childhood photo of you Mom kept, and I *will* post it to my one thousand, two hundred and eight social media contacts."

Then there was silence on the other end, and Ginnie knew she'd been schooled.

Stupid brother.

With a scowl she wanted to think was as rebellious as Mr. Lip Ring himself, but knew probably couldn't pass for more than cute, Ginnie downed what was left of her beverage, then signalled the bartender for another.

Two

Quinn cursed his own stupidity and kept his eyes on his too-frothy beer.

It was her. He knew it, even though the blurry picture Jase had shown him didn't do those green eyes of hers any justice at all.

Button-up blouse. Check.

Severe skirt, each calf-length pleat pressed to a perfect fold. Check.

Polish-free hands, closing on a third – at least from what Quinn had seen – drink. Check.

"She's not supposed to be here," he snarled, just loud enough that a man two tables over jumped.

Quinn shot him a toothy grin, and the guy quickly looked back at the cellphone in his lap.

Yeah, sucker. Go back to your Internet porn, Quinn thought snidely, then sighed.

The job was supposed to be easy – find Ginnie, keep a distance, keep her safe.

He was tempted to hurl most of the blame at Jase's feet. From everything his friend had told him, he'd assumed a bar was the last place he'd find Ginnie Silver.

Sweet. But painfully straight-laced.

Those were the exact words Jase used to describe his adopted sister. Yeah, she had that look. No makeup, no pretension.

When she looked at him, though, Quinn was damned sure that ponytail was just begging to be set free, that those soft, pink lips were just begging to be kissed. A nice, clean woman who needed to be messed up. Badly.

The way she'd examined him, bottom to top…It hadn't had any of the detachment he would've expected. It wasn't even as though she was just undressing him with her eyes.

No.

It was more like he was a glass of water, and she hadn't had a drink in a week.

By the end of her slow, almost ravenous surveillance of his body, Quinn's mouth had gone dry and his pants were a little too fucking tight. When her eyes hit his, he'd had the sudden feeling that if he grabbed her right then and there, and tossed her across the bar and hiked up that pleated skirt, she would've welcomed it.

All that, and she hadn't even spoken a word.

Christ. Why the hell did I take this job?

The simple answer was that Quinn was bored. Retirement at twenty-nine was surprisingly uneventful. He had a lot of time on his hands, and while hard partying didn't interest him much, neither did lawn bowling or backgammon. A little bodyguard work on the side seemed like a good distraction. The fact that he was guarding Ginnie's body *secretly*…That was just a bonus. Quinn liked working undercover. It's what he was used to. What he'd been good at.

So the complicated answer to why he'd taken the job was…Well. *Complicated.*

When Jase – one of the few people who knew the ins and outs of the double life Quinn had been leading for the last ten years – had first approached him about keeping an eye on Ginnie, Quinn's instinct was to say no. The last thing he needed was to get straight back into the game. *Any* game, however innocuous. As Jase talked about her, though, something gave Quinn pause.

His two-bit criminal of a friend actually cared about the girl. Yeah, she was legally his sister, and yeah, the guy seemed to think of her as flesh-and-blood, but there was more to it than that. It was like Ginnie gave Jase a softer, kinder side.

Quinn was envious as hell. Which surprised him. He'd never wanted a damned thing to do with being soft. It didn't matter if it was family, or relationships, or work. Soft equalled weak.

Quinn's last girlfriend moonlighted as a call girl, and it hadn't bothered him in the least. Not in the whole six years they were together. When he'd walked away from the Black Daggers and lost her along with them, he'd barely blinked.

His job – his life – was about deception, riding that line between what *had* to be done and what was the *right* thing to do, and they were rarely the same.

As far as family was concerned, Quinn had none to speak of. Nothing about him was soft. But suddenly he wondered if there were parts of him that *could* be.

So whether he chose the simple reason or the complex one, it didn't matter. Both landed him here in this bar, watching as the girl slammed down another drink, looking mad and sweet at the same time.

Quinn's phone chimed, and he yanked it from his pocket and found a message from Jase.

We still on?

Quinn's finger moved slowly across the touch screen, cursing the need for this particular medium of communication. He hated the damn thing. Hated texting and talking and doing things virtually in general. There was something to be said for face-to-face, and his calloused hands were made for tasks far less delicate than this one. He took so long to type his reply that another message came through from Jase before he even finished.

U there man?

Quinn gritted his teeth, deleted his first, partially complete text and typed something simpler.

Yeah.

I think my sister's drunk.

No shit.

There was a long pause before another message popped up.

No shit? What do u mean? Are u there already?

Yeah.

This was supposed 2B covert!

Quinn rolled his eyes. Why did the man have to text like a twelve-year old girl?

Not anymore.

U saw her?

Yeah.

She saw u?

Relax, Naval. It's under control. Quinn stared down at his screen. Naval? What the hell. Stupid fucking autocorrect. Another reason to hate the phone.

Jase didn't seem to notice anyway. *Tell me you have a plan.*

Quinn punched in a lie, and told himself that Jase wasn't *really* his boss, not in the strictest sense of the word anyway.

Yeah.

What r u going 2 do?

Quinn's tongue darted out, found the reassuring bit of metal on the edge of his lip and clicked against it as he considered his next move. He shook his head at the fact that he had to think about it at all. Clearly, six months of bed rest followed by a year and a half of boredom had dulled his ability to think on his feet.

He'd planned every detail for how things *should* go, from the plane that arrived just fifteen minutes after hers, to the hotel room at an adjacent casino, to the reservations at the time share presentation. He was going to be Ginnie's shadow.

Now all of that had to be completely scrapped.

Even the clothes he'd packed were going to be useless. He'd brought nothing but blend-in-with-the-crowd suit jackets. The kind that could be buttoned up over his ink and make him stand out less than usual. That wouldn't matter much now that Ginnie had seen him *sans* disguise. He couldn't even pretend she wouldn't recognize him again if she saw him.

The repeated chiming of his phone didn't help him focus, either. Jase had managed to send him three more messages in under a minute. Quinn flipped through them.

The first one made him want to throw his phone across the bar as hard as he could.

I'm paying u to help me.

The second one made him roll his eyes for what felt like the hundredth time since picking up the phone in the first place.

U can't let her get on the plane drunk!

The last one, though…It actually did get to him.

C'mon, man. She's vulnerable as hell. I love her, but she's got no idea what's good for her. And it's my fault for telling her to take the trip. Please.

Quinn growled. It didn't matter that the text could very well be a manipulation. Jase was a conman by nature, but that didn't mean his words weren't true.

Ginnie's back was to him, her focus on her drink. She didn't look all that vulnerable right that second. In fact, she looked the opposite. More determined than anything else. Rising above. That was something Quinn could relate to. Something he admired. It made her already pretty face all the more attractive to him. If he was another kind of man, it might've been enough make him walk up to her, offer to buy her another drink, and charm his way into her life. Which would also solve his problem of sticking close enough to her to keep her safe.

The only issue with that plan was that Quinn *wasn't* charming.

Persuasive? Yes. In control? Absolutely. Ruthless when necessary? Definitely. Charming? Hell, no.

Ginnie adjusted a little on her stool, scooping her skirt up a little tighter, hugging the curve of her ass. Quinn's eyes rested on it for a moment, then moved down to the bit of newly exposed leg. Smooth and lean, long and supple. It was the kind of leg that deserved to be wrapped around a good man. A mental picture formed in Quinn's head, and his body responded to it with an overwhelming amount of force.

He couldn't shake his attraction to her. Hell. He wasn't even sure he wanted to. It had been quite a while since he'd felt anything like this toward a woman.

Too long, obviously.

Ginnie wasn't even his type. Case in point, the call girl. Fast, trashy, easy to let go no matter how long they stuck around. *That* was Quinn's preferred set of characteristics. Not newly divorced, pursed lips, crossed at the ankles sweet.

But when she tipped her head to one side, giving Quinn a nice view of her creamy throat, blood shot straight to his groin once more.

Jesus, she was hot.

Too hot.

For the first time in his life, Quinn wished he *was* that kind of charming.

Quinn had to consider what that meant in terms of the job. He looked down at his phone, loathe to admit that his underused libido might mean having to admit defeat.

His gaze sought Ginnie once more. Her stool was empty.

Shit.

Any and all thoughts of quitting went straight out of Quinn's head. How the hell had she slipped away so quickly? Disappointment hit him like a shot, and he wasn't even sure why. He had no intention of speaking to her directly. People didn't get this kind of gut-rot regret from losing a piece of eye candy. Or they shouldn't, anyway.

At least it laid out the truth for him. No way in hell could he do the job. Not objectively. Which meant no way in hell could he do it at all.

Quinn eyed the now-unoccupied stool, and his lips twisted to match the bizarre feeling in his chest. A pink, jewel-studded phone case stuck out of her abandoned highball glass.

Abruptly, a narrow-shouldered man in a pinstripe suit blocked Quinn's view. It somehow cut off whatever lingering connection he held to the woman, and the dull ache in his heart expanded.

Quinn willed the other man to move, and it only took him a second to figure out why he hadn't.

Pinstripes' hand had closed around the discarded phone, and he was looking toward the glass doors, a hopeful expression on his face.

Oh, hell no.

The girl was *his* target. Her so-called vulnerability was *his* to protect.

No way was Quinn letting anyone but himself go after her.

With a grim smile, he stepped up to Pinstripes – entirely closer than necessary – and held out his hand. In a heartbeat, Quinn was headed for Departure Gate 32, the bejewelled phone in his pocket.

Three

Never in a million years did Ginnie think she would ever be standing in front of a ticket agent, arguing against her right to a First Class seat. But at that second, it was exactly what she *was* doing. Loudly and vehemently.

Did vehemently automatically imply loudly? she wondered, knowing the errant thought was a direct result of the amount of gin in her system.

In fact, probably the whole conversation with the so-perky brunette in front her could be linked to the liquor coursing through her veins. Normally, Ginnie bordered on painfully polite.

"Ma'am?"

Ginnie narrowed her eyes, sure that the agent was being deliberately condescending.

"It's miss," she corrected.

"What?"

"I'm barely a week over twenty-four," Ginnie snapped. "It's safer to assume I'm a *miss* and not a *ma'am*, wouldn't you agree?"

At least the girl had the decency to look taken aback. But then she glanced down at the screen on her desk, and when she looked back up at Ginnie, her mouth was set in a line. Not quite annoyed. But almost.

"You're listed as a *Mrs.* Genevieve Michaels," she stated coolly.

"What's *your* name?" Ginnie replied.

"Leila."

"All right, Leila…Tell me something…" Ginnie lifted her left hand and waved it in the girl's direction. "Do you *see* a ring on my finger?"

Too late, she realized her mistake. Lawrence's ring – just like his ring*tone* – hadn't been deleted from her life.

She remembered pulling the damned thing from her purse just to give it a dirty look. And must've unconsciously slipped it on.

Now, the flawless, one and a half carat diamond, set in its sparkly, white gold band, caught the fluorescent light and shimmered accusingly back at Ginnie. At *them*. If she counted Leila. Which at that moment she didn't particularly want to do.

"Ma'am…Are you *drunk*?" The ticket agent's voice no longer held any pretence of friendliness.

Ginnie opened her mouth to ask how it was possible that the other woman had just noticed her inebriated state *now*, when a deep voice interrupted.

"She can have my seat."

Ginnie didn't even have to turn to know who it was. That voice – it was the kind that deserved a feather pillow wrapped in satin. And matching, mussed up sheets. The kind that would tear a hole in said pillow in the throes of passion, and rip through a pair of lace panties with a single word.

A warm hand cupped her shoulder, and from the corner of her eye, Ginnie caught sight of a tattoo in the shape of a curved knife blade.

Oh, hell.

It was definitely the picture-him-naked man from the bar.

"Are you okay, hun?" he asked.

For a second, Ginnie was so enamored with his bend-you-over-the-counter, like *right now*, rumble that she almost didn't notice he'd tossed out an endearment.

But it hadn't slipped by Leila, the not-so-friendly agent.

"You the husband?" she wanted to know, doubt evident in both her voice and the up and down look she gave Mr. Boxers-or-Briefs-nope-Commando.

"The rebound," the tattooed man corrected.

Ginnie's face flamed, but Leila just gave a shrug that said *makes sense*.

"Name?" she prompted.

"Quinn Mcdavid."

While Leila tapped away on her keyboard, Ginnie took a breath and worked up enough nerve to turn and face her would-be savior.

"The rebound?" she whisper-yelled.

He raised an eyebrow, and his tongue flicked out to tap the ring in his lip. Ginnie had to force her gaze to focus anywhere but there.

"Do I look like the *husband* type?" he countered.

Oh, crap. His voice was even sexier when he dropped it low like that. And, no. He sure as hell didn't look like any husband that Ginnie knew. Except maybe a few rock-gods who happened to be married to a reality star or two.

After a moment, Ginnie realized she was just staring at him – *Quinn, god even his name sounded a little too rock star to be true* – with a scrutinizing frown on her face.

She forced herself to speak. "I don't know about *husband* type, but I do know about *my* type, and you're not it."

He didn't look offended. In fact, a slow, self-assured smile spread across his face instead.

"Do you think women typically choose *their* type for a rebound?" he asked.

No. Not if the way she'd so eagerly undressed him *with her eyes was any indication.*

Ginnie shoved down the mental concession and snapped, "I wouldn't know."

"I guess it's a good thing I'm not a real rebound then." Quinn's smile widened and he leaned a little closer. "But. Just for the record…I'm of the opinion that most rebounding women choose someone with a little bit of a different…flavor."

When he said the last word, his eyes fixed on Ginnie's mouth, and she found herself wondering exactly what he meant by *flavor*. Was it a metaphorical comment? Or something intended to be quite literal? And how *would* the big man in front of her taste? Would that piercing of his add something metallic to his kiss?

Ginnie's mind filled with a mental picture.

His mouth pressed to her mouth. Her tongue tasting that ring.

Get a hold of yourself, she commanded silently.

But now that the image had crossed her mind, there was no way to look at his mouth without bringing it to the forefront once more.

And come to think of it…What *else* could that ring do?

Crap.

She had to work far too hard to shove down the next image that threatened to overtake her tipsy brain.

The ticket agent cleared her throat, cutting off Ginnie's rapidly dirtying mind.

"Mr. Mcdavid," the other woman said. "I'm afraid you're not actually booked on this flight. You're on the next one."

"I'm aware," Quinn replied.

"You're aware?" Ginnie said.

"Of course I am, hun." Quinn rested an elbow on the counter, shot Leila a wink, and whispered, "Before I was the rebound, I was the affair. Arriving separately is just a habit."

Ginnie's mouth dropped open, and a heated blush crept from her neck to cheeks.

Oh god. I've blushed more in the last five minutes than I have in the last five years.

Leila's critical gaze found Ginnie again. "Do you want to take the later flight then?"

"No!" she declared at the same second Quinn said firmly, "Yes."

The girl at the counter pursed her lips and looked from Quinn to Ginnie, and then back again, which immediately drove Ginnie's irritation to a new high.

How dare she assume that he has the final say?

"No," Ginnie repeated, sounding more than a little strangled. "I do *not* want the later flight."

After a disapproving *tsk,* Leila went back to her keyboard, punched in a few furious clicks, and looked at Quinn.

"There's one seat on *this* plane," she stated.

Ginnie put her hands on her hips. "You said it was full."

"No," Leila corrected. "I said that *Coach* was full. This seat is in First Class."

"I'll take it."

At Quinn's pleased exclamation, Ginnie gritted her teeth.

"He will *not* take it," she argued.

The words came out so unintelligibly that Leila just stared at her blankly.

Ginnie forced her jaw to loosen. "Excuse us for a second?"

Leila shrugged. "Sure. Priority boarding starts in five minutes. And due to small mechanical glitch – soon to be repaired, don't worry! – we'll be entering through the rear doors today."

Quinn chuckled "Rear – "

Ginnie cut off whatever dirty thing the tattoo-happy man had been about to say with a look, then grabbed his arm and dragged him across the small waiting area. Once they reached a relatively empty spot, she rounded on him.

"*What* are you *doing*?" she demanded.

He shoved his hands in his pockets and shrugged. "Trying to help you."

Ginnie shook her head. "You can't help me."

Oh, she heard the quiet desperation in her voice. It was the same tone in which she'd answered her phone, thinking it was Lawrence. And she knew immediately that her statement had somehow managed to encompass things far beyond the fact that she was stuck on a First Class flight when all she wanted was the cramped anonymity of Coach. And Quinn – hot tattoo model slash dude who was very likely on probation for *some*thing – obviously picked up on it too.

His fingers were suddenly on Ginnie's chin, tipping it up so he could meet her gaze. His eyes were the sweetest shade of brown she'd ever seen – really, really almost amber – and they were full of concern. For *her*.

"I think I *can* help you," he corrected.

His tone was sure, and full of dark promise and not *quite* cocky, and for a second, Ginnie wavered. Was it so wrong to want to try a different "*flavor*"?

Maybe there was a chance he could help her after all.

But how?

Ginnie could only think of one possible scenario, and that way was the *wrong* way, she was sure. She would only wind up more wounded than she already was. And Quinn, oozing his sexual surety the way he did, would just wind up disappointed. Lawrence had made it plenty clear enough that Ginnie wasn't a savant in the bedroom.

But she was good at lots of other things.

Like taking charge, telling it like it is, and not needing to be rescued.

And that was what she had to channel right that second.

"The thing is, Mr. Mcdavid," Ginnie said, glad that her voice came out without a tremor. "I don't *want* your help. And even if I did…I have no interest in trading flights with you. It would just put me behind schedule. And if you're *really* trying to help me, getting on this plane doesn't do that. So unless you're a) the kind of man who forces himself on women who don't want him, or b) the kind of man who lacks the intelligence to admit when he's in a no-win situation, then I think we're done."

Ginnie stepped back, pleased with the way she'd woven him into a tiny, wordsmith's box from which he could not back out without either looking like a complete ass, or calling himself stupid.

Ha, she thought. *Put that in your pipe and –*

Ginnie's inner, self-directed high five was cut off suddenly as Quinn grabbed her hands roughly and shoved her against the wall. She barely had enough time to gasp in shock as his lips crushed hers. Fire whipped through her blood, and her knees almost gave way. The only thing that kept her from sinking to the ground was the fact that Quinn's arm snaked around her waist and held her upright as he kissed her.

And holy shit.

The little ring that looped through his lip was *warm* too. Not metallic at all. It was sensual, and radiated that warmth outward, lighting up Ginnie's mouth. The heat flowered, and when Quinn's tongue exerted just the tiniest bit of pressure, Ginnie's lips dropped open to welcome it. And then she wasn't just letting it happen; she was kissing him back. For all she was worth.

Her arms came up and settled on Quinn's shoulders, and her fingers toyed with the very bottom edge of his faux-hawk. Her spine curved so she could push into him. And her mouth worked across his, with his, inside his...Tasting each bit of him. She deepened the kiss further, and found another piece of warm metal in the center of his tongue.

Dear god.

The mere thought of what other parts of him might be pierced made Ginnie gasp, and she sucked in a much needed gulp of oxygen. Quinn pulled away.

"What the hell was that?" Ginnie demanded, unable to cover her breathlessness.

Quinn ran a finger down her cheek, then leaned toward her again. And instead of doing the smart thing, Ginnie closed her eyes and tipped her mouth up in anticipation.

Stupid, treacherous body.

But he didn't give her another kiss.

He stopped just short of lip-to-lip contact, and whispered, "*That* was me, proving you wrong."

Ginnie's eyes flew open. "What?"

Quinn shot her a smug smile. "I have absolutely no need to force myself on you, and I'm sure as hell not ready to concede a loss. Enjoy your flight, hun. See you in Vegas."

Sonofabitch.

With her face as red as the setting sun, Ginnie spun on one of her sensible heels and stalked back to Leila and her fake smile and the goddamned First Class seat.

Four

Quinn waited until Ginnie and her sweet, tempting ass were completely out of sight before he sagged against the wall. Not that very many parts of him were *saggy* at that moment.

Christ.

He had no clue what had come over him.

One second, the ticket agent with the shiny veneers and over-plucked eyebrows had her figurative claws dug into the visibly-wobbly Ginnie, the next Quinn was swooping in to rescue her. Like some asshole superhero, saving her from her own damned smart-mouth.

Yeah, and not two minutes after that, you were sucking that same smart-mouth right off her face.

Quinn suppressed an unexpected grin. Her mouth *was* hella smart. Quick and clever. He hadn't been expecting that at all. Demure and well-mannered. That's what her brother had called her. Quinn remembered it well, because he'd never heard the word *demure* used to describe an actual, living, breathing person. Ginnie was alive, no goddamned doubt about it.

And breathing...

Yeah, she'd been breathing all right. Panting, hot and heavy as she melted underneath his mouth.

Thank god he'd decided not to take the job.

Apparently, pleated skirts and button-down blouses were his asshole-superhero kryptonite.

Quinn shifted his mind to his usual type – his usual *flavor,* trying to remind himself again that he liked tight-ass jeans, cleavage all over the place, makeup just shy of screaming *clown.* Girls who weren't embarrassed to admit they were after him for his reputation, body, or just a quick fuck. Even when he wasn't willing to give it.

Two years.

That's how long had gone by since he cut the last girl loose along with his assumed life, and truth be told, he hadn't felt an urge to seek another. Not that he was a eunuch, but hell. Even his gratuitous viewing of some televised bikini contest last week hadn't piqued his interest. Nothing had. Until this girl and her hot-and-cold routine.

If she hadn't been a job, Quinn would've dragged her off – caveman style – to some dirty corner and shown her a hell of lot more of what she was missing by sending him packing.

His tongue flicked out irritably to tap the ring on his lip, and that didn't help at all. Ginnie had practically devoured it, sucking on it to the point of exquisite pain.

Why hadn't he stuck to his plan?

Just drop the phone at the goddamned counter and – oh, shit. The fucking phone.

He pulled it out of his pocket. It had gone completely out of his head. As he stared down at the ridiculously pink and sparkly case, the stupid thing started to ring, a jazzed up version of some eighties love song that made Quinn groan. How could he possibly be attracted to a girl who listened to *that*?

A woman standing nearby – and she was pushing ninety, Quinn could swear it – began to hum along with the tune. She waggled an eyebrow at him, and if he'd been the kind of man who got embarrassed, he sure as hell would've died of it just then. Luckily he was the shameless type instead, so he just slammed down on the answer button and waited.

Jase's voice floated over the air. "G? You there? Hey, am I on speaker?"

"Not on purpose," Quinn growled as he searched for the key that would switch the call back to handset mode.

He didn't get to it quick enough.

"Quinn!" Jase hollered. "Why the *fuck* do you have Ginnie's phone?! Jesus, can she hear me? G-dog?"

Finally, Quinn found the right button, gave it a smack and replied, "*She* can't hear you, but the rest of the goddamned airport can."

On the cue, the grey-haired granny nodded and winked.

Quinn smiled a toothy smile, and spoke to her instead of Jase. "Sorry. My boyfriend is a little uppity."

"Boyfriend?" Jase yelled. "I'm not your – "

Quinn held the phone away from his ear, and widened his grin, then added loudly, "Maybe more than a little."

Granny gave him two thumbs up, and Quinn let out a real chuckle before bringing the phone back to his face.

"You're an asshole," Jase was saying.

"Is that a nice way to speak to your man?" Quinn countered.

"I have far better taste than that. Where's my sister?"

"She dropped her damned phone in her drink. I picked it up to give it back. Thought it might be a nice icebreaker."

"You weren't supposed to talk to her at all."

Too late, Quinn thought, but what he said was, "Doesn't matter. She's on the plane, I'm in the terminal, and I'm not finishing the job. She can buy a new phone in Vegas."

There was a pause. "What?"

"I can't do it, man. Sorry." Quinn kept his voice even. "Why not?"

Because you're sister's too fucking hot and just thinking about her makes me want to hang up the phone so I can – Quinn forced his mind up and out of the gutter. "Doesn't suit me. Turns out I'm a terrible undercover bodyguard."

"I'll double your pay."

It was Quinn's turn to pause. Jase wasn't paying him much, but Quinn didn't really need the cash, either. His dual pension – hush money, he liked to call it – more than took care of his living expenses.

"What the hell is going on, Jase?" he demanded.

He heard the other man take a breath before he answered in a rush. "Her ex didn't cancel the room reservations."

Quinn narrowed his eyes. "And you know this because…?"

"Because I'm monitoring the asshat's computer," Jase snapped. "And yes, I'm well aware it violates my probation. But the dick deserves it."

Quinn exhaled. He had no real obligation to report his friend's illegal activities. It just pissed him off that a man who'd been out of jail less than twelve months was so willing to risk his freedom all over again.

"Are you there, Quinn?" Jase asked impatiently.

"Yeah. I don't want your money."

"At least get her the phone." The other man was practically begging.

"No. I'm not going to chase after your sister just because her ex forgot to cancel a room. Hell, maybe she'll get there and be able to use the room herself. Call it alimony."

Jase sighed. "Listen, Quinn. Lawrence didn't just *forget* to cancel. He upgraded and ordered a very expensive bottle of wine. Along with a few other…goodies. The man is going to *be* there, and he's not going to be alone. If Ginnie walks in on that…it'll destroy her. If she can't reach out to me…"

Quinn felt an unusual squeeze in his heart. Apparently, the dick *did* deserve to be spied on. He also deserved a serious ass-kicking.

"Quinn?"

"You are one needy boyfriend, you know that right?"

"So you'll do it?"

"Just the phone part."

"Thank you."

Quinn pressed the end call button, pocketed the phone again, then strode back toward the ticket counter. The last of the upper echelons of the plane clientele had just finished boarding.

Leila smiled at Quinn, those fake teeth glinting in the fluorescent light, and spoke to him like she'd never seen him before in her life. "General boarding begins in ten minutes, sir."

What the actual hell?

"Yeah, I know."

He waited for her to say something else, but she just stared back. Quinn gave in and spoke again.

"My girlfriend forgot her phone." His heart beat weirdly as he said the G-word. "Can you call her off so I can give it to her?"

Leila blinked, smile never wavering "I'm sorry, sir. Once a passenger's ticket has been scanned and he or she's on the plane, we're not permitted to allow them to leave."

Quinn rolled his eyes. "Fine. Can I get on the plane and give it to her myself?"

"Definitely not!"

Quinn forced himself to grin that sideways grin that always impressed girls but made him feel like a shitty Elvis impersonator.

"Definitely, *definitely*? Or just definitely?"

Leila's smile faltered, just enough that her teeth disappeared for a minute. Then they reappeared.

"Sir, the only way for you to get on the plane is to buy a ticket."

"I *have* a ticket," he reminded her.

"For the next flight."

Quinn didn't bother pointing out that she'd just proved she remembered him. He just proffered the sparkly phone.

"If you won't let me on…Could *you* give it her?"

Leila recoiled from the phone like it was a bomb.

"I'm sorry, Mr. Mcdavid. That's strictly forbidden."

"Lucky for both of us, forbidden is my second-favorite f-word," he stated.

She wasn't buying into his falsified charm any more than he'd bought into hers.

Quinn sighed. "Help me out here."

"The only way to get your *girlfriend* her phone is to take it to her yourself," Leila told him. "And the only way for you to get on *this* plane is to pay the fare difference between *your* ticket and the First Class one that's available."

"Jesus Christ," Quinn muttered. "How much?"

She clacked away on her stupid keyboard for a minute, then smiled at him. This time it was a genuine one, and Quinn knew he was totally screwed.

"One thousand, two-hundred, forty-two dollars. And ninety-three cents," Leila said, then added brightly, "I can waive the fifty dollar change fee."

Well, shit. No wonder the seats up front had the extra goddamned legroom.

"You still have the original credit card on file?" Quinn managed to ask.

Clack. Clack. Clack.

Another bright smile. "I do. But it's for a Mr. Jason Silver. *He* would have to sign for it."

Quinn's teeth closed around his lip ring furiously. With a barely disguised snarl, he reached into his pocket and yanked out his coup-de-grace. A slightly flawed coup-de-grace, but a certain victory nonetheless. He slapped the leather case down on the counter, and Leila jumped back.

The badge on the counter glinted brighter than even her teeth would dare to do.

Why the hell he'd even brought the damned thing out of storage for this little trip was a mystery. Some weird compulsion to feel legitimate, maybe. Now, though, he was glad he had it.

Leila eyed it, then him, then it, and Quinn grabbed it up again before she could note that the wallet was that of a retiree. Then he shot her his own very real smile.

"You can charge Jason Silver for the ticket, or you can *not* charge him. I don't care. Just let me on the damned plane so I can give my damned *girlfriend* her phone, or I'm going to throw your damned yoga-zumba-step-class-doing ass in airport jail. Please."

Quinn had no idea if there was an airport jail or not, and he didn't care. He was tired of playing nice.

"And Leila…I'm going to need my damned bag off the other plane, too."

The ticket agent's eyes had gone wide and her mouth was pinched. She banged hard on the keyboard once more.

"You're clear," she told him in a strangled voice, her face almost purple.

Quinn didn't bother with a thank you; he strode past her onto the plane, walking so hard he nearly crashed directly into Ginnie in the flesh. She'd stopped at the curtain between First Class and Coach, and was staring at a couple who were sucking face in the front row of coach.

Quinn knew immediately why she was watching them.

The man – the asshat, the dick, the dirty sonofabitch – with his lips locked to the barely-legal girl with a shirt so low it showed nipple…was her husband. The man standing beside her in the photo Jase had given Quinn. There was no doubt about it. Somehow, the sleazebag had managed to bypass the priority boarding.

And Quinn only had one, run-together sentence of a thought as he worked his way toward Ginnie.

Letmeatthatmotherfuckersolcanbreakhisface.

Five

Ginnie's feet wouldn't move.

Silently, she willed them to keep going. But they were disturbingly disobedient, apparently as transfixed by the scene if front of her as her eyes were.

Dr. Lawrence Michaels.

Stupid, sexy name.

Stupid perma-tan and perfect hair.

Stupid girl in his lap.

Twelve weeks had passed since she'd seen him last. And even then…It had been from across a boardroom. At the end of the longest table in the world. He'd had his four lawyers on his side. She'd had Jase – a furious look on his face – on hers. Both had acted as wall between them.

Now, she was close enough to touch him. To break through the bullshit restraining order he'd put into place when she tried to ask him why he *really* wanted to call off their life together. The only thing between them was the large-breasted, poofy-haired girl. She didn't look anywhere near as formidable as his lawyers. In fact, she didn't even look old enough to drink airplane champagne. Which was very likely the reason he hadn't seated the two of them in First Class. That. And the fact that Ginnie was booked into the second-to-last available seat, of course.

Shit. Speaking of First Class…

She was going to have to go directly past Lawrence and Miss Barely-Eighteen just to get to her own seat. And her feet still wouldn't cooperate.

Then two simultaneous, horrifying things happened.

Lawrence looked up and saw her.

And a bag fell from the overhead bin and knocked Ginnie in the head.

Ginnie honestly didn't know which was worse. Which was more embarrassing. She only knew that she wanted nothing more than to sink into the hideous airplane carpet. Or maybe to vomit up all those gin and tonics from the airport bar.

Then another bag fell from above, making her stumble, and one of her heels got caught on the in-floor lighting track. And down she went. Her rear end hit the ground with a thud that was hard enough to bring tears to her eyes.

Ginnie shot her gaze heavenward and realized that four more bags, each as precariously balanced as the next, were poised and ready to rain down on her.

What were all those bags *doing* there, anyway? No had even boarded the plane yet.

But worse than that, when her eyes flicked back toward Lawrence, Ginnie saw that he'd extracted himself from the beauty queen's arms, and was moving in her direction.

Please! Ginnie prayed. *If there was ever a time to be smote…It's now! God?!*

Then, abruptly – thankfully – a warm hand found her elbow and pulled her both to her feet and out of the line of fire. And an already-too-familiar waft of subtle cologne hit her nose.

Quinn bloody Mcdavid, king of the lip ring.

"You okay, baby?" he asked.

Baby? Baby?!

It was worse than hun. Almost.

Ginnie opened her mouth to sputter out something about the fact that she was full-grown woman who did *not* appreciate the diminutive, but had to slam it shut again when she saw that Lawrence was just a step or two away. She refused to embarrass herself any further. She wriggled a little in an attempt to free herself from Quinn's grasp so she could make her way through to First Class with as much dignity as possible. But the tattooed gorilla didn't let her go. Just the opposite, in fact. His wide palm slid down her elbow to her forearm, and his other hand landed on her hip. He pulled her into him, then leaned down and spoke directly into her ear.

"Work with me here," he said.

Work with h –

Ginnie's thought cut off as he spun her around and kissed the exact spot - on her head, not her rear end – where she'd bumped just a minute ago. He did it with perfect, believable tenderness. Then he tipped up her face and gave her lips the same attention.

This kiss was different than the one he'd claimed from her just a few minutes ago. Oh, it sent waves of heat through her in the same way. And it made light explode behind her eyes in the same way too. But it was far less urgent. Far less demanding. And unbelievably good.

The world slipped away from Ginnie as she sank into Quinn's embrace. No. Sank wasn't the right word. She *melted.* Swooned. And sweet tendrils of desire seeped from his lips to hers, then down through her chest and lower, pooling between her legs.

When he finally pulled away, Ginnie was trembling.

And her former husband was gawking at her.

"Thanks for coming to help her, man," Quinn said, and clapped Lawrence hard on the shoulder. "But as you can see…I take good care of my baby all on my own."

"Ginnie…" Lawrence trailed off, like he had no idea what to say.

Not that Ginnie could blame him; she was utterly speechless herself. Quinn though…He was *full* of it. And himself.

"You know this guy, baby?" he asked, an eyebrow raised like he couldn't quite believe it. "Friend of your dad's, or what?"

Lawrence's mouth worked silently for a second before he blurted, "She's my *wife!*"

Quinn's eyes darted from Ginnie to Lawrence, and then his lips peeled back into an amused grin. "No shit. You married, baby? Sorry, man. Name's Quinn. Guess she forgot to tell me about you last night when we were – "

Ginnie finally recovered enough to reply. "No!" she protested, then took a breath and added coolly, "Not even close to married."

And she slid her hand into Quinn's and dragged him forward. When she reached the First Class section, she snapped the divider shut and rounded on him, unsure if she was about to shower him with thankful kisses, or if she was preparing to unleash a tirade on him. Either way, he beat her to the punch.

"You're welcome," he said smugly.

"My *welcome?*"

"I'm assuming that douchebag out there is your husband, even though you claimed otherwise. And I'm assuming that brunette isn't his sister. So I'm pretty sure I just did you a big favor. So. Yeah. You're welcome."

At his too-loud speech, several other First Class passengers turned in their direction, and Ginnie's face reddened.

"He's not my husband," she retorted in a whisper.

"Uh huh."

Quinn moved past her, folded his thick body in seat 1B, and stretched out his long legs so far that they almost hit the wall in front of him. Somehow, he made the decently-sized space look small.

Quinn tossed her an expectant grin. "You coming?"

Ginnie glanced down at her ticket. 1C. And there *was* no 1A.

"You've got to be kidding me," she muttered.

She gave his feet a dirty look, climbed over his ankles, and sat on the very edge of her own seat.

She refused to look at him. But no matter how hard she stared out the window, she could still feel his looming presence beside her. And no matter how she shifted, his knee kept brushing hers, sending unnerving ripples of awareness up her thigh.

And you like it.

Ginnie shoved down the snide voice in her head and squeezed as close to the window as she could. She was thankful that for the moment, Quinn was silent too. In fact, he didn't speak to her at all. Not as the flight attendant gave her safety speech, not as the plane pulled onto the tarmac and not when it roared to life and climbed into air.

He stayed so quiet that Ginnie couldn't help but steal a sidelong glance of his profile.

He was faced forward, eyes closed, body still. His lashes were enviably long, and the barest hint of stubble covered his cheeks.

God, he was hot.

There was no getting around it.

Hair so dark it was almost black, cut short at the sides and spiked up in the middle. And that lip ring. And *inside* his mouth. That tongue ring.

What would it feel like, to have it slide down the sensitive skin on her neck? To have it trail to her collarbone and down further to trace the curve of her lace bra?

Ginnie's nipples tingled at the thought and she swallowed nervously. But her mind didn't want to stop there, either.

She tried to halt it by pulling her gaze from his mouth, but that didn't help at all, because her eyes landed on his hands instead, and damned if they weren't hot, too. Rough and masculine, nails clipped short, and a wide, silver band on one pointer finger. And Ginnie knew just how warm they would be on her back as they unclipped that same lace that his lips were tasting.

"Ex?"

His voice cut through the fantasy, and Ginnie jumped. He was watching *her* as she watched *him*, and she realized she'd leaned back in her seat, and her knees had parted a little too, just enough that she was touching him. Again.

She jerked away.

"Genevieve?" His named wrapped around her full, proper name with an unreasonably perfect French accent.

So damned sexy.

"Ginnie," she corrected automatically.

"Ginnie," he agreed softly. "Is the douchebag your ex?"

"Sort of," she admitted, not sure why she felt so compelled to tell him the embarrassing truth.

Maybe it was the way those caramel eyes stared straight into her. Like he knew her secrets already, and was just waiting for her to speak up.

The flight attendant came by with an offer of drinks, and Ginnie waved her off. Clearly, the last thing she needed was to consume anything more.

She cleared her throat. "He's my *former* husband."

"And that's different because…"

"Because we didn't get divorced. He had our marriage annulled."

One thick eyebrow went up. "Annulled?"

Ginnie nodded. "So it's like it never happened."

Quinn didn't look convinced. "Former and ex are kind of the same thing, though, aren't they?"

"It just sounds more fitting."

That same, I-call-bullshit eyebrow of his went up. "I don't see the difference."

Ginnie crossed her arms over her chest irritably, then uncrossed them again as soon as she realized it drew attention to her breasts. And Quinn was helping himself to an eyeful.

"Are you always this argumentative over semantics?" she grumbled.

"No. In fact, I rarely argue over semantics at all." She was sure he was trying to cover another grin, especially when he added, "I get the feeling you don't like me very much."

Ginnie colored. "That's not true."

"So you do like me?" he teased.

She rolled her eyes. "Could you get anymore high school?"

This time, Quinn didn't hide his smile. "As a matter of fact…I could. But I've decided on a way I can definitely help you. I'm kind of leaning toward a revenge scheme. And come to think of it…That's pretty high school, too."

"Revenge for what?"

"Annulment."

Ginnie was going to argue. She really was. Revenge wasn't high on her list of priorities. She'd gone ahead with the vacation – solo – as a part of her plan to prove that didn't care about Lawrence at all. But the truth was…she did care. At least a little. It ticked her off that he'd come on their vacation, too. Not even because he had the ridiculous arm candy at his side. No. It was because it felt like he'd stolen something *else* from her. Ginnie had *owned* this trip to Vegas. With the encouragement of her brother, she'd made it hers.

So even though she knew it was a bad idea – that it would only lead down some dim path that she'd probably never be able to return from – she turned an expectant eye in Quinn's direction.

"What did you have in mind?" she asked.

And a totally devious, totally sexy, one-sided smile crept up the rock-god-esque man's face.

Six

Oh, Christ.

Those startlingly green eyes stared up at Quinn, and every protective fiber in his body stood on end. He saw the hope there, hung on his vague promise of revenge. He saw pain, too, and when she'd confessed about the annulment, he'd seen a hint of guilt and a shitload of self-doubt.

Annulled. Hell.

She didn't deserve that.

What kind of shit-for-brains man made a girl like that question her own worth?

"Quinn?"

She said his name emphatically. Short and sweet, like an important piece of punctuation. And it reminded him that he was supposed to be telling her something.

Right. Revenge.

Quinn leaned forward, looked around conspiratorially, and whispered, "Jealousy."

"Jealousy?"

"Oldest trick in the book," Quinn confirmed.

"But why would he even get jealous?" Ginnie wanted to know. "He wants to pretend our marriage never happened." She shook her head. "Even when we *were* married, he wasn't exactly possessive."

Quinn gave her another onceover. Any man who got a chance to bury himself in that creamy skin – or even one who got a taste of those so-soft lips, like he had – was going to earn a jealous streak as wide as the Grand Canyon. He could see Ginnie didn't believe it, though.

"Trust me. I can smell green a mile off. He's jealous as hell," Quinn stated firmly. "If you want proof, think of this…The man just dumped some girl off his lap to run over and tell me you were his *wife*. Which you're not."

He watched as Ginnie's mouth opened, then closed.

"Fine," she said a little grudgingly. "Tell me your plan."

Quinn grinned and said the first thing that popped into his head. The thing that would drive a thick-skulled, self-centered sonofabitch like Ginnie's "former" husband crazy. Quinn wanted to punish him too.

"You ever heard of the Mile High Club?"

Her eyes went wide and her face went crimson. "The – yes. Of course I have. But I'm *not* having sex in an airplane bathroom!"

Quinn's smile widened, mostly because her protest had been about the accommodation, not the company.

Freudian slip? he wondered.

He decided not to draw attention to it.

"I'm not talking about *actual* sex," he told her instead.

The red didn't leave her cheeks. "Fake sex?"

Quinn nodded. "Mm hmm."

"I can't do that."

"Really?"

"No."

Her eyes were on her hands, though, and Quinn knew she was lying.

"You're telling me you've never *faked* it before?" he asked teasingly.

"Err…"

He'd never heard a more awkward noise.

If a blush had a sound...that noise would be it, he decided.

It was cute as hell though, and Quinn couldn't resist an urge to reach out and tip her chin up so that she *had* to meet his eyes.

"Not once?" he asked.

"Maybe once," she admitted softly.

Oh, that blush.

"Good. You'll know what to do then," Quinn said, and he unbuckled his seatbelt. "I'm going to go in the regular seating area. All the way to the rear washrooms."

"We're doing this *now*?"

"Yep. In less than two minutes, you're going to follow me. Make sure you grab your not-husband's attention."

"How?"

Quinn shrugged and stood up. "Smile at him. Bump his seat. I don't care. Just make sure he knows you're going by."

"Okay." She said it like she couldn't quite believe she was agreeing to do it.

Quinn didn't blame her. He couldn't believe it either. It was a very bad idea. With a capital bloody V and capital damned B, topped with a cherry.

That didn't stop him from leaning down, his face just an inch from her sweet-smelling hair, and saying, "Ginnie?"

"Yes?"

"If you were *my* wife, I'd make sure you *never* had to fake it."

He heard her little gasp as he strode through the plane without looking back.

Jase was going to kill him.

The girl deserves a goddamned break, he growled internally.

She'd been handed a shit deal. Her brother said he wanted Quinn to help her. Well. Maybe not quite like this.

Okay, not at all *like this,* he amended.

But hell. Quinn was used to doing things his own way. Why should this be any different? If anything, he was doing *more* than Jase asked him to. He wasn't just protecting her. He was pulling her from the mire of baggage she was carrying around. On top of that, he was putting the asshole ex in his place.

And speaking of the asshole…

Quinn caught the other man's eye as he walked by his seat. He shot him a knowing grin, made a show of checking out the ample cleavage of his lap-candy girlfriend, then offered him a thumbs up before making his way to the bathroom.

"Jase should give me a fucking medal," he muttered as he opened the tiny door and entered the stall.

Maybe she won't even come. Maybe she'll realize it was a shitty plan and tell you where to stick it.

The thought made Quinn's heart lurch unexpectedly. He tamped down the unusual emotion and forced himself to focus on counting off the passing seconds instead.

Two minutes or less.

And on the seventy-seventh second, a hesitant tap told him she hadn't chickened out after all.

Quinn swung open the door. There she was, flushed cheeks, perfect ponytail, and chest rising and falling nervously.

Quinn's body reacted automatically, and he wondered briefly just how the hell he was going to hide his obvious arousal in such a closed space.

"Can I come in?" she asked.

The breathlessness in her voice made it that much worse. His jeans were already uncomfortably tight.

"Quinn?" she persisted.

He cleared his throat. "Did Captain Douchebag see you?"

Ginnie's eyes flicked sideways. "He's a doctor, not a captain. And he's looking now," she whispered.

Of course he was.

"Let's give him something to watch then," Quinn suggested.

He took a small step out of the stall, making sure he was visible up the aisle, and placed a hand on Ginnie's waist possessively. He bent to her ear.

"Giggle," he ordered.

"What?"

She tried to pull away and he held on tightly.

"A little laugh," he said.

"I can't giggle on command!"

"Are you ticklish?"

He didn't wait for her to answer. He yanked the bottom of her blouse out of the waistband of her skirt, slipped his finger under blouse, and poked her ribs.

"Oh!"

Her exclamation was loud enough that several people looked their way. The asshole was definitely paying attention too. Quinn could feel the burn of his gaze.

Good.

He dragged Ginnie into the bathroom and reached around her to close the door. Then he locked it firmly and stared down at her.

"Well," he conceded. "That wasn't a traditional giggle. But I guess it did the trick."

She gazed up at him, her eyes unblinking, her pretty mouth pursed thoughtfully. Quinn's memory stuck on the softness of those lips and how they felt against his. How they resisted for just a breath, then succumbed. Then became a willing accomplice.

He wanted it again, but he didn't dare take it. He might not be able to control himself if he did. He focused on the puzzled look on her face instead.

"What's wrong?" Quinn's voice was husky.

"Nothing. I'm just trying to figure out if you're a good guy, or a bad guy."

Quinn chuckled. "Is there no gray area?"

Ginnie shook her head, gold ponytail bouncing. "Not in my world."

"That must make your world a tough place to be."

"Not at all. It's easy."

"So…What…You put everyone and everything into their little boxes and that's that? Then they stay there, just waiting for you to unwrap them?" he teased.

"In a far less sarcastic, clinical-sounding way, yes. I like to know where I stand."

"In relation to what?"

"Everything."

"Sounds…confining."

A little smile curved her lips sexily. Quinn's heart thumped with a desire to run his tongue along that curve. Her next question didn't help matters either.

"More confining than being trapped in an airplane bathroom with a strange man?" she asked.

"Am I strange?" he countered.

"You'd prefer another adjective? How about...unusual. Unpredictable. Unexpected."

He grinned crookedly, enjoying the word play. "That's a lot of 'uns'."

A strand of hair snuck out of her elastic and dangled over her cheek. Ginnie reached up to brush it away, but Quinn beat her to it. He tucked it gently behind her ear.

What he really wanted to do, though, was pull it all out and see it tumble down her shoulders. Thread his fingers through it, pull it back and sink his teeth into her throat.

As he pictured it, his tongue darted out to tap his lip ring, and he heard the little catch in her breath as her eyes focused on his mouth. Her eyelids fluttered, almost to a close, and Quinn had a funny feeling she was picturing it too.

He couldn't help but wonder what would happen if he actually did it. If he closed the miniscule space between them and did what every part of him was longing to do.

Knock it off, he told his libido irritably.

Out loud he asked, "Should we get down to business?"

Her eyes moved away from his lips with visible reluctance and sought his gaze again. "Business?"

He raised an eyebrow. "The fake sex business."

"R-r-right," she stammered, then recovered quickly, and asked in a serious – *very* down-to-business – voice. "Should we just wait for a few minutes? Maybe ten?"

"Ten minutes? That's pretty damned insulting."

"Sorry. But, I mean – shouldn't it be a quickie? It's a bathroom stall, right?"

"There's a quickie...And then there's a waste of time. Besides which, we're going to put on a show."

"No can see us," she reminded him.

"Nope," he agreed. "But they can hear us."

"They can – wait. What?"

In reply, Quinn grabbed her by the hips, lifted her up, and turned to set her on the sink. Ginnie squealed.

"That's a good start," he told her. "But you should *probably* fill your screams with delight instead of terror. I don't want people to think there's a murder happening in here."

"You actually want me to scream?"

She was squirming in her seat, trying to find a way to keep her skirt down. She was failing, and a little bit more leg got exposed with each wiggle. The movement was making Quinn a little crazy.

Hot. But crazy.

"Can you stop that?" he grunted.

"Stop what?"

"Moving."

"Not exactly."

"Your knees are in my stomach," he said.

"You're the one who put me up here," she pointed out. "And my butt happens to be a little bit stuck in the sink."

He pressed a palm to each of her legs and pulled her forward. "Better?"

Ginnie said nothing, but when she glanced down quickly, and Quinn followed her gaze, he saw that he was practically sandwiched between her thighs. Her skirt was now well above her knees, and the view was enticing as hell.

Shit.

Blood rushed through him, fast and hard, and all of it pooled in his groin. Any second, Ginnie was going to notice exactly how much *better* Quinn's body thought it was. He tried to pull away, but there was really nowhere to go.

He was losing control. Quickly.

Only one way to stop it.

"This was a bad idea," he announced.

His hand shot backwards, but before he could grip the door handle, Ginnie's fingers found his forearm.

"Please," she said softly. "I really do want Lawrence to pay. Just tell me what to do, Quinn, and I'll do it."

Damned if he could say no to that.

"Show me what you've got," Quinn ordered softly. "Moan. Scream. Yelp."

"Just, um…like that?"

"Yes."

"I can't."

Quinn repeated himself, biting off each word with a click of his lip ring.

"Moan." *Click.* "Scream." *Click.* "Yelp." *Click.*

Her eyes stayed trained on his mouth, and when he finished speaking, a tiny noise *did* escape from her lips.

Quinn didn't know which of the three it was, but he sure as hell knew it wasn't fake. And he wanted her to make it again.

Shit.

"That was good," Quinn said quickly, careful to keep his face impassive. "But make it louder."

"All right."

She opened her mouth, and nothing came out. She tried again, and managed a small, unconvincing whimper.

"That's fine," Quinn said. "If you're imitating a *mouse* having sex."

She rolled her eyes. "What do you suggest?"

"Close your eyes."

She shot him a doubtful look. "So you can help yourself to a look at me?"

Quinn fought a grin. He had a perfectly good view of her in the mirror above the sink, but he wasn't going to point it out.

"You said you'd do what I told you to do," he reminded her. "Are you a liar *and* a shitty faker?"

"I'm not a – " Ginnie cut herself off, shook her head, then said, "Fine."

Truthfully, Quinn was actually relieved when she squeezed her lids shut. It gave him a momentary reprieve from her intense stare.

Why the hell is this so important to you, Quinn? he wondered.

He stared at her face, trying to figure it out. Her lips were parted. Not sexily, but awkwardly. For some reason, it still made him as hard as a rock.

He willed himself to fight it, and he closed his own eyes for a second too, but a pig-like squeal made them fly open again.

"What the hell was *that*?" he demanded.

"A sex noise!"

"Seriously? That's the *worst* sex noise I've ever heard."

"I'll take that as a compliment," she retorted. "And it was a *fake* sex noise, remember?"

Quinn shot her deliberately cocky grin. "Right. I guess I've never heard one of those before."

Ginnie rolled her eyes again. "Shut up."

"Listen," he said. "I realize we're doing this to induce jealousy, but I'd appreciate it if I walked out of here looking like an accomplished lover. Not a farmer who's a little too fond of his pigs."

"That's gross."

"My point exactly."

"I'm doing my best."

Quinn opened his mouth to tell her what he thought of her so-called best, but he caught the slight tremor in her lip and the trace of insecurity in her eyes.

Dammit.

"Oh, hell," he muttered. "Just make it a little more authentic. Think about it the same way you would think about a *real* orgasm. Build and release."

"I don't – " Ginnie cut herself off, mid-sentence. "I've actually never had to fake an orgasm."

An unreasonable surge of jealousy shot through Quinn. She'd never had to fake it with Dr. Husband. Damned if she was going to have to fake it with him. Not if he could help it.

Seven

Ginnie's face was warm, and she was afraid to meet Quinn's eyes in case he guessed what she'd been about to say.

Because the truth was she had no idea if she'd *ever* had an orgasm for real. Not given to her by someone *else* anyway.

Which was ridiculous.

She'd been with Lawrence for six years. Since her freshman year in college, when she was just barely eighteen. And before she met him, she hadn't been much for casual dating. She was focused on school, on her scholarships, and not much else. Besides that, she'd been *waiting*.

And as much Lawrence had liked sex, things between them were pretty routine. He'd never stopped to check if she liked it too.

And maybe she hadn't.

Maybe when Lawrence cited their lack of compatibility in the bedroom as the primary reason for annulment, it shouldn't have surprised her so much.

But right that second, it was *exactly* what had made Ginnie think pretending to join the Mile High club was the *perfect* piece of revenge. Lawrence *hated* being wrong. If thought he'd been wrong about this...

Except it wasn't going to be so perfect if Quinn figured out her secret.

He would have a field day with it, she could tell.

Married, orgasm-less woman.

There was a damned good punch line in there somewhere.

"You know what?" she said, and made herself meet his eyes. "You were right. This was a bad – "

Abruptly, his hands landed on top of hers, and her protest died on her lips.

"Let's try something else," he suggested.

"I don't – "

"Now, Ginnie."

She fixed him with an irritated glare. "You're awfully bossy."

He ignored the insult. "Just give me a tiny bit of trust."

"Trust? We just met."

"So? No reason *not* to trust me right?"

Ginnie narrowed her eyes. "Not exactly infallible logic, Quinn."

The big man grinned. "How about you give me a little leeway instead then?"

Yeah, right, Ginnie thought. *Give* you *an inch, and you'll overrun the whole damned city.*

Quinn went on like she'd already agreed anyway. "I know what your problem is, Ginnie."

She colored. "I do *not* have a problem."

"Yeah, you do. You're too tense."

"Of course I'm tense! I'm locked in a bathroom with a man I don't know, trying to – "

Quinn's hands reached up, closed on other side of her face, and he slammed his lips into hers. She wanted to fight him. Ought to have fought him.

Instead, her shoulders dropped, her legs turned to jelly, and the rest of her became molten lava.

Why the hell did he have to be such a good kisser? she wondered as he eased away.

It made it impossible to focus.

Which, it turned out, was his whole game.

"Better," Quinn said his voice indescribably soft and sexy. "See how easy it is to relax when you're not thinking about anything else? You can't fake an orgasm if your body's that tense. Even a faked one is about *releasing* tension. Letting it out. Build. And release."

"It is?"

"Mm hmm. Build," he murmured, then brushed his lips against hers. "And release. Try saying that."

"Build and release," Ginnie repeated, hoping her voice didn't sound as breathy as it felt.

"It's all about mind over matter. And maybe looking the part, just a little bit more."

His hands landed on the back of her neck, and his fingers buried themselves in her ponytail. The elastic band holding the tendrils so carefully in place snapped open.

Ginnie stifled a gasp.

"Close your eyes again," he instructed, and she did as she was told. Then Quinn spoke again, and his voice was right next to her ear. "Stop holding it in."

Ginnie swallowed. "Okay."

"Relax your hands."

Her palms dropped open obediently, and Quinn turned them up and pressed his thumbs to their centers.

Another little gasp built up in her chest, and this time she couldn't have held it in if she tried. It *flew* from her throat.

"Much better," he said.

Quinn continued to make circles on her skin. They were so tiny that they should have been nearly indiscernible. Instead, they were all-consuming. And heat soared from Ginnie's hands to her forearms to her shoulders to her chest, making her nipples come to attention under the lace of her bra.

Just because he's touching your hands *and* talking *to you?* she scolded herself.

But as much as her brain thought she should pull away from the attention, her body had zero interest in cooperating.

No thinking! she ordered herself.

"All right?" Quinn wanted to know.

"Mm," she mumbled.

He released her hands and set them, palm-down, on the top of her knees. Then he reached up to smooth her hair into a soft fan across her back. His fingers brushed her shoulder blades pleasantly before he pulled away. Every part of her body was on high alert, waiting for his next move.

Ginnie's eyes crept open, but Quinn shook his head.

"Keep them closed," he instructed. "Less pressure for both of us."

"Okay," she agreed again, even though right that second, she almost wished she could stare into those unusual eyes of his.

But when he spoke again, she realized his voice did the trick just fine too.

"Imagine your favorite actor is across from you, his hands on your knees."

Actor?

A half a dozen names crossed her mind, but their images were slippery and generic.

This isn't going to work.

"Got it?" Quinn asked gently.

"Yes," she lied.

"Good. Now imagine his hands are moving *up,* taking your skirt with them."

Ginnie tried, but the backs of her lids kept flooding with images of Quinn's lip ring and flashes of his dark tattoos.

"You with me, Ginnie?"

With him.

Yes, and that was a problem. No actor could do for her what the mere first glimpse of Quinn had done.

"Genevieve?"

Oh, and the way he said her full name with that perfect accent. It was far better than being the queen of her own sexy movie.

So she gave up. She let herself imagine *his* hands on her knees instead. And her breath caught immediately.

Now I'm here.

"It's working," she murmured.

"Good. Because your imaginary Romeo is having a hard time keeping his hands down near your thighs."

Ginnie could very easily visualize Quinn's thick fingers creeping eagerly under the synthetic fabric. Warm and firm against her skin.

She shivered, enjoying the fantasy.

"Try it now," Quinn said, his voice filling the tiny space with its rumble. "Let some of that imaginary, pent up sensuality out."

A low moan built in Ginnie's chest, and she didn't even realize she *had* let it out until Quinn affirmed its worth.

"Perfect, baby."

And now the endearment didn't bother her at all. In fact, she kind of liked it. She imagined him saying it again. Against her throat. Against her collar bone. Down where his imaginary hands were.

"Your fantasy man has leaned down," Quinn told her. "And even though his hands are busy – almost at your panties now – he wants a little more. So he's using his teeth to unbutton your shirt. All right?"

"Yes," Ginnie replied, hearing the eagerness in her reply and not caring at all.

She could practically feel Quinn's mouth working open the white buttons, practically hear his lip ring hit the plastic. Her chest tipped forward. Her breasts begged to be free for real.

"Oh, god," she groaned.

"Very good," Quinn said.

"So good," she agreed, her voice rising.

"He's got the top three undone, baby. But he's a little excited and he wants to see you. So you reach your own hands up to help him. You undo your bra. Quickly."

Ginnie slipped her hands from her thighs and gripped the edge of the sink so she wouldn't do it for real. God, how she wanted to. She actually wasn't sure she'd *ever* wanted something so badly.

And it's not even real.

She shoved down the thought.

"Tell him what you want," Quinn commanded. "He wants to hear it."

"More!" she demanded loudly, using the game as an excuse to express what she wanted to ask for in actuality.

"Anything you say." Quinn sounded pleased, and a little husky, too. "You bra is loose now, and you're so eager to be touched – to be tasted – that your breasts are aching. Throbbing with need, Ginnie. Do you want him to kiss them?"

"Please!" she cried.

She was sure that the whole plane must be able to hear her, and her natural instinct was to be embarrassed, to bite back the animalist sounds that wanted to leave her mouth.

No, she reminded herself. *This is the whole point.*

"His mouth finds your nipples – they're swollen and pink and perfect," he said. "And he sucks each of them slowly, while his fingers finally find the edge of your panties. He's glad they're lace because he can feel you underneath them as he strokes you overtop of them."

Ginnie's legs fell open, wetness soaking her real underwear as Quinn talked about the fake ones.

Holy shit.

How could Quinn not be feeling what she was feeling? Was it even possible?

"Soon, baby."

His soft comment brought her to the edge. She was too far gone to care. Her insides were coiled tightly, eager for release.

"One finger pushes the lace aside," Quinn said. "And the other…It slides inside of you, where you're hot and wet and ready to be touched."

Part of her couldn't believe he'd just said that. But most of her was so glad he had and wanted to hear more.

"It feels good, Genevieve."

Yes, it sure as hell did.

Unable to help herself, Ginnie tossed her head back and let out a cry.

"He wants you, Ginnie. Really fucking badly," he murmured.

"Yes!" she moaned.

"But this is about you, not him, and he's not a selfish man. So he thrusts that finger into you, just deep enough, just firm enough. His thumb gives your clit the attention it wants, circling around, bringing you closer and closer."

And Ginnie could feel it build.

Build.

And build.

And build some more.

"Now!" she commanded, completely losing herself in the fantasy. "Please!"

"All right, baby. He pushes into you, finding that sweet spot."

"Yes!"

The plane bounced, just hard enough to slam her right into Quinn, and under his jeans, his was diamond-hard, clearly as turned-on as she was. But Ginnie didn't have time to stop and think about what that meant. She was far too caught up in the moment.

Build. One final time. And release.

Ginnie's body exploded with pleasure, heat rocking her to her core. She shook with it.

Holy god.

Every part of her was pulsing. Spent. She could barely breathe. She wanted to collapse into Quinn's arms and stay there. Maybe cry a little. Definitely kiss a lot.

No way in *hell* had she ever experienced something like that. Not with Lawrence, not ever before.

Was it like that every time? She kind of wished she could just ask.

"Ginnie?"

Her eyes opened slowly. There he was. Shit. Why had she let herself get carried away like that, with him at the center of it? Why hadn't she pictured some rom-com actor like he'd suggested?

"You back with me now?" he wanted to know.

I never left you, she answered silently.

"I'm here," she managed to get out.

"That was the best fake sex I've ever had," Quinn stated.

Ginnie had recovered just enough to narrow her eyes at him. If he was mocking her, he was hiding it well. His heated gaze did rake over her body once – very quickly – then focused on her face again.

"Was it believable enough?" she asked, cringing because the question felt so deceptive.

"Incredibly believable. Actually…I feel like I should've bought you dinner first."

Ginnie flushed. She couldn't decide whether to be insulted, or flattered. The only thing she was sure of, was that she was glad he didn't seem to have noticed her own intense, momentary break with reality.

Thank God.

"You ready to face the masses?" Quinn wanted to know.

"You think they heard it?"

"I think they heard it. And I think the men are wishing they were me and the women are wishing they were you."

Definitely a compliment.

Ginnie inhaled. "Okay. I'm ready."

She started to slide to the floor, but Quinn stopped her.

"Wait. One more thing," he said.

"What's that?"

"Your underwear."

Ginnie frowned to cover the blush that crept up her cheeks. "What about them?"

"Take them off and give them to me."

"No!"

"Yes."

"Why?!"

Quinn smiled crookedly. "Because I'm going to go out first. And I'm going to drop those underwear on the floor directly in front of your former husband's seat."

It was brilliant. And devious. And the perfect climax to their little revenge plot.

Well. Second *most perfect climax,* she corrected mentally.

The only problem was…The underwear in question were thoroughly soaked from her not-so-fake-after-all orgasm.

She couldn't do it.

"Ginnie?"

"Yes?"

"If you don't take them off yourself, I'm going to take them off for you."

Ginnie's eyes widened. "You wouldn't."

But she knew he would. Maybe he even *wanted* to. God knows just minutes ago she would've been happy to let him.

"Better hurry," Quinn warned.

Quickly, Ginnie jumped from the counter to the ground and pulled the panties down to her knees without even lifting her skirt. Then she shimmied them down to her ankles, kicked them off one ankle, and angled the other foot up awkwardly to slip them off.

"Here," she muttered as she handed them over.

She was ridiculously glad she'd opted for a pretty pair of panties. Pink. New. Hole-free.

And lacy as hell.

But Quinn barely glanced at them. If he noticed their embarrassing dampness, he didn't say. He just balled them up in his meaty fist, making them disappear completely.

"Thanks, baby," he said teasingly.

"You're welcome. I think."

Quinn leaned in, kissed her lips with easy familiarity, and swung the door open.

"Remember. It's fine if you're blushing. It's fine if you look a little guilty. We *were* naughty, after all." He winked. "Just keep your head up when you hit *his* seat. Make sure you smile at him. See you in a minute."

Ginnie watched Quinn's receding back as he disappeared up the aisle, admiring its impressive width. In spite of her recent release, warmth crept up between her thighs again anyway. It got even worse – or was it better? – when she remembered she was panty-less. And the fact that those panties were in his hand...

She shook it off, and moved after him, walking slowly, hyper-conscious of her commando state.

She had no problem with the first two things he'd mentioned – the blush and the bit of shame. Her face was hot with embarrassment, and the heat doubled when a retirement-age couple gave her a knowing nod. And when a young mother with a toddler in her arms shot her a dirty look, her shoulders dropped guiltily too.

But when she hit Lawrence's row, she couldn't work up the nerve to even look at him. And she almost got past him without having to. Until his hand shot out unexpectedly and grabbed her wrist, giving her no choice but to face him.

"What the hell was that?" he demanded in a whisper.

Ginnie gave him and his question a cursory assessment.

He looked and sounded mad. Confused. And very, very jealous.

Yes! Quinn was right.

And Lawrence's other hand was closed tightly around something.

Her underwear.

Her former husband's hand was nowhere near as big as Quinn's, so the pink lace poked out everywhere.

"Ginnie, explain this!" he ordered.

She felt no compulsion to comply. In fact, his voice – and his touch – did nothing for her at all. They evoked almost no emotion, and the only physical reaction was something that bordered on revulsion.

Even the girl he was with – who currently had her head resting on Lawrence's shoulder and her hand right on his crotch while she snored away – didn't make Ginnie feel a thing.

I was in love with him, just three months ago. Wasn't I?

"Ginnie!"

Now she did meet his eyes, as she shook off his hand and replied coolly, "What the hell was *what*?"

"That display."

Ginnie bent down, making sure that Lawrence, and Lawrence alone, could hear her reply.

"I believe that's what they call *getting fucked.*"

Then she smiled a very sweet, very genuine smile, stood up again, tossed her hair over her shoulder, and flounced straight to First Class without looking back.

Eight

As Quinn waited for Ginnie to make her way back to the seat beside his, he didn't know if he was pleased with himself, or disappointed.

Probably both.

Okay, it had been his goal to get her genuinely going, but he was surprised at his success anyway. Quinn was damned sure that Ginnie's sweet, shuddering orgasm – created by his *words,* for God's sake – had been far from fake. Not that he couldn't dirty talk with the best of them. Hell. He'd received more than a few compliments on his abilities in the bedroom in the past so he knew he was a more than passable lover. A virtual orgasm with almost no touching at all, though?

Except for the end, when the plane propelled her forward and straight into his waiting body. She must've felt it. Realized how badly turned on he was.

I should still be in some kind of book of records, Quinn thought.

Then he shook his head.

She was either so tightly wound that an explosion like that was inevitable, or she was one hell of a faker.

Her mouth open just that little bit…Her eyes closed and her head thrown back. Utter release.

No one is that *good of an actress,* he thought.

Those gasps. Those moans.

Who the hell had she been picturing as it happened?

Quinn wished he hadn't planted the idea of using her celebrity crush as a source of eroticism.

Yeah, because you *want to be the one she was thinking of.* You *want to be the one making those soft, sexy panties all wet.*

There wasn't even a point in denying the internal accusation. The response was a resounding *hell yes.* He did want those things.

And there isn't anything wrong with that, he told himself.

He was a red-blooded, woman-loving man. Who hadn't seen any action in quite a while.

And Ginnie…

Well. Under that slightly prim, put-together appearance, she was hot as hell. Sexy, toned thighs. Perky breasts, pressing against the thin material of her blouse. Soft skin, soft hair, and soft, plump lips, made for kissing. Made for sucking.

Quinn adjusted a little uncomfortably in his seat. His erection – which hadn't seemed to subside since the second he laid eyes on Ginnie, if he thought about it – pressed insistently against his zipper.

Yeah, he wanted her all right. His body was a clear indication of his insistent need to set her free.

As though he could sense her entrance, his eyes flicked up to the divider between First Class and the rear of the plane just as she walked through. Her hair was still down, slick over her shoulders, and crowning her head like a halo.

Quinn sighed and muttered, "And *that's* what makes it wrong."

She had a bit of sass, but what Ginnie really *oozed* was niceness. Goodness. Politeness. Qualities which were probably compounded even more when she was in a normal state of mind and not led astray by Quinn and his bad habits and not-so-nice ideas. Qualities which Jase had hired him to protect.

He studied her as she paused to smile at and speak to one of the flight attendants, the brightness in her eyes evident even from where Quinn sat. The flight attendant nodded at Ginnie, and she looked to Quinn. She was full of post-imaginary-coitus sparkle. In fact, her face was glowing, and she even shot Quinn a happy-looking wave.

Jesus.

The orgasm he gave her shouldn't have been like that. It shouldn't have been kiss-free, hands-free…It shouldn't have happened for the first time in a bathroom stall, thirty-five thousand feet above ground. It shouldn't have happened because she wanted to punish her ex-husband. Ginnie sure as hell shouldn't think that's all there was to it. To him. She shouldn't be looking at him like he'd done something *nice* for her.

A lot of "shouldn'ts", Quinn thought, his tongue reaching for the comfort of his lip ring. *When what she needs are a lot of "shoulds".*

Like she *should* be with some guy who was planning on sticking around for more than a weekend. Who was capable of it.

"I'm an asshole," Quinn muttered as Ginnie got closer, and he saw that she was carrying four miniature bottles of champagne and two glasses gripped in her delicate fingers. "A really big asshole."

"It worked!" she announced gleefully.

She balanced the drinks on the wide armrest, then strapped herself into the seat, talking excitedly as she got settled and popped the bottles open.

"Lawrence – that's his name, I can't remember if I told you before – was royally pissed. Hopping mad. In all the time I was married to him, I don't think I ever saw him so angry. Not even when I destroyed the three-thousand dollar rug in his home office."

Who the hell had a three-thousand dollar rug?

Quinn forced a casual smile. "So he was jealous?"

Ginnie took a triumphant sip of champagne, and handed him a glass too. "*So* jealous. I had my doubts, but you were right Quinn. He even kept the underwear."

Quinn almost spat out his drink. "He *what*?"

"Kept them."

"Why'd you let him do that?"

Ginnie's face became quizzical. "Was I supposed to ask for them back?"

"Yes!"

"Why?"

"Because..." Quinn trailed off, not sure what to say.

Because I don't want that prick to be walking around with your panties, while true, seemed...inappropriate. Possessive.

Inappropriately possessive. Which was totally unreasonable on every level.

Ginnie was already moving past it, and she waved a hand dismissively. "I wouldn't wear them again anyway, not now that the two of you have manhandled them."

"Right," he muttered. "Manhandled panties are the worst."

Internally, Quinn gritted his teeth. He hated that she'd lumped him in with the douchebag. Even as a joke. Then he gritted them harder, annoyed with himself for letting it get to him in the first place. Clearly, his desire for the girl sitting with her knee pressed casually against his was clouding his ability to think straight.

"You know what?" Ginnie said, still smiling. "I know someone who would *love* this. He'd probably even *pay* to see it."

He?

Another prick of jealousy stabbed at Quinn, and even though he forced it aside, Ginnie picked up on his consternation immediately.

"What's wrong?" she asked.

Was he that easy to read? He'd always thought of himself as good – better than good – at assessing his audience, finding the right way to blend in. Hiding his true feelings.

Yeah, because you're good with drug dealers and scumbags. Not so much with pretty doctor's wives.

"Quinn?" she prodded.

Quinn tried to relax as he shot back his reply with a wink. "Nothing's wrong, baby."

"You're a liar. And I told you not to call me baby."

"You told me not to call you *hun*. Baby you seemed fine with," he corrected. "And I'm not sure what makes you think I'm lying."

"Oh, please," she scoffed. "Every time your tongue hits that lip ring of yours, I know you're thinking hard about *some*thing."

Quinn grinned and tried not to be distracted by the fact that she was so interested in what his tongue was up to. "Are you saying I have a tell... baby?"

She gave him an eye roll. "Yes."

Quinn tapped the ring with his tongue, sucked it for a second, then said, "Hmm. Maybe I should just take the damned thing out, then."

Ginnie's eyes fixed on his mouth for a moment, her own bottom lip visibly moist. "Don't."

Quinn stifled a groan. The way she exhaled the bossy little command had a hardline to his crotch.

"Why? You think I should leave it in so you can keep reading me so easily?"

She muttered something that sounded like, "I need *some* way to keep you in line."

Quinn stifled a chuckle and told a half-truth. "Nothing is *wrong*. I was just wondering what kind of *friend* would pay to watch you get hot and bothered just to piss of your husband."

She pursed those pretty lips of hers in a way that Quinn was sure was meant to cover a smile. Her own little tell.

"I think you mean *fake* hot and bothered."

Quinn shot her a sly grin. "You sure you didn't like that a little bit for real?"

"Are you sure *you* didn't like it?" she countered.

"No. I'm quite sure that I did, actually."

A flush crept up from under her tight collar, and she took a big gulp of champagne before answering.

"I was talking about my brother, actually. Jase hates Lawrence. He'd love to see him put in his place."

Jase.

Quinn had all but forgotten his obligation to the man. Guilt hit him in the gut, full force.

Paid to look out for her, but lusting after her instead.

"Brother?" he replied innocently.

"Yeah," Ginnie said. "My big, protective brother. A little too protective sometimes, actually."

No shit, Quinn thought. *He'd want to throttle me if he knew how I was thinking about you.*

And just like that, he realized that he needed to put the parameters back up. Quickly.

She was the target. He was the shield.

Be the undercover bodyguard you're being paid to be. Not the need-to-get-some-action fool. Jump into the role and see it through. No more thinking about putting her on a sink. Naked. Pants around your ankles and –

Quinn cut off his thoughts forcefully.

He just wasn't sure how the hell he was going to manage it. He needed her to like him, too. At least enough that she wouldn't send him packing before the end of the weekend.

What a place to be stuck. Between a rock and a...soft place.

"So," Quinn said slowly, "If big brother Jase is so protective, how come he let you take a trip to Vegas by yourself?"

She arched a critical eyebrow at him. "*Let* me?"

Quinn crossed his arms. "Uh huh. If I had a sister as sweet and pretty as you are...I doubt I'd let her out of my sight. Never know what kind of weirdos and perverts are out there."

She gave him a pointed look. "I think you know *exactly* what kind of weirdos and perverts are out there."

He grinned. "Hey. I'm not the one who enjoyed myself a little too much in bathroom."

Ginnie's face glowed pink, and for a second, Quinn thought he'd won this particular round. Or that he'd crossed a line. Then she snapped open her purse, pulled out a tiny bottle of airport-approved hand lotion, and held it out.

"What's that for?" Quinn wanted to know.

"For you."

"For me?"

"So you can go back to the bathroom and enjoy *your*self. And just FYI...your hands are a little rougher than you think they are."

Quinn narrowed his eyes and clicked his lip ring. He had a half-dozen snappy replies at the ready, but she didn't turn his way, and she was wearing a pleased, self-satisfied smile that he couldn't stand to wipe off her face.

You're a big, giant suck, Quinn.

Slowly, deliberately, he opened the bottle of lotion and sniffed it. Its scent was Ginnie's. Or at least the top layer of her heady, intoxicating smell. Quinn had been close enough to her to know that underneath that was a sweeter, feminine scent that was completely her own.

He took another big inhale, then squeezed out a generous dollop of lotion into his palms. He set the little bottle in his lap and began to rub his hands together. He did that slowly, too, for her benefit. She might be pretending not to look, but he was sure she was watching. So he worked the cream between his knuckles, across the backs of his hands, then up his wrists. There, he focused the rub into a lazy back forth motion reminiscent of one thing and one thing only.

You want auto-erotic, you get *auto-erotic,* he thought smugly.

He snuck a glance at Ginnie's profile.

Yep. Definitely paying attention. She'd sucked in her bottom lip and her chest was rising and falling a little quicker than was normal.

Quinn started to tell her she shouldn't dish it out unless she could take it, but the plane jerked abruptly, sending the remaining champagne flying.

Frightened cries – including a little yelp from Ginnie – erupted throughout the plane, and then the fasten seatbelts sign flashed, followed by the captain's voice over the loudspeakers.

"Attention passengers," he said, his words calm. "We've hit a large pocket of turbulence."

The plane bucked again, the speaker cut off, and a second generalized murmur of concern rose from the seats around them. The cabin vibrated heavily for several seconds, then smoothed out again. The calm only lasted for about twenty seconds before everything started to shake for a third, far longer period. Long enough that even Quinn got a little nervous.

His eyes sought Ginnie. Her face was frozen straight ahead, her body stiff, and Quinn forgot about his own worry.

"Hey," he said softly. "We're going to be fine."

She didn't look at him. "I *am* fine."

"You look a little tense."

"I'm fine," she insisted. "My dad was a pilot. I know exactly how safe we are."

"You dad was?"

"Yes. When I was a kid – back before my mom died – he used to take us all over the world. I think I must've missed a whole year of school over the course of my childhood."

Then she snapped her mouth shut and turned away, like she couldn't quite believe what she'd said.

Quinn was really tempted to ask a few questions. She had to be talking about her biological father. Which made Quinn very curious. In the time he shared a cell with Jase, the other man had spoken to him ad nauseam about the foster parents he shared with Ginnie. Dad worked construction, Mom was a book keeper. In all those conversations, Jase had never brought up his own biological parents, and he'd definitely never mentioned hers either.

He could feel the pain of the tiny bit she shared and Quinn wanted to know more.

So you can do what? Kiss it better?

The loudspeakers squawked, and the captain spoke again, still even-toned. "Sorry folks, but it looks like this turbulence is being caused by a very sudden, severe winter storm. We were hoping to skirt around it, but it's become unsafe to do so. As a precaution, we're going to be making an unscheduled stop at a small airport here in Huntingdon, Colorado. Your flight attendants will be through in a few moments to collect any trash or unwanted items. We should be on the ground within forty minutes. Further information on overnight accommodation and rescheduled flights will be available at the ticket desk in the airport. We do apologize for the inconvenience."

Before the captain even finished his speech, the cabin filled with noisy complaints.

Not that Quinn could blame them. Anyone on his or her way to a what-happens-in-Vegas weekend wouldn't be thrilled about losing a night of debauchery.

He stole another glance at his companion. She was looking a little green, and the hand closest to Quinn was opening and closing nervously.

And he didn't care what she said – something had clearly scared her.

Nine

The plane rumbled under Ginnie. It made her chair vibrate. Then it bumped hard enough to make her strain against her seatbelt.

And she was glad.

It gave her an excuse to keep her eyes forward and her mouth shut.

Which she needed help with. Apparently.

She had no clue why the comments about her parents had slipped out. She hadn't seen or heard from the man in over a decade, and she could count on one hand the number of times she'd brought them up voluntarily. Because Ginnie had one, simple – very solid – rule about discussing her biological parents.

Don't do it. Ever.

Even Jase, who knew nearly every little thing about her, wasn't well-acquainted with the early years of her childhood. And she liked it that way.

She'd overcome the troubles in her past. Just like she was about to overcome the ones in her present.

So why had she mentioned her mother at all, let alone the father she hated? Why had she used a man she hadn't seen since she was eleven years old as an excuse to not be affected by a bit of strong turbulence? She could've easily said that she and Lawrence flew all the time. Because that was true, too. Hawaii, Whistler. Even South America. They'd done plenty of travelling.

But she *hadn't* said any of that.

And that's what scared the shit out of her.

She cast a sidelong glance at Quinn.

His lids were down, but she had a funny feeling he was keeping his eyes closed for *her* benefit. To give her the space she needed in the claustrophobic state brought on by her offhand remarks about her dad being a pilot and her mom being dead.

Which was silly. Because how the hell would he even know that she needed the space?

Ginnie prided herself on being able to maintain a cool exterior under even the most strenuous circumstances. Like having her marriage forcibly ripped out from under her. With the exception of what she'd shared with Jase, she'd kept the details to herself. Kept her emotion in check.

Somehow, Quinn – a virtual stranger – made that impossible.

And for some reason, she also had to keep reminding herself that Quinn *was* a stranger. Because as much as his presence unnerved her – *well, unnerved her* body *anyway* – she also felt oddly at home with him. Warm. Easy. It made no sense at all.

Just like the way her body responded to him. To the sound of his voice. The way he'd brought her to the brink, then sent her over the edge, inside that tiny bathroom.

Unnaturally natural.

But she didn't want that undeniably satisfying physical encounter to be the reason she'd dropped her guard. It was ridiculous. Weak. Plenty of people had meaningless sexual escapades. Especially when a little under the influence, on vacation, and on the rebound.

But inside, Ginnie knew she wasn't most people.

She was a girl who had just discovered that her life had been barren of sexual satisfaction for twenty-four years. All the experience she'd built up with Lawrence had been…nothing. She'd been missing out. And Quinn had given her a glimpse of something better.

Even right that second, as the plane started its rapid decent, she had to fight an urge to reach out and clasp his open hand, which rested between them.

His well-moisturized hand.

God, had *that* been distracting.

His fingers working over the back of his hand. And the palm of his hand. Rubbing up against the nails and over the knuckles. Kneading and smoothing.

A trickle of renewed need wriggled through Ginnie, from her lips all the way down to her knees.

She could easily picture those hands of his working open the button of his jeans, reaching in to close around his erection. It would be supple and hard. And his hands would be smooth from the lotion she'd mockingly tossed his way. The perfect contrast.

The plane bumped to the ground, sending Ginnie's skirt flying, and as she remembered that she wasn't wearing any underwear, another image popped into her head. It was of herself, turning to Quinn, straddling him right then and there.

She closed her eyes, but it only made the vision more vivid.

Her thigh wrapped around his hips, his hands on her waist. His pierced tongue caressing her body. And the jostle of the plane, thrusting them together, again and again.

The trickle of desire threatened to become a raging river.

"Ginnie?"

"Shit!"

The enticing vision flew away as Ginnie realized that Quinn's eyes were open now, and he'd fixed her with a half-concerned, half-amused smile. "You all right?"

"Yes!" *It wasn't quite a gasp. Was it?* "Why wouldn't I be all right?"

"Because I just said your name and the response was a curse?"

"I thought you were sleeping. You startled me."

"Uh huh," he replied, disbelief clear in his voice. "Just so you know, …they announced a full minute ago that we're allowed to get off the plane now."

A full minute?

Ginnie glanced around and saw that First Class was nearly empty already. Even the flight attendants seemed to be missing.

"You're a very bad First Class passenger," Quinn observed, still sounding amused. "We're supposed to be allowed to priority deplane."

Ginnie narrowed her eyes. "If we're allowed to get off the plane, how come *you're* still sitting there?"

Quinn's smile grew. "Maybe I was waiting for you."

"Or maybe you were just waiting to use that line."

"Only one way to find out. Get up and see if I follow you."

In spite of the way she screamed at it not to, Ginnie's heart skipped a beat. She unbuckled her seatbelt, came to her feet, and looked down at Quinn, her arms crossed over her chest.

"Hmm. Now it looks more like *I'm* waiting for *you*," she stated.

Quinn stood up, too, his wide body taking up most of the space between the seats. He lifted his arms up in a lazy stretch. It provided a momentarily distracting view of one lean hip.

Dammit.

"Still waiting," Ginnie said, forcing her eyes up to his face.

"Just the way I like it."

"Ha."

Ginnie spun away and marched up the aisle, but Quinn was hot on her heels. Literally. She could feel his warmth as he followed closely behind her.

His hand found her elbow, stopping her hurried flight. Familiar. Possessive. Enticing.

Heart-thumping-ly terrifying.

"You making big plans here in Asscrack, Colorado?" he asked.

"I think the pilot said it was called *Huntingdon*," Ginnie corrected dryly.

"The pilot also said we were going to Vegas," he reminded her. "So I'm not sure we can trust him to be right about *any*thing. And if you don't have big plans..."

"My plans involve pajamas and a hot bath."

Quinn's eyes dragged over her, and Ginnie warmed. Was he picturing her in her pajamas? Or in the bath? If he was...Did he like what he saw?

His gaze steadied after a second, and he winked. "You sure you won't be needing me again?"

"Again?" she countered. "I wasn't aware that I needed you in the first place."

"Right. I forgot that you have your lotion."

"The lotion doesn't do it for me."

It wasn't what Ginnie intended to say. She'd meant to vehemently deny any kind of need whatsoever. And Quinn picked up on the slip right away.

Without warning, he slid his hand from her elbow to her wrist, twisted her sideways, and pushed her against a row of seats. He pressed his body flush against hers.

Ginnie glanced up and down the aisle. They were alone.

Where had all the other passengers gone? And where were the damned flight attendants? Where was her shield against the intensity in Quinn's amber eyes?

"Genevieve?"

"Yes?" she whispered.

"What *does* do it for you? What *do* you need?" he asked, soft and sexy.

Ginnie swallowed nervously. "Need is a strong word.""

"Now who's arguing semantics?" he teased.

"I'm not – " She cut herself off and tried again. "I don't need anything."

"So you didn't need me back there in that bathroom? You merely *wanted* me?"

"Has anyone ever told you that you're pretty damned good at twisting people's words?"

"Yep."

"Are you going to let me go anytime soon?"

He inched closer. "Nope."

"No?"

"Not until you agree to indulge my desire to hang out with you here in Asscrack."

"You realize how wrong that sounds?"

"Yep."

"And if I say *no* to indulging you?"

"I'll follow you around until you have no choice but to say yes instead."

"I'm pretty sure that even Asscrack, Colorado must have a law against stalking."

He grinned a lopsided grin. "And *I'm* pretty sure I can find my way around that law."

Ginnie shook her head. "I should've known the second I laid eyes on you."

"Known what?"

"That you were a criminal."

He reached up to trace a lazy finger down her cheek. "Would that bother you? If I was on the wrong side of the law?"

"Yes."

It was a lie. At that moment, she wouldn't have cared if he was a trained assassin, out for her blood. All she wanted was for his hand to continue its gentle ministrations. Cupping her cheek, sliding to the back of her neck...Then those fingers of his found her jugular and she knew he must be able to feel the way her pulse was thrumming.

"You sure about that answer?" he asked teasingly.

No.

The word popped into her mind. But it didn't make it out. Quinn's palm slid to her chin and his lips crashed into hers and his tongue drove through her mouth in a ferocious exploration that made Ginnie's head spin and her toes curl.

But its intensity was short-lived.

Quinn jerked back, and Ginnie's eyes flew open to see a thick hand on his arm, yanking him away. A firm but authoritative voice accompanied the aggressive maneuver.

"If I were you, I'd keep my mouth shut and my eyes to myself. And let go of the girl. Quickly."

A protest built up in Ginnie's throat, but died quickly when Quinn gave her a quick headshake as his arms dropped to his sides.

Why?

He didn't seem like the kind of guy who would just lie back and take it. Whatever *it* was.

And then Ginnie got a full view of the man who'd issued the warning.

He was a cop.

Or something like it. An airport official with a uniform and a sidearm and a two-way radio fastened to his shoulder and a patch on his chest that said is name was Gilligan. TSA, maybe. Probably.

And when he moved slightly, Ginnie realized he wasn't alone, either. Three other men accompanied him. Two stood back with their hands resting a little too casually close to their weapons. And a final one, who reached for Ginnie, closed a none-too-gentle fist on her elbow, and pulled her even further away from Quinn.

And she was too surprised – and too scared – to protest as the tight-lipped guards stepped between them – deliberately she thought – and shuffled them from the plane.

No one said a word as they marched down the stairs directly onto the tiny tarmac. The ground was coated with snow, and it still fell from the sky. The blank scenery and the cold air momentarily distract Ginnie.

Asscrack, Colorado.

And they really did seem to be in the middle of nowhere. Unlike the airport she'd come from, and presumably the one where she was supposed to be headed, there were no twinkling city lights on display. The only sign of civilization was a few dull glows in the distance.

She paused for a second to stare out at the nothingness, and the airport security man gave her an impatient tap on the shoulder.

"Move," he grunted.

All this? Seriously? For a little bathroom action? What are they going to do, throw us in jail? Shit. What if they do throw us in jail? What if we're labeled as sex offenders? Shit with a cherry on top. If I get a police record because of this...Maybe they'll just fine us. But what if it's a big fine? Like, hundred grand. I don't have *a hundred thousand dollars to...*Ginnie's thoughts trailed off as they got closer to the rundown air terminal, she saw that what they didn't lack was an audience. A line of passengers from the plane stood waiting at a counter. And every one of them had his or her eyes fixed out the window, gawking at them.

Ginnie scanned the crowd, automatically seeking out Lawrence. It only took a second to find him. There he was, the brunette wrapped around him, her face pressed into his neck. And he was looking right at Ginnie. And her unwelcome entourage.

Immediately, Ginnie's face flamed. A smile – visible even from the distance between – tipped up her former husband's mouth, making Ginnie's feet begin to drag. Then they stopped moving completely once again.

The guard on her arm gave her a little pull, but she couldn't make herself respond. He shoved her a bit harder, making Ginnie's feet slip.

And a snarl from Quinn let her know that at last he'd reacted.

Ten

Truthfully, Quinn had been holding in his fury and frustration since the second the short, stout man named Gilligan had grabbed him.

Not because the man wore a gun he could probably yield, and not because TSA was the shit at the airport – and they were probably *more* than the shit at this tiny terminal – and sure as hell not because he was scared of any of them.

It was something more refined.

Professional courtesy. Respect.

Simple as that.

Even though it sucked to be hauled from the plane. Even though he hated the way the passengers were scrutinizing them as it happened. Even though the other man's hand on Ginnie's arm was making him crazy, he *continued* to hold it in. He'd decided to wait until they got inside, wait until they were out of the public eye, then speak to them calmly. Like colleagues. Like equals. Work out just what the hell was going on. He knew he'd have an easier time of convincing them to tell him if he played nice.

But Quinn didn't get a chance to follow through on his plan. Halfway across the tarmac, he saw the guard shove Ginnie, and the girl stumbled.

What the hell?

It was too much. His self-restraint and his training could only take him so far before protective instinct took over.

Yeah, it was stupid and reckless. Yeah, it was get-yourself-shot-in-the-ass-worthy.

Quinn knew it and he didn't care.

Instead, he let emotion rule, allowed it to guide his actions as he spun away from the half-assed hold his own guard had on his arm and dove toward the man holding Ginnie.

In a heartbeat, Quinn had him pulled close to his body, had his gun out of his holster, and had dropped the weapon to the icy ground.

Not so tough now, are you, jackass?

His smugness at his own quick move only lasted a moment. A click behind him told him that one of the other guards had drawn a gun, and the little whimper from Ginnie told him the man must have it trained in his direction. Then a rough grip closed on his collar and yanked him off.

The first guard – Gilligan – spoke in a low, measured tone, right at Quinn's ear. "We're a small town, and right now we have an audience. Not to mention that half those nitwits watching us also probably have their cell phones on video mode. I don't want the bad publicity, so I'm not going to consider firing. But *you* don't want to try my goodwill, either, so you're going to step *back* from Mr. Jones, you're going to step *between* Mr. Riles and Mr. Farisi, and the three of you are going to walk into the airport. *I* will take Mrs. Michaels in separately. Are we clear?"

The man's use of the word *I* instead of the word *we* placated Quinn. At least for the moment. So long as Jones-the-Asswipe kept his hands off of Ginnie.

"Are we clear?" Gilligan repeated.

"Clear," he agreed gruffly.

Quinn stepped back, cursed his unusual lack of control, and shot Ginnie an apologetic look. Whatever was going on was likely his fault. She was holding very still, her face a mask of impassivity, an emotional wall up.

Shit.

Quinn tried to take a step toward her and Gilligan held him in place. Quinn automatically bucked against being restrained, and when he tried to yank himself away, the other man slapped a pair of cuffs onto his wrists. Tight. Then he pushed Quinn to the snowy ground and shot him a frown.

"Dr. Michaels," Gilligan said calmly. "I thought you told me we were clear."

Quinn flipped his head toward the other man.

"I'm not Dr. Michaels," he snapped.

For the first time, the guard looked a little put out. "You're not Dr. and Mrs. Lawrence Michaels?"

"Do I look like a fucking doctor?" Quinn countered.

"In my business, experience has taught me that looks are often deceiving," Gilligan replied.

Then Ginnie spoke up. "I'm Genevieve Michaels. But Quinn's not my husband."

Why the hell did those words make Quinn want to punch something? Why did the tremor of embarrassment in her voice make him feel so furious?

"You wanna tell me who you *actually* are, then?" Gilligan asked.

"Nobody, apparently," Quinn muttered, just barely shy of bitter.

Gilligan sighed irritably, then nodded toward one of the other officers, who moved forward to reach into Quinn's pocket and pull out his wallet. He held it open for Gilligan, who scanned it. His eyes went from Quinn to the ID, then back again.

"All right," he said with another sigh. "Mr. *Mcdavid*, you're with Fasiri and Mrs. Michaels is with me. Jones and Riles, you can head back to your stations."

As the senior officer stepped close to Fasiri to issue some hushed instructions, Quinn's eyes sought Ginnie. Her expression was now completely unreadable, and she refused to look at him.

"I'll fix this," Quinn vowed. "I'll sort it out and find you."

As soon as the promise was out of his mouth, he realized he meant it. He had to protect her. Far more than he had to keep his commitment to Jase. Quinn was damned sure that he was directly responsible for the stiff way Ginnie held herself. The fiasco in the bathroom was his fault, and he was determined to undo it. As soon as possible.

Then the guard assigned to handle Quinn finished speaking to Gilligan, grabbed the cuffs and pulled him to his feet, then slapped his hand onto the back of Quinn's neck, and began to guide him roughly across the remainder of the tarmac. He didn't release him, even when they were well-within the terminal. Instead, he led Quinn through the airport and past the little crowd gathered there. Then kept going even farther. Across the dated linoleum floor, wide around the baggage carousel, and all the way to a corridor marked *Emergency Exit* in bold red letters. They took a few steps into the hall, then finally stopped.

Quinn's anger dissipated into momentary confusion, and he frowned. "What the hell is this?"

"Waiting on instructions," Fasiri told him.

"Here?"

"I just do what I'm told." Then the guard snapped his mouth shut and focused his gaze anywhere but Quinn.

Conversation over.

Quinn tapped his lip ring, frustration nearly overriding common sense once again. He'd been on both ends of this deal before, and he knew the stoic-faced guard wouldn't be budging on his silence any time soon.

If it was Jones-the-Asswipe…

That would've been a different story. Self-important people like that guy – criminal *or* cop – could be goaded into giving away almost anything. It almost made Quinn wish Gilligan had sent the hothead with him instead of Fasiri.

Just a minute or two went by, and then a nervous-looking flight attendant approached them, Quinn's bag in tow. She set it down, then hurried away. Quinn's eyes flicked from his luggage to the retreating woman's back, then to the guard.

They're letting you go.

Which made no sense. Quinn's frown deepened and he bit his lip hard enough to hurt.

"What the *hell* is this?" he repeated, sounding as puzzled as he felt.

"This is us, keeping our town safe."

The statement came from behind Quinn, and he spun to see that Gilligan had joined them again. He stood just a couple of feet away, his arms crossed.

He was noticeably alone. No Ginnie. No Jones-the-Asswipe, either.

Worry spiked Quinn's temper and his jaw tightened. "Where the – "

Gilligan cut him off. "Relax, Mcdavid. Mr. Jones is still occupied, and Mrs. Michaels is in holding, supervised by one of our female TSA officers."

"She's – what?"

Gilligan inclined his head toward the other guard, and Fasiri took his silent order in stride, disappearing back up the corridor. Once they were out of sight, the stocky agent dropped his arms and moved so that his body blocked the way back into the main part of the terminal.

"Mrs. Michaels is going to be questioned in regards to some items in her baggage. *You* on the other hand, are being escorted to the hotel."

"She's not really *Mrs. Michaels,*" Quinn corrected irritably, clueing in for the first time that whatever this was, it might have little to do with him. "She's *Miss* Silver. And there's no way in hell she has anything questionable in her bags."

"You know her well?"

Quinn considered lying, then thought better of it. He was dug in far enough. No need to hand the TSA a shovel.

"No," he replied. "We actually just met."

"So you weren't travelling together, then?"

"Not officially."

"Unofficially?"

"I thought you weren't holding me."

"We're not." Gilligan's voice remained impassive, but he also showed no sign of letting Quinn go by.

"So you're not holding me, but you're questioning me?"

Gilligan echoed Quinn's own words. "Not officially."

"And you're not going to let me talk to her?"

"No."

Quinn ran a frustrated hand over the buzz-cut side of his head. "What the hell could you possibly want with her?"

"Do you know her husband?"

"*Former* husband. And also no."

What the hell did that douchebag have to do with this particular situation anyway?

Gilligan wasn't telling him. "Those tattoos of yours...They have a special meaning? The knife, maybe?"

Quinn refused to allow himself to lift his hand to cover the dagger on his wrist. There was no shame in the life that he'd lived. Everything he'd done had been in pursuit of justice.

"Don't worry. I'm retired," he stated.

"I'm aware. And if I believed that you posed a threat, I wouldn't be ushering you out the door."

"Then why *are* you trying to get rid of me?"

Gilligan shrugged. "I'm thorough. I have good access to records. And yours tells me your loyalties are skewed, your temper is hot, and keeping you around would just plain be a bad idea."

Quinn narrowed his eyes. Was the man implying he knew something about his undercover role?

Unlikely. But also not the point of this conversation, he reminded himself.

"Where's Ginnie?"

"I'm not at liberty to disclose any further information, Mr. Mcdavid."

"Of course you aren't," Quinn muttered, then added, "Who *is* at liberty?"

"No one."

"Then I'm staying right here until you're done with her."

The TSA officer sighed, showing his first true sign of impatience. "Listen to me, Mr. Mcdavid. You may think you landed your ass in some Podunk town and that I'm some hick cop with little to no authority over you, but you're wrong. Just the fact that you laid a hand on one of my colleagues give me reasonable cause to toss you in lockup."

"Wouldn't be my first time behind bars," Quinn retorted.

Gilligan crossed his arms and said softly, "No. But it would be the first time you were behind bars and your *roommates* were aware of your actual occupation. And we don't have a big place here. Just a wide open cell. Wanna guess how long you'd last in there once they found out how little allegiance you have to that tattoo of yours?"

So the man did know about the police work. And about Quinn's association with the gang. He was eight steps ahead of everyone else, then.

How had he found out? The records were sealed.

Then a very recent, very irresponsible memory crashed down on Quinn.

The ticket agent. The goddamned retirement-issue badge.

Right. Quinn had whipped it out – and not in a flash-her-from-behind-a-trench-coat kinda way either.

Shit. Yet again.

Quinn knew perfectly well how convicts dealt with cops, and he sure as hell didn't have a death wish.

Could he leave Ginnie, though? Even to protect himself? Not that he'd be any good to her if he was bleeding out on a concrete floor in some small-town jail.

The bigger question was…Would this guy *actually* rat him out? He didn't have the high-on-power vibe that Jones-the-Asswipe gave off, but he was quietly authoritative. More genuine.

Yeah, he'd turn you in, Quinn decided as he examined the other man's cool expression. *But he might feel bad about it.*

Which Quinn could relate to.

Damn.

This thing with Ginnie, a girl he barely knew, was throwing him the curviest of curve balls. He opened his mouth to tell Gilligan he would take his chances, but the other man beat him to it.

"I'm not unappreciative of the service you've done, Mcdavid, and I can tell that even though you just met this woman, you care what happens to her." Gilligan's expression lost its hard edge for just a second, but returned quickly. "But let's be real here. You don't know her, she doesn't know you, and neither of you owes the other a thing. And I have a job to do. A job I think you understand. And you can't tell me a man in your position hasn't made a decision that puts career and public safety over personal wants a dozen times."

Quinn ground his teeth together. Every word of what the other man said was true, even if he didn't want it to be. Quinn *did* understand. He'd become a cop because he respected the law and wanted to uphold it. Of course, he'd also become a cop to protect the innocent. His current situation wasn't the first that made doing both seem im-fucking-possible.

The agent went on. "Listen...I'm willing to offer you my word that I will personally deal with Genevieve Michaels, that I'll personally look out for her until this thing is resolved. And you...You can do what you want and give us both a headache. Or you can do what you *should* do and save me the trouble of arresting you."

Quinn considered the other man's suggestions as if they were viable options.

Walking away felt wrong. Charging in and breaking laws felt right.

But it won't do any damned good.

Then Gilligan asked a question that made his decision a little easier. "She know you're a cop? And what things you've done in that capacity?"

"No," Quinn admitted.

"You want her to?"

For one second, Quinn thought the other man was threatening to tell her. Then he realized he was merely making a point. Just off the top of his head, Quinn could think of a dozen things he'd hate for her to hear about. A dozen things that would turn her stomach. Make her wish she'd never met him. He might not be ashamed of his past, but it wasn't exactly wine-and-cheese conversation material, either.

What the hell had he been thinking, dragging her anywhere near that?

It's not what *you were thinking,* he corrected. *It's what you were thinking* with.

There was still time to undo what he'd done to her, though. All he had to do was walk away.

And just like that, Quinn made the decision. A clean break. One of the things that made him good at working undercover, at working in situations that required quick thinking and a detachment from emotion.

Pretending not to feel a nagging sense of doubt – pretending not to feel anything at all – Quinn snapped up his bag, and met Gilligan's eyes with an unwavering stare.

"Is someone outside, waiting to take me to the hotel?" he asked.

"Dark hair, navy blue suit," the TSA officer confirmed.

Quinn strode down the hallway and pushed through the exit without looking back.

Eleven

Ginnie worked at keeping her eyes from flitting around the little room nervously. In the too many minutes since the airport guard had left her alone, she'd already noticed that the table was bolted to the floor, that the door had no inside handle, and that there was no clock on the yellow-stained walls. And she was pretty sure that the big mirror straight across from her was one of the one-way kind. She felt like she'd walked straight into an eighties cop show.

And somehow I'm on the wrong side.

And speaking of wrong sides...What had they done with Quinn? What was he telling them?

When he'd dived for the man holding her, she'd had a weird, hopeful moment. One where she'd pictured the big, tattooed man scattering the airport police like bowling pins, then sweeping Ginnie off her feet – literally. And then the two of them had gone running off, Bonnie and Clyde style. Into hiding. Maybe holing up in some hotel somewhere with nothing to do but –

Ginnie cut off her thoughts before they could go any further.

"What is *wrong* with me?" she muttered under her breath.

Before she could stop herself, Ginnie glanced up to the mirror in an attempt to see if the change was something visible.

I look like hell.

Her hair was a nightmare of curls, loose around her shoulders and damp from the melting snow. This morning before leaving the house, she'd meticulously applied just enough product to tame its wildness. But any trace of the smooth ponytail was gone. Destroyed by Quinn's strong fingers. Made worse by the walk through the storm.

Ginnie's clothes were askew, too. The top two buttons of her blouse had come undone, exposing a glimpse of her collarbone, and throwing off her usually prim appearance even more. A flush had settled under her skin, and she wasn't certain if it was a result of her current incarceration, her thoughts of Quinn, or the change in temperature – warm, then cold, and now almost stifling. Either way, the brightness of her cheeks showed no signs of settling down.

I look like hell, Ginnie thought again. *But…in a good way.*

She wasn't sure what made it true, and she stared at her reflection a few seconds longer, trying to figure it out.

One of her hands came up to smooth something – *anything* – back into place. Instead, her fingers found a loose strand of hair, wrapped around it, twisted it up, then let it drop again. The curl landed softly against her throat and teased its way to the gap in her blouse.

Inexplicably, the sight of the gold tendril against her skin sent a rush through her.

What had *Quinn* seen, when he freed her hair? A glimpse of the wantonness that now seemed to dominate Ginnie's features? Something that made him push her up against the seat in the airplane and tear into her mouth with his own?

Ginnie's breath caught as the tingle under her skin flourished, and she forced her eyes away from the (really, seriously possibly one-way) mirror.

God. You're locked up for having sex on an airplane – but not really having sex at all – and still all you're thinking about is sex.

She placed her hands back on the bolted-down table and folded her fingers together, then crossed her legs in an attempt to resume a demure appearance. But the motion reminded her that her underwear weren't where they should be, and her mind slipped to the way Quinn had seemed so annoyed by the fact that she'd left them in Lawrence's possession.

And Ginnie realized that she wasn't just thinking about sex. She was thinking about sex. And Quinn.

Just buy a damned vibrator and get over it.

The thought was so unexpected that Ginnie snorted a laugh.

But maybe she really would do it. Maybe when she got to Vegas, she would pop into the first sex shop she saw, and buy the biggest, shiniest one she could find.

Wait. Did they come in shiny?

Does it matter?

She was going to lock herself in her hotel room and find out what else she'd been missing.

If she ever made it to Vegas, and didn't just wind up in prison in Huntingdon instead. Although if what she'd seen on TV was true, and she *did* get sent to prison, she'd get a whole other kind of sex education pretty damned quick.

Oh, good. Now you're not thinking about sex with Quinn. You're thinking about vibrators and lesbian sex with fellow inmates instead.

She really needed to get a grip. She was going to have a hell of a time convincing the authorities her Mile High encounter had been an act if she was squirming like this.

"What's taking them so long, anyway?"

Ginnie jumped as the door swung open and a dry voice answered the question she hadn't meant to ask aloud.

"Sorry, Mrs. Michaels. We're just not accustomed to processing potential felonies here in Huntingdon."

Ginnie whipped around to face the security officer. It was the same one who'd intervened when Quinn grabbed the man who pushed her. The same one who'd locked her in the room in the first place. Gilligan. And he looked totally serious.

"Felonies?" Ginnie repeated, trying her damnedest to keep the worry from her voice.

Ginnie's eyes followed the stocky man as he crossed the room. When he seated himself across from her and gave her a short nod, a cold sweat broke out on her upper lip.

"Felonies," Gilligan confirmed.

Was sex in public a felony? It couldn't be. Could it?

"You're in a serious amount of trouble," the airport official told her.

"But it wasn't even real!" Ginnie gasped. "I swear."

"I know."

"You – what? What did Quinn tell you?"

Gilligan shrugged. "He had nothing *to* tell us. He couldn't have known ahead of time what you were planning."

"What *I* was planning?"

The agent sighed. "All right, Mrs. Micheals, let's start there, then. Even a fake one, undeclared, is considered an offence."

Undeclared? What did that mean? And wait a second…He'd said a fake *one.* Which meant he was talking about her orgasm. Which hadn't actually been fake at all. *Shit.* He had to be lying about Quinn telling them nothing. Which meant that Quinn knew and…*Oh god.* Could someone actually die of embarrassment?

"It was so real even I was fooled," Gilligan added.

At those words, Ginnie's face heated up, and her mouth snapped shut. He'd been there, on the plane, listening.

"Do you have anything to say?" Gilligan prodded.

"Not particularly," Ginnie stated, her voice sounding a little faraway to her own ears.

"I think telling me what happened would be best."

He wanted *details?* This was a nightmare. The worst kind of humiliation.

But under that, a spark of anger was lighting.

"Quinn didn't take *any* responsibility?" Ginnie asked.

"No. But we know you weren't travelling together, so we had no reason to hold him responsible."

"Where is he now?"

"You should be thinking about yourself, not him."

"Where *is* he?" Ginnie repeated, the seed of fury growing.

"He's left the airport, Mrs. Michaels."

So he really had thrown her under the bus.

Fine, she thought. *I can do that, too.*

"It was his idea," she announced.

"His idea?" Now Gilligan was frowning at her.

"Yes!"

"But you had never met before today?"

"No."

Gilligan shook his head. "Back it up, Mrs. Michaels. I feel like I'm missing something."

"Quinn thought having a fake – you know – was a good way to get revenge on my husband."

The TSA officer leaned forward. "And how were you going to *get* that revenge?"

"Um…Loudly?"

"And he was going to help you?"

"He *did* help me."

"Tell me…When – precisely – did you meet Quinn Mcdavid?"

"Right before I got on the plane."

"So this was before you checked your luggage."

Ginnie shook her head. "After."

"So how did he put it in there then?"

Ginnie just about choked on her next breath. "How did he – he *didn't*. I told you…It was fake. I had a few drinks, got in an argument with the flight attendant, and there was Quinn."

My knight in shining ink. Yeah, so much for that.

"Are you sure it was just a *few* drinks?" Gilligan asked.

Ginnie shot him an indignant glare. "There's no law against getting tipsy. And I'm not even sure there's a law against airplane sex. So if you're not going to…" She trailed off as the officer's eyebrows shot up so far that they disappeared into his hairline. "What?"

Gilligan jumped to his feet and rapped on the mirror.

Ha! Ginnie thought. *One-way. I* knew *it.*

Seconds later, the door swung open once again, and another TSA agent came in, rolling a familiar, black and grey bag behind him. He lifted the luggage, set it at the edge of the table, then exited silently.

"Recognize this?" Gilligan asked as soon as the door was closed.

"It's my bag."

"Yes, it is."

The TSA agent stood up and unzipped the suitcase. Then he flipped the top open and pushed it toward Ginnie, whose face reddened immediately. The contents was a mess of lace and silk and was that a pair of handcuffs? And a big, plastic police badge attached to a distinctly blue shirt. And yes, it looked like vibrators did indeed come in *shiny*.

She reached up and shoved the bag a bit farther away.

"That's not – " But Ginnie cut herself off as the stuff in the bag shifted and she spied a plastic evidence bag and *its* contents.

A gun. What the hell?

Gilligan reached in and yanked the bag out. He held it up.

"*This* is the fake I was talking about," he said. "I don't know how it got missed in the bigger airport, but it was the first thing we saw when it came through our screening department. So, Mrs. Michaels…Do you have something to say now?"

Ginnie's gaze strayed back to the suitcase. Leather. Lace. Toys. A police costume and a gun.

And then Ginnie figured it out.

"It's a prop," she blurted.

"A prop?"

Ginnie was sure that every drop of blood in her body had managed to settle in her face. "For the, uh, bedroom."

Gilligan blinked once. "I see."

Great, Ginnie thought. *Now I'm a woman who has fake sex on airplanes* and *carries fetish items wherever she goes.*

Except the bag wasn't actually hers. It just *looked* like hers. Exactly like it.

Very quickly, she scanned the tag attached to the suitcase. *L.W. Michaels.*

Oh. Ew.

"Mrs. Michaels?"

Ginnie brought her eyes back to the airport guard. Should she tell him that the bag really wasn't hers? Or would it just create a headache and generate paperwork and stall her even further? Would he even believe her? She knew who the…err…items belonged to. And Lawrence would definitely recognize Ginnie's own stuff the second he unzipped her real suitcase. He was more than familiar with her standard look of crisp blouses and tidy skirts.

And there was the added humiliation factor to consider.

Sorry officer, that bag isn't mine after all. It belongs to my former husband's hoochie. Looks like they were gonna get kinky. My bad.

No. Far too embarrassing.

And the TSA officer wasn't quite done yet anyway.

He reached into his pocket and yanked out a second evidence bag, this one full of slips of papers.

"These," he stated, "Concern me even more than that replica."

Ginnie squinted at the red-tinted bag.

The look like…Prescription pads. What the hell?

"Are those Lawrence's?" she asked.

"You tell me."

Ginnie took a breath and put on her game face. "Were they in my bag?"

"They were. And I'm sure your husband is aware that he'd be violating several laws if he used these inappropriately."

I'm sure he would, Ginnie thought, then wondered, *Is this still so embarrassing that you'll get arrested on Lawrence's behalf? Just turn him in for…Whatever dumb thing he was up to.*

But she wouldn't do it. She wouldn't stoop to his level. What she needed was to stay cool, calm, and collected, and talk her way out of this situation.

She knew she could do it. She was good with words, when she put her mind to it. The past couple of hours had just temporarily clouded her memory. Clouded her course.

"I'm really sorry," she said slowly. "But there's been a misunderstanding. Lawrence and I aren't travelling together any more than Quinn and I are."

The agent pursed his lips. "Who *are* you travelling with, Mrs. Michaels?"

"Myself."

"Yourself?"

Ginnie lifted her chin. "I can't be the first recently divorced woman to head to Vegas for a wild weekend."

"I suppose not. But you're travelling alone, and your husband just happened to be on the same flight? Seems a little too coincidental to be true."

Ginnie sighed. "You're telling me. But my husband and I *did* book this trip together, and apparently both decided not to lose out on what we paid for."

"And he just happened to leave a giant stack of his prescriptions in your bag?"

"We shared a life for five years, so some of his things are bound to have been mixed up with mine."

Gilligan should her a dubious look from across the table. "Some things?"

"Do I need a lawyer, Mr. Gilligan?"

Gilligan looked at her like he was carefully considering both her words and her expression. Ginnie sensed that he was swaying in her favor. She smiled – not smugly, but agreeably.

"I suppose not," he finally said.

Ginnie let out a mental breath. "And I apologize for the fake gun. I truly didn't realize it was something I had to declare."

"Both the real thing and replicas need to be identified at check in."

"Now I know."

"Now you do," Gilligan replied, still examining her as he tapped his fingers on the table. "Huntingdon is a safe community."

"I get that."

"No one – including me – is happy about this little waylay from Sin City."

"No."

"And I'd prefer for all of this to be over quickly."

Ginnie nodded. "Me, too."

"I'll need to keep the prescriptions."

"Please do."

"Is it safe to assume that you'll declare the gun next time? Or better yet…Leave it behind altogether?"

"Yes! And if you need to confiscate it too, that's fine."

And even if you don't…I'm tossing the damned thing out the second I get away from here.

Gilligan tapped his fingers on the table, then turned, nodded toward the one-way mirror, and face Ginnie once more. The door squealed open, and relief made her entire body sag.

Gilligan zipped up the bag, then pushed it toward her.

"We'll let it go," he said. "Chalk it up as something for the bloopers reel."

"Thank you."

Eager to get out before he could change his mind, Ginnie rose to her feet and snagged the handle of the suitcase, then dropped it down and took a step toward the door. Gilligan's voice made her pause, one foot out and one foot in.

"Mrs. Michaels?"

"Yes?"

"The other thing you claim that you were faking…You may want to consider leaving *that* behind, too."

Ginnie's face flamed as she nodded.

No way would she be doing that again. Especially not with Quinn, who she damned well hoped she never laid eyes on again.

With her mind stewing and her stomach churning, Ginnie made her exit as swiftly as dignity would allow.

Twelve

Quinn kicked off his boots and sunk his toes into the area rug under his bed. He was trying his damnedest to settle into the hotel room. Which was decidedly hard considering that he felt a bit like he was being held under lock and key.

He might've left behind the stone-faced man who led him to the hotel door, but he had a feeling that if he made a move – back toward the airport, in particular – the guy wouldn't be far behind.

Might as well have settled for an overnight in lockup, he thought irritably.

Truthfully, he probably *would* have felt more comfortable in jail. Or just about anywhere with a little less curb appeal and a little more grit. Some place where he'd feel a little more at home and not like if he bumped something the wrong way, it was going to fall and break.

He shot another critical look around the hotel room. Nothing would make it comfortable. It was clean and tidy and meant to look homey. Luxury in the guise of old-fashioned charm.

Quinn, though, was accustomed to far more Spartan conditions. Less than Spartan.

During his undercover time on the streets – working his way up from the rank of low-level thug to trusted advisor of a minor drug lord – he'd stayed in his share of shitty places. Actual crack houses. Pay by the hour hotels.

Later, when he was incarcerated, his undercover stint in the prison system taught him to live with even less luxury. A thin mattress, a seat-less toilet, and plain walls.

Then the injury and the hotel room.

Lack of comfort had become so normal that when Quinn finally moved on, when he was finally free from both prison *and* the police force, the outside world had been overwhelming.

So his apartment at home was as minimalist as possible. No cushy damned bathrobes or baskets of fake flowers or soothing paintings.

Sometimes, it was *still* overwhelming. Especially when he was faced with an emotionally draining day or situation.

Like today.

With an annoyed grunt, Quinn sank down onto the bed, resting his elbows on his knees. He yanked on the tips of his faux hawk, then flopped backwards on the mattress. As he landed, something dug through his pocket and into his ass. He reached to adjust it, then stiffened as he realized it was Ginnie's phone.

Goddammit.

Why was she still permeating his existence? He'd let her go.

Quinn stared up at the too-white ceiling.

Let her go? You practically abandoned her, he scoffed guiltily. *Admit that there's more to it.*

Which was very likely the real reason he couldn't get comfortable.

Genevieve Silver – and her sweet, curved ass and her sweet, curved smile and all her other potentially sweet, curved parts – had somehow managed to get under his skin.

He was sure the airport security had figured out they'd made a mistake, and that Ginnie was somewhere ironing the stupid pleats back into her skirt and smoothing out every bit of kink brought into her life by Quinn and his generally bad influence. By his jacked up libido and his need to keep her safe.

"Shit," he said out loud. "I'm such an asshole."

He threw himself back forcefully again, hoping to knock the stupid from his body. Instead, the pillow was silky smooth, just like Ginnie's skin.

He hoped like crazy she was okay. And maybe that she'd understood why he left her there.

"Double shit," Quinn muttered. "Now I'm a sentimental douchebag too."

Yeah, he knew *sentimental douchebag* seem oxymoronic. But he wasn't in the mood for logic. He was in the mood for slipping off his clothes, slipping under the covers, and slipping into Ginnie.

Christ.

His emotions weren't just drained – they were on a runaway train. Right along with his sex drive.

Quinn rolled to his side and caught sight of the TV. It was an older model. Maybe close to an antique. There was a rental box on top, though, so there was a high probability he could get some kind of porn. Not his usual cup of tea, but hell. He clearly needed to get it out of his system.

Very briefly, his mind slipped to the young woman at the hotel's front desk. The daughter of the manager. Who'd smiled at him like the TSA agent wasn't standing beside him. What had she said her name was? Kelsey? No. Chelsea. She'd made it abundantly clear that Quinn was *her* cup of tea. She'd asked three times about tattoos, touched his arm several times, and hinted fairly emphatically that she was just a call away, and that she was off in a half hour.

Chelsea had been pretty. Ish.

But she's not Ginnie.

With a self-directed eye roll, Quinn stood and moved toward the ancient television. As he took a few steps, though, he spied the bathroom door, and behind that, the promise of a marble tub.

A bath.

Ginnie had said she wanted one, he remembered. Maybe she was settling into her own hotel room now, running her own bath. Maybe she was thinking of him, as she slid her off her robe.

The remembered smoothness of her skin filled his mind again. It expanded with his imagination. Her shoulders and her back. The bend of her waist and the swell of her hips.

Quinn groaned. "Fuck, man. Get a grip. If they already let her go, she probably hates you. Which is what you wanted."

The idea of soaking in a steaming pool of water was suddenly very appealing. He hadn't had a bath himself in years. A decade or more.

He could lose himself in it. In more ways than one, if he chose.

And it's getting to be less and less of a choice.

He was thick with bottled up need.

"All right," he muttered, and came to his feet. "Take a bath, Quinn. It's better than staring at the ceiling and tormenting yourself. And right after that…Stop fucking talking to yourself."

Quickly – so he wouldn't change his mind and go back to brooding – he set the taps to hot and stripped down.

He stepped in and let the scalding water lap at his toes. It burned against the bottoms of his feet, then the tops, pleasantly punishing. The slight pain was a welcome distraction, and it suited his mood perfectly.

The heat reached his ankles, then his calves, massaging away the ache. Or maybe just driving it higher.

Why hadn't he held Ginnie's hand a little more forcefully? Why had he been so stupidly stubborn? If he'd stuck around, he might've had her here now. Underneath him, waiting.

He started to sink down, to let the water consume him, but the bedroom door squeaked open, and he froze as blast of frozen air accompanied by a gasp carried across the room.

"Quinn!"

For a desperate second, he was sure his brain had simply conjured up a very vivid memory of her voice.

He turned slowly and blinked.

There she was, straight across the room, and straight out of his fantasy.

Well. Almost. This Ginnie was fully clothed. The fantasy version of Ginnie would *definitely* have walked in naked.

And she wouldn't look near *as pissed off.*

Not that she wasn't still sexy as hell.

Her hair was speckled with snow, and the flakes that had already melted had turned the tendrils around her face into clinging curls that licked her cheeks and throat. Quinn was *so* glad she hadn't tamed it with another ponytail. The wildness suited her.

Her eyes were flashing, and damn was she vibrant with how mad she was.

In spite of her obvious anger, Quinn couldn't help but drink in the rest of her appearance, and white hot lust quickly overrode his other emotions.

Ginnie's cheeks were pink with cold, and her clothes were soaked, hugging every curve. The wetness had turned her blouse see-through, and her bra was pink lace. It matched the panties she'd handed over earlier.

Panties she isn't wearing now, Quinn remembered.

Suddenly, that was *all* he could think about. Creamy, wet skin. Bare ass. Just a few feet away under that prim skirt. Which Quinn wanted to tear off. Preferably with his teeth.

Even the cold air that still swept through the room wasn't enough to dampen his desire. His very *obvious* desire.

Shit.

She was staring right at it, her face turning from pink to an alarming shade of red. Well, hell. She'd walked into *his* room, not the other way around. What right did she have to be staring at him like he was doing something wrong?

Quinn was torn. Part of him was tempted to drag her into the bathtub. To kiss the living hell out of her. To make her beg for more, to show her how that bullshit, talk-you-through-it orgasm in the airplane bathroom couldn't come close to the real thing.

Very fucking tempted.

Then she crossed her arms over her chest, momentarily blocking his view, and sending a trickle of sense back into his head.

You already decided you were no good for her, he reminded himself, then added, *Yeah, after you promised to sort everything out.*

He needed to get rid of her. Nicely.

Because two seconds alone with her, looking like that...

Her eyes narrowed as though she could hear his thoughts.

"Can I help you?" she asked coolly.

"Can *you* help *me?*" Quinn replied.

"You're in my room."

"*Your* room?"

She lifted an old-fashioned key – one that was an exact match for his – and shook it at him.

"*My* room. And stop repeating everything I say." Her voice was just imperious enough to piss him off.

He stepped from the tub, ignored the way she gasped and leaped away as he strode by her, and – still bare-ass naked – snatched up his own key from the night stand. And *he* waved it at *her*. Mockingly.

Then he echoed her words and her superior tone, too. "*My room.* Come in and close the door, Ginnie. And you can tell me what you're doing here."

She opened her mouth like she was going to argue, then closed it, and turned to slam the door shut with entirely more force than necessary. When she spun to face him again, two dots of pink highlighted the center of each cheek.

"Look," she snapped. "There's obviously been a mistake. The woman at the counter said this was the last available room."

Quinn raised an eyebrow. "Maybe you should've been more specific about what you meant by available."

Her lips pressed together irritably, but after just a second, her gaze betrayed her by straying to his still-on-display masculinity.

Quinn just barely managed to keep from grinning and asking her if she wanted to take a picture.

"Can we be serious, for just a second?" Ginnie asked in a strained voice, clearly being careful to look anywhere but south.

"Sure we can," Quinn replied. "If you wanted a little more fake action, you should've just asked nicely."

"Quinn!"

"What?"

"I meant it about being serious. And for the record...I didn't want *any* action, fake or otherwise."

Quinn crossed his arms over his chest. "I think you mean any *more* action. And you could've fooled me."

"Can you at least put some pants on while we sort this out?" She was almost begging.

Quinn wasn't giving in. Not even to that incredibly desperate, incredibly cute look on her face. He shook his head slowly.

"Hell no. This is my room. You may have talked Chelsea into giving you a key, but it's me you'll have to talk into letting you stay. I hope you're feeling creative."

"Talk you into…" She trailed off, her eyes wide. "I am *not* staying here. And who the hell is Chelsea?"

"Chelsea. The pretty redhead downstairs. And if you're not staying here…Try not to let the door hit your ass on the way out. Wouldn't want to bruise those sweet cheeks of yours."

"Quinn!"

"Third time you've called out my name since you came in, and we haven't even made it to the bed yet."

Her face flamed again. "Your bed is the *last* place I'm going to wind up tonight."

Quinn suppressed a smile. "And the *first* place you'll wind up in the morning, too."

"Qu – Ugh! You're an exasperating man."

"I know."

"Pants? Please?"

With a sigh, Quinn relented. He snapped up his jeans and slid them over his hips. Then flopped down onto the bed, lifted his hands to put them behind his head, and closed his eyes. He could still feel her gaze.

And finally…the room felt comfortable.

"Genevieve?"

"What?"

"Now that you've got me where you want me…What are you going to do with me?"

Thirteen

The arrogant son of a bitch.

He'd left her alone in the airport, where she could very well have wound up on the unpleasant end of a rubber glove.

He'd accused her of purposely turning up in his room.

My *room,* she corrected.

And now he was insinuating that she was just going to jump into bed with him – and not only that, but that it was *her* idea to do it. That somehow, she was calling the shots and this was the result.

Ginnie's temper flared.

She wanted to deny vehemently that he was where she wanted him. But she knew that's what he was waiting for, so that when she *did* deny it, he could turn it around and point out that she'd asked him to put the pants on, and suggest that maybe she wanted him to take them off again.

So she kept her mouth stubbornly closed and stared down at the big man who was stretched out like he owned the place. And – of course – he thought he did.

Ginnie waited for him to notice her pointed silence, to open his cocky mouth and say something that would incriminate himself rather than her, but he stayed quiet too. His breathing evened out, and as Ginnie studied the rise and fall of his wide, well-inked chest, she thought maybe the jerk had actually fallen asleep.

Which was what she was dying to do herself.

Ginnie narrowed her eyes, and considered screaming, just to find out if he really had drifted off. But she had a feeling that wouldn't go over so well. She could picture – far too easily – the tattoo-covered giant overreacting, grabbing her, and pinning her down to prove he was still the one with the upper hand. And she was a little worried that she might even like it.

She bit her lip and glared at his reposed form. He was taking up entirely more space than was necessary, even for his big body.

So even if you were *considering winding up in his bed, there isn't much space for you.*

The thought made her blush. But it irritated her too. It was supposed to be *her* bed, dammit.

She gave him and his stupid muscles another dirty look.

Clearly, he couldn't be forcefully removed. And as far as manipulation was concerned…Ginnie knew full well that she was out her league here. Quinn held her body enthralled, and the time they'd spent together had shown her that she wasn't strong enough mentally to overcome that.

You could just give in, nagged a little voice in her head. *Forgive him. Climb into that bed. See how far you can get. Slip your hand into those jeans, help yourself to more than a handful…But no.*

For some reason, she was sure that the second she succumbed to her body's will, her heart would follow. And while Ginnie might not know Quinn Mcdavid well at all, she *did* know a few things. He was the kind of man who knew how to use his sexuality properly. Who kissed a girl – a stranger – just to shut her up. Who faked sex in a bathroom on an airplane like it was no big deal. And who took off the second things got a little awkward.

Oh, yeah. Let's call getting held under suspicion of terrorism a little bit awkward, the nagging voice said to her mockingly, then it asked – a little too acerbically, *Would* you *have stuck around for* him?

She shoved the voice away again.

If he was really interested, he would've made a move. An effort. And he hadn't. All he'd done was make her a promise, then renege on it.

So as much as she might be tempted…Quinn Mcdavid was *not* the guy for her. Not for a bit of gratification, and not for anything else, either. In fact, he was the exact opposite of everything she wanted.

Case in point, his ink.

She could see now that the tattoo on his neck – the one that screamed prison-love – was an intricate sunburst. Below that was a tree, its branches curved below the sun, its trunk dipping down his bicep. The tree's roots were visible, too, spreading down to form a cocoon over a small knife, then wrapping around his arm completely.

Ginnie's gaze moved up the tree again. At the end of the branches were leaves, so real they looked like they were twisting in the wind as they spiralled down from his pecs to his ribs.

Ethereal.

That's the word Ginnie would use to describe that particular piece, even if the word didn't suit the rest of Quinn at all. The rest of him was the opposite.

Impossibly solid.

She flushed as the visual *solidity* of him popped to mind.

Part of her wondered how he managed to walk around all day comfortably with *that* impressive display of manliness between his legs. He'd had a hard-on that would put a Chippendale dancer to shame.

Not that Ginnie had ever *seen* a male exotic dancer. Or a female one for that matter. But if she *had* to picture one. A male one, that is then…Yep. It would be like that. Or less like that, she guessed, if averages were considered.

She tried to force her gaze up, but his abs grabbed her attention again before she could stop it from happening. Chiseled. Washboard. Mouth-watering.

He shifted a little and the unbuttoned jeans – which already hung *so* low on his hips – slipped down ever further, highlighting the sexy 'V' that pointed straight from his chiseled abs down to his hard as a rock –

Oh, hell. Bloody, freaking, oh, my God hell. What is wrong with me?

She was standing in a hotel room, mentally devouring a sleeping man. Whom she'd just barely met. Out of character didn't begin to describe the silent perusal of his assets.

And. He *was* still hard. She could see it right through his pants.

If he didn't want her…he sure as hell wanted something. Someone.

It could *be me.*

Ginnie shuffled a little in place as desire made her damp. Try as she might, she couldn't make herself *not* want him.

"Genevieve?"

Her name, spoken in the sexy, sweet, ridiculously perfect French accent just about made her jump out of her skin.

So much for being asleep, you big phony.

She swallowed. "What?"

"Tell me something…How'd you get so wet, anyway?"

Ginnie's face burned. "Excuse me?"

Quinn's eyes opened, and he shot her a puzzled frown, then chuckled knowingly. "Your clothes. How'd your *clothes* get so wet?"

"Oh." The blush didn't subside in the least. "I slipped on a patch of ice. Landed in the snow."

"Ouch. You okay?"

Did he actually care? He sounded like her might. Of course, he'd also sounded like he meant it when he told her he'd sort things out at the airport.

"I'm fine," Ginnie said coldly.

"Not as interesting a story as I was hoping for."

"Really? Because my day has been a little *more* interesting than *I* was hoping for."

"You wanna sit down and talk about it?"

"Um. No. I think I'm just going to go."

He sat up, looking serious for the first time since she walked in. "Go where?"

"Does it matter?"

"Yeah, it does."

"Fine," she sighed. "I'm going to go anywhere but here."

"C'mon, Ginnie. You're soaked. And Chelsea told me this was the very last room available in all of Huntingdon. You'll just wind up sleeping in the lobby. And I know you'd hate that."

Chelsea again. Dammit. For some reason, hearing the other girl's name made Ginnie's throat constrict. Who was she? Besides some pretty girl?

Prettier than me? Ginnie wondered petulantly.

Dammit with a side of ice cream.

And then he did it again. "Let me just call Chelsea and – "

Ginnie cut him off. "I know I look a little worse for wear, Quinn, and I probably don't seem like the kind of girl who's comfortable sleeping in a chair for a few hours, but I've spent the night in worse places. Don't let me ruin your date."

She turned to go, but only made it halfway up before Quinn was on his feet and on *her*, his warm but vicelike grip clasping her shoulders and spinning her around to face him.

She wished she could shake him off. She wished the tips of his fingers didn't send tiny explosions of heat in her skin. She wished she didn't have that raw, ready-to-cry burn in her throat.

But her body didn't care what her mind wished. It just remembered the feel of the orgasm tearing through her as she'd listened to him talk.

Dammit, body. Get your shit together and start listening to your head.

Even her annoyed, self-directed command didn't make it easier to cooperate.

"Ginnie," Quinn said softly. "What *exactly* is it you think is going on here?"

She swallowed and tried to speak without a telltale catch in her voice. "It's none of my business."

"I want to hear it anyway."

"Fine. I think I'm crashing the party, third-wheel style."

He frowned and his dark-lashed eyes tossed a pointed look around the room. "Little hard for there to be a third wheel when there's only two of us in here."

"But when Chelsea gets here…"

"Chelsea? Why the hell would she come in *here*?"

He sounded genuinely confused, but before she could stop herself, Ginnie glanced toward the bathroom and the steaming tub. And Quinn caught her look. Of course. And her drift.

"You thought that…" He trailed off and one side of his mouth tipped up in a sexy, crooked smile. "And you're jealous."

"No."

"No?" The reply was weighted with disbelief.

"It's fine, Quinn," Ginnie lied. "I get it. And I'm not jealous. I just don't want to wreck your night."

He reached over and grabbed her chin, lifting her face gently so she had no choice but to look him the eyes. "I do *not* have a date, Ginnie. Not with Chelsea. Not with anyone."

God. Why did she want so badly to believe him? Why did she want to forget that he'd taken off and left her at the mercy of Gilligan and his accusations and just sink into his arms? Drown in those brown-flecked, amber eyes? Be seduced by his voice as he continued to speak, his voice dropping lower and lower, sexier and sexier, begging to be believed?

"Hell," he added. "I haven't been on a date in two years. The most action I've seen in all that time was a little bit of fake Mile High Club, all right? As I recall, you were there for that. And for the record, I was getting into the tub with nothing but my thoughts."

And Ginnie saw the raw hunger his gaze. It was evident in the dilation of his pupils and the eager way his tongue touched his lip ring. It was clear in how he moved closer again, and how his hands scooped away her wayward hair and slid down her throat and across her shoulders.

He was definitely primed and ready, and his attention was all on her.

A fan of warmth seeped into Ginnie's core. Her heart rate quickened and her breath caught as he inclined his head.

He was going to kiss her, and this time it was going to be different. It wasn't going to be the shut-up kind, or the make-your-ex-jealous kind. It was going to be something more genuine. Something potentially amazing.

Ginnie's eyes drifted shut. And unbidden, the image of Quinn in the tub floated to the surface again.

He'd been alone.

With his thoughts.

Naked.

Erect.

And looking the tiniest bit embarrassed.

Then Ginnie clued in.

Oh.

He might not have had a date, but he'd been planning a party all right. For one.

She pulled away just as his lips brushed hers. It didn't matter how badly she wanted this. She had no illusions about what kind of lover she was – Lawrence had made sure of that. And she would never measure up to whatever fantasy Quinn had created in his mind.

"Seriously," she said, smoothing her skirt and working to keep any trace of her desire – or disappointment – out of her voice. "You don't have to make excuses."

He moved toward her, reached for her. And Ginnie put her hands up. Her breath caught as her palms grazed the hard lines of his chest. Very quickly, she slid her arms back to her sides and took a step back. The space gave Ginnie just enough room to breathe. Just enough room to miss his nearness.

"Quinn, you don't owe me anything."

"Owe you…" He trailed off, shot her a puzzled look, then shook his head and tugged on his hair.

"It's okay," Ginnie told him far more firmly than she meant it.

This time it was Quinn who put a bit more space between them, his brows knitting together and forming a soft crease in the center of his forehead. The thoughtful expression somehow made him all-the-more sexy.

"Are you one of those girls, Genevieve?" he asked softly.

"One of which girls?"

"Who says things she doesn't mean, just to make someone else feel like it's okay to treat them like shit?"

"No."

"So tell me the truth then."

"You tell me something first."

"Whatever you want to know."

Ginnie tipped up her chin, feeling again like she might cry and wanting not to, desperately. "Why did you leave me at the airport?"

"Because I'm not good enough for you," Quinn said, his voice rough and sincere at the same time. "And quite frankly, I'm afraid that the more I get to know you, the less that's going to stop me from taking you."

And Ginnie's heart stopped for a moment, then tripped over itself as it started up again at double time.

"Quinn," she whispered. "I'm pretty sure it's the other way around."

Fourteen

Quinn stared down at Ginnie's sad, bright eyes.

What in God's name would make her think she didn't measure up to *his* worth?

He couldn't think of one damned thing, and she wasn't giving much time to consider an answer anyway. She was on the move. She snapped up her suitcase from the hotel room floor, spun toward the door, and had her hand on the handle before Quinn even realized what was happening. In the time it took for him to collect his slow thoughts – *Is she leaving?* – the door was open and she was almost gone.

Shit.

No.

Without thinking about it any further, Quinn vaulted across the room.

Ginnie was only two steps into the hallway when his arms closed around her thighs. In the same split second he made contact, he realized his tackling instinct was a bad one, and abruptly took the only alternative available. He scooped her from the ground and tossed her over his shoulder, caveman style.

Ginnie let out a startled shriek, and her bag dropped to the ground.

Luggage be damned, Quinn thought.

He spun to take her back to the room, but her hand found a doorknob on the other side of the hall, pulling them both of them forward instead.

Quinn wasn't expecting the resistance, and it threw him off. He stumbled backwards, and when he tried to slow the momentum, succeeded only in changing their course slightly. He stumbled again, this time toward the wall.

In a frantic attempt to keep Ginnie's perfect, round ass from taking the bulk of the impact, Quinn adjusted again, letting her slide down his chest. He slammed his palms into the wall behind her, leaving them inches apart. Quinn could feel each of her curves pushed into his bare chest. Her clothes were damp and cool, but under that, she was tantalisingly warm. She took a breath and Quinn had to beat back a groan as her nipples bumped his skin and sent all the blood rushing to his groin.

Holy God, this woman has power over my body.

For ten long, perfect seconds, she stayed there, sandwiched between him and the wall, her eyes wide and her lips parted. Then she wriggled and made an attempt to slip under his arm.

Automatically, Quinn slid his hands down, blocking her in.

"I really don't think so," he murmured.

Ginnie glared up at him, her face pink and her chest still rising and falling rapidly. "What the hell are you doing?"

"Keeping you from running off."

"You're holding me hostage?"

Down the hall, a door squeaked open. Quinn ignored it.

"I'm stopping you from hurting yourself by taking off in a snowstorm in a town you don't know."

"It's not up to you to decide whether or not I'm going to hurt myself!"

Quinn bit the inside of his mouth to keep from smiling. "So you admit that you're endangering yourself?"

"No, I – just let me go!"

Quinn shook his head. "Uh-uh. You forgot the magic word."

"Please," she snapped.

"That wasn't very nice."

"And you *are* being nice?"

Another hotel door swung open. This one drew Ginnie's attention. Her eyes flicked to their growing audience, then back to Quinn.

"I'll scream," she warned.

"Try it," he countered, his eyes fixed on her lips. "See what happens."

Hell. He *wanted* her to yell. He *wanted* an excuse to slam his lips into hers. He leaned in, daring her to make a sound. She returned his stare, her breathing getting quicker by the second, her pupils threatening to drown out the green of her eyes. When she did speak again, it wasn't a scream. It was barely more than a whisper.

"People are staring."

"Come back in the room then, Ginnie," he suggested, bringing his arms closer together – close enough that any move on her part was going to initiate contact. "No one will have anything to stare at anymore."

She sucked in another breath. "I *can't*."

"Can't? Or just plain *won't*?"

"I can't, Quinn." Her voice was almost ragged. "I can't possibly live up to what a person like you expects."

Something about her statement made Quinn draw back. "What kind of person do you think *I* am?"

"I have no idea," she told him.

"I didn't ask you if you *knew*...I asked you what you *thought*. I know you've got me pegged in some way in that head of yours or you wouldn't be running away like this."

"That's not true," she replied, the lie clear in her the deepening of her flush.

"You haven't shoved me into one of those mental, black or white boxes of yours?"

"No."

"So then how do you know what I'm expecting?"

"Because – " She stopped, pulled her bottom lip between her teeth in a way that made Quinn want to growl, then exhaled and started again. "For starters, I'm not the kind of girl anyone calls *baby*."

"You're the kind of girl *I* call baby," Quinn pointed out.

"I'm the kind of girl you *think* you want to call baby."

"Are you trying to control my thoughts, baby?" he teased.

She didn't laugh. "I don't just want to control your *thoughts*. I want to control everything."

"Now *that*...I see."

"So why are we standing here, having this discussion?"

"Because you refuse to come back inside."

"You don't really want me to do that."

"I always know what I want, Genevieve."

Her color deepened. "That's not what I meant."

Quinn raised an eyebrow. "What then?"

"I was talking about me giving you the wrong impression."

"Which impression is that? That I can call you baby?"

"That. And making you think I'm the kind of girl you should fantasize about in the bathtub," she blurted.

At that, Quinn couldn't hold in a chuckle. "What makes you think that's what I was doing?"

There was blank silence for a second, and then Ginnie's face went impossibly crimson, and she wouldn't meet his eyes. "I'm sorry. I don't know why I assumed…Just forget it."

He let her squirm for another moment, then growled in a low voice, "I was doing exactly what you think I was doing. I was *about* to do exactly what you think I was about to do."

"Quinn – "

He cut her off. "I was thinking about how you'd feel, pushed against me like this. I was thinking about your lips. On my mouth. On *me*. How it would be if what happened between us on the plane was real."

Ginnie gasped, but she still shook her head. "But it wasn't. And I'm not the girl who does crazy things in airplane bathrooms and seeks revenge on her former – *ex* – husband."

"I never thought you *were* that kind of girl."

"So why the hell are you bothering with me?"

His hands slid down, then in, and he placed his palm in the small of her back. She arched into him, and her body fit his like a glove.

"Ginnie?"

"Mmph," she mumbled back.

"You think you've got it all figured out, and you don't. I want to show you that's okay. Since the first second I saw you in that bar, *all* I've wanted is to get you here, like this. You're the sexiest, most desirable woman I've ever met. And if you don't come inside with me right this second, I'm going to prove it in front of all these people."

Quinn bent down to seal the truth with a kiss, but paused as a tear leaked from first one of Ginnie's eyes, then the other.

She was *crying*?

"Hey," Quinn said, wiping a big, wet tear from her cheek. "I know that I kind of suck at this serious stuff, but I don't think I've ever made a girl *cry* by calling her sexy."

He wasn't the kind of man who felt compelled to smooth out a woman's insecurities, or the kind of man to shower a woman with compliments just to stroke her ego. But staring down at Ginnie's face, he didn't think either thing applied to her.

"I'm *not* sexy, Quinn," she whispered, her voice shaking. "You just think that because you don't know me."

She sounded like she genuinely believed what she was saying. Truly thought that he was wrong to want her.

He fought the urge to tell her that he knew far more than he needed to form an accurate picture of who she was. That Jase had supplied him with a shitload of information – quirks, abandonment issues, favorite foods.

He knew admitting that right this second would send her running in the other direction. No way was he letting that happen.

He took the easier road – the safer one – and offered her a crooked smile. "You're not Genevieve formerly-known-as-Michaels?"

"I mean the person *inside*."

Quinn opened his mouth, but she beat him to the punch.

"Don't you *dare* say something about what should or shouldn't be inside me."

"Would I do that?" he replied innocently.

"Yes!"

"Okay. I *would*," he conceded. "But I won't right this second."

"Thank you."

"Only because I still need to convince you that you're sexy as all hell."

She made an exasperated noise. "If I *were* sexy…My husband wouldn't have left me and cited my lack of ability in the bedroom as the primary reason for the annulment."

Quinn went very still. "He did what?"

"He said we weren't compatible in the bedroom. That I wasn't capable. He told a roomful of lawyers that I was – and I quote – unfuckable."

"Ginnie, that's he most ridiculous thing I've ever heard," he said it slowly and quietly, but a tirade raged through his mind.

What kind asshole was this guy? Doctor Fucking Lawrence Michaels. What was he the doctor *of?* Douchebaggery? Who the *hell* took a girl with a history like Ginnie's and then crushed her like that? Based on a pack of flaming bullshit no less. Quinn had been forced to work alongside criminals for years. He'd befriended them as part of his job. Drug dealers and thieves. During his undercover time at the prison, he'd even been temporarily housed with an accused murderer. But for some reason this…*this* filled him with a fury like no other. He hated people who knowingly honed in on others' weaknesses. Who manipulated them.

"Quinn?"

Vaguely, he heard the worried tremor in Ginnie's voice, but it couldn't quite cut through the anger surging through Quinn's veins. He'd dropped his hands from the wall and balled up both into fists. In fact, his whole body was tense with fury. He breathed in and out, trying to even out his mind along with his inhales and exhales.

Sneaky, underhanded, self-centered, soul-sucking sonofabitch.

If Quinn ran into the man again – ever – he wasn't going to give him a phony high five. He was going to throw a fist straight into his face.

"Quinn."

This time, Ginnie's call was a little louder, a little firmer, and it managed to bring his attention back to the moment. Back to the emerald eyes, full of concern. For him.

Oh, hell.

It was supposed to be the other way around. He was supposed to be looking out for her. And Quinn knew exactly how he wanted to do that. To show this girl just how wrong she was about herself.

Anger morphed into passionate need.

With a growl, Quinn reached down, gripped her ass, and lifted her to his waist. He pushed her against the wall, hard.

Ginnie's legs closed on his hips, and she tipped her head up, her eyes already half-closed in anticipation, and Quinn allowed himself a moment to peruse her face, devouring her features with his gaze. Graceful neck. So supple, so delectable. Arched cheeks, beautiful and highlighted with that perma-blush. And those lips.

Oh, fuck. Those lips.

He had to taste them. To claim them. Now.

As he leaned down, a door somewhere up the hall slammed, and her eyes flew open.

Goddammit.

Ginnie opened her mouth, and Quinn braced himself for another protest.

"Please," she said. "Please take me back to the bedroom, Quinn."

He'd never been happier to hear the magic word in his life.

Fifteen

Coherent thought had left Ginnie's brain, and Quinn had taken up residence instead. She wasn't sure what it was that pushed her over the edge – if it was the fierce look in his eyes before he swooped her from the ground, or the raw sexuality in every move he made, or the easy way he tossed out sly smiles and clever banter. All she knew was that he filled her senses and still she wanted more.

Hurry, she thought as he carried her to their hotel room.

Their room.

Yes. It solved the dilemma around whose it was. It could belong to both of them.

The realization sent further tendrils of warmth through her already aching body. Her thighs tightened on Quinn. She loved the way he felt between her legs; she hated the fabric that separated them. She shifted, trying to push aside the denim of his jeans and the pleats of her skirt. Quinn drew in a hissing breath as Ginnie succeeded just enough to feel the bare flesh of her inner thigh graze the skin of his hips.

Why was five feet of hallway taking so long?

"Hurry," she urged, this time out loud.

"Bag," he replied with a grunt.

"Not mine," Ginnie murmured automatically.

But Quinn ignored her, and paused to grab the suitcase. And she forgot about her protest, because when he bent to pick up the bag, she slid down his body and straight into his erection. For a dizzying second, Ginnie got a glimpse of how the real thing was going to feel. Her head spun. Her lips tingled. Her pulse throbbed. And all of it drove an incredible awareness, right between her thighs.

She heard Quinn's remembered voice in her mind. *How'd you get so wet anyway?*

She wanted to cry out, *You.* You *make made me this wet.*

She bit down on her lip to keep from doing it. They were at the door now, and Quinn shouldered it open – thank God it wasn't one that closed and locked automatically – then used his bare foot to kick it shut behind them.

The bed was just steps away.

And thank God for that, too.

"Baby."

The word was a throaty rumble, like it had been drawn not just from Quinn's mouth, but from his whole chest. Or maybe even deeper. From his gut. From his entire being.

Ginnie shivered.

"Please, Quinn," she said, not sure how exactly to ask for what she wanted. What she needed.

"Yes," he replied, like he knew anyway.

Then he loosened his grip on her bag, and it fell to the ground. The soft-sided suitcase landed with a thud, followed by a decisive pop. A satiny pair of panties, tag still attached, flew upwards, then floated down again and landed on the edge of the bed. And suddenly the whole floor was littered with lingerie. Lace and leather and slips of fabric that were far too small to cover *any*thing.

The plastic badge.

And the handcuffs.

Why, oh why, hadn't she tossed those away?

Then something rolled – *thump, thump, thump* – along the floor.

Oh no.

The blood drained from Ginnie's face as she watched Quinn look down, puzzlement furrowing his brow. In slow motion, Ginnie aligned her stare with his, stared at what it was that made him bite down on that lip ring of his.

A big. Shiny. Purple. Dildo.

There was no mistaking what it was, no mistaking its all-too-real shape resting on top of Quinn's toes. His quizzical gaze lifted to meet Ginnie's horrified one.

Good job, she thought. *You just invented an entirely new level of embarrassment.*

And every ounce of abandonment faded.

"This has *got* to be a sign," she muttered.

"A sign?" Quinn echoed.

"That this is a mistake."

"Ginnie…"

"Oh, come *on*," she said, then realized it would be hard to take her seriously while she was still wrapped around him and added, "Can you put me down?"

He set her very gently on the floor. "This isn't a mistake."

But being on solid ground stabilized Ginnie's thoughts even further, and they came tumbling out. "We pretended to have sex on a plane. The plane had to make an emergency landing. We kissed on that plane. I got taken into custody. We do this and…" She trailed off and waved her hand around the room. "The universe is telling us to stop."

Quinn looked around the room again. "You think that the universe used your underwear to tell us not to have sex?"

"That's not *my* stuff."

"Oh. You're just holding it for a friend?"

"Not exactly. Just – Never mind." Ginnie sighed. "That stupid bag is what got me detained at the airport."

"So which is it?"

"Which is what?"

"Is it this *bag* that made Gilligan stop you, or the universe?"

"It's the same thing!"

Quinn crossed his arms over his bare chest, and his jeans slipped down, and Ginnie had to forcibly keep her eyes on his face. Especially when he took a step closer and she could see every detail of his tattoos over every detail of his muscles.

"Ginnie," he said. "The snowstorm wrecked our flight, that bag got you stopped, and as far as sexy panties flying around the room go…Not what I'd call a turnoff on my end."

Ginnie felt like her stomach was going to cave it. "But they're *not* my sexy underwear."

"You were serious about that?"

"Somehow, my bag – which is the Dr. Lawrence Michaels special, apparently – got mixed up with this one. Which must belong to the girl he's with." Ginnie sank down on the bed and added bitterly, "On the plus side…At least now I know what I was lacking in the bedroom."

Anger flashed across Quinn's face. "You're not lacking *anything* in the bedroom."

"Except imagination."

Ginnie felt ridiculous, arguing with him about it when the proof was spread out across the room. She sank down to the edge of the bed, then began to shake. Without the heat of desire dancing through her, she was freezing.

In a heartbeat, Quinn was at her side, drawing the quilt up from the bed and wrapping it around her shoulders.

"Did he tell you that, too?" Quinn's voice had an edge that conflicted heavily with his tender actions.

"N-n-no," Ginnie replied through chattering teeth. "He d-d-didn't even t-t-tell me about th-th-this."

"He didn't tell you about his fantasies?"

"N-n-no."

"So he didn't even give you a chance."

Quinn muttered it so quietly that Ginnie wasn't even sure he intended her to hear it. She answered anyway.

"It d-d-doesn't matter," she said.

"Of course it matters."

Quinn slid backwards on the bed, then pulled Ginnie back, too. When she resisted, he sighed loudly.

"Don't fight with me," he said. "I'm just trying to stop you from getting hypothermia."

"R-r-right."

"It's a choice between cuddling like this and stripping down and using body heat, Ginnie. You pick."

Her face warmed. "N-n-not much of a ch-ch-choice."

"C'mon, Ginnie" he cajoled. "You're wrapped in a grandma-blanket and telling me about your *former* husband's fantasies. I can't think of anything less sexy. I should be able to control myself."

Ginnie opened her mouth, then closed it. He'd done that thing again. The one where anything she said could – and would – be used against her.

"F-f-fine," she conceded, and slid a little closer.

"Let's not leave hypothermia to chance," Quinn said, then dragged her up between his thighs, cocooned her in the blanket, and slid her arms around her body. "Better?"

She wished she could lie and say no, but the second her back molded into his chest, her teeth stopped banging together and warmth seeped into her body.

"Much," she admitted, then added – just to show that she could be adult about him being right, "Thank you, Quinn."

"You're welcome." He gave her a firm squeeze. "See how a little communication goes a long way? You can't just keep your needs to yourself and expect someone to guess what you want."

"Easy for you to say. Since you *always* know what you want, apparently," she grumbled.

"Are you going to try to convince me that you're shy about what *you* want? Because I'm not gonna believe it."

"I thought we were talking about Lawrence," Ginnie replied.

"Were we?"

"Yes."

"Hmm. Tell me then… How could you know what he wanted if he didn't tell you? Maybe you would've come through."

"That might be true. If you happened to be talking about anything other than cops-and-robbers in the bedroom."

Quinn chuckled. "If he *had* shared his little fantasy with you…What would you have done?"

Ginnie started to exclaim emphatically that she would have complied with whatever Lawrence wanted, but all that came out was a noise that sounded like, "Ugh."

"That enthusiastic, huh?"

She didn't even blush. She was too busy wondering why the mere thought of playing a dirty version of cops-and-robbers with Lawrence had about much draw as…

A grandma blanket and talking about one of Quinn's *exes?* her mind filled in. *Wait. Does Quinn have a lot of exes? Why does the feeling that he probably does make me want to pick up that shaded lamp and toss it across the room?*

"Ugh," Ginnie said again, this time on purpose.

"So you would've told him to take his handcuffs and shove them up his ass?" He sounded thoroughly pleased with her disgust.

"No," Ginnie replied, the smallest smile turning up her lips. "He might've *liked* that."

Quinn laughed again. "All right. So your fantasies weren't in line. Still not grounds for being a total douche."

"I didn't *have* any fantasies," Ginnie blurted.

"Everyone has a fantasy or two."

"Yeah, okay. I had one. To marry a doctor. Look how that turned out."

Quinn's chest shook behind her, and she knew he was laughing even harder.

"It's not funny," Ginnie told him. "My marriage ended because of this."

Abruptly, Quinn stopped laughing. He slid his hand under her knees and spun her sideways, then put two fingers on her chin.

"Tell me one of your actual fantasies," he commanded.

And something did pop into Ginnie's head. But it was embarrassing in its tameness.

What does it matter? she thought. *Tell him anyway. Twenty-four hours from now, you'll never have to talk to him again.*

"Ginnie," he prompted.

She exhaled. "Okay. When I was twelve, I moved in with the Silvers. They'd been fostering for years, and they were in their sixties and decided that they wanted to adopt. I spent my teenaged years with them, and they were great. But they were used to having a lot of troubled kids come through, and they picked their battles carefully. One of the things they didn't care about was letting me have boys in my room."

Quinn tapped his lip ring. "I'm not sure I want to hear about the boys in your room."

"Why? You jealous?"

"Extremely."

Ginnie inhaled sharply. She'd been expecting him to deny it, and the fact that he didn't...It made her tingle.

"You have to be patient," she told him. "I'm getting there."

"Patience isn't my strong suit."

Ginnie rolled her eyes. "I didn't *have* a lot of boys in my room."

"Some?"

"Stop that!"

He growled out a, "Fine," and Ginnie suppressed a sudden urge to make up some sordid details, just to get an even bigger reaction.

"There wasn't a *point* in bringing boys home, because they didn't care."

Now Quinn shot her a lopsided smile. "No thrill?"

"Exactly," Ginnie said with a blush. "And I guess I always wondered what it *would* be like to have that thrill."

Quinn's smile became a cat-like grin. "So..." he dragged out the word, turning it from a single-syllable conjunction into lazy, sexy purr. "You want to know what it feels like to have some hot-bodied, shouldn't-be-there hunk of man in your bedroom – in your *bed* – while you're just *waiting* to be caught?"

As teasing as the question was, it sent a battalion of butterflies to flight in Ginnie's stomach, and the rapid beat of their wings didn't create a breeze – it created friction. Hot, *work its way down to her panty-less crotch* friction.

"Yes," she whispered.

"That," he replied. "I can do."

"You can – "

He cut her off. "My bag's just inside the bathroom. Help yourself to something dry, then meet me back here."

Ginnie stared at him, her eyes wide. She was on fire. Everywhere.

"Ginnie?" he said softly.

"Ermph?" she mumbled.

"Hurry."

Sixteen

Quinn stared after Ginnie for about ten seconds, wondering what kind of game life was playing with him.

If he believed in fate, even a little bit, he'd say the opposite of what she had said. The universe wasn't tossing them signs that they *shouldn't* be together. It was just plain tossing them together. However the fuck it had to.

But you don't *believe in fate,* he reminded himself.

Perseverance, hard work. Tangible, measurable results. Those were real. Not fate.

Unconsciously, Quinn fingered the scar just up and to the left of his heart.

If fate were real, it had a lot of shit to answer for.

Then he heard his suitcase unzip, and the sound was sexy as hell, and his questions went out of his head.

He snapped up the phone from the side table, pressed zero to speak with reception, and issued a request in a low voice. When he was done, he slid into his T-shirt, then flicked out the lights.

And just as he climbed into bed, Ginnie opened the bathroom door. She stood just fifteen feet away, her petite but well-curved frame drowning in a pair of pajamas that Quinn didn't even remember packing.

In the dim light, she looked small and needy, scrubbed and perfect. She'd wound her hair into a tight bun at the nape of her neck, and she was the opposite of everything Quinn found attractive in a woman.

But holy shit.

She was still the most beautiful damned thing he'd ever laid eyes on.

"Quinn?"

Her voice was soft – unsure but not wanting to admit it. Just like her. And also just like her, it had a hardline to his groin.

"I ordered room service."

"What?"

"Twenty to thirty minutes. I told them to walk right in."

"But – "

"Get in the bed, Ginnie," he ordered.

"In the – "

"Quick. Before someone catches us."

He lifted the quilt, and Ginnie scurried across the room. She jumped into the bed and tucked herself in, and Quinn grinned as he realized how careful she was being to leave a foot between them.

None of that.

He reached across the space and pulled her flush against his own body.

"Hi," he said softly.

"Hi," she breathed back.

She felt just right, against his chest. Like something he could get used to.

Jesus, he wanted her.

"Do you think anyone heard me sneak in?" he asked in a conspiratorial whisper.

"No." She still sounded a bit nervous, but she cleared her throat and added, "My parents are out. At least for the next half hour or so."

"That's both good and bad," Quinn replied.

"How do you figure?"

He then leaned back, ran his finger along her cheek, and dropped his voice. "Because I plan on making you scream in the most pleasant of ways. But I sure wish I had more than thirty minutes."

Ginnie drew in a sharp breath, and her chest rose. Her nipples were erect enough that he could feel them pressed against him through both the light cotton pajamas and his T-shirt. It made him eager to free them, to undo those buttons and drop his mouth to their waiting firmness. So eager that he almost forgot what role he was supposed to be playing and went for it.

Then Ginnie tipped up her head and scrunched her face into sweet little frown. "Maybe you should go then. Before they come home."

Quinn flicked his tongue to his lip ring and gave it a slow, deliberate poke. "Maybe I should convince you to let me stay instead."

She shook her head. "You know what? I'm a nice girl and – "

He cut her off with a deep kiss, forcing her lips apart with his tongue and plunging it into her mouth. He dragged the titanium ball from his tongue stud across every surface inside, then gave her bottom lip a solid nip before he pulled away.

"*You* know what?" he countered. "Nice girls don't let boys like me sneak into their rooms in the middle of the night, do they?"

She shook her head and mumbled, "Mm," while keeping her eyes on his lips.

Quinn grabbed her chin and forced her gaze up. "I've seen the way you look at me in math class. There are definitely some not-nice thoughts running around in that pretty head of yours."

"Math class?" Ginnie repeated, her face screwed up again, this time like she was trying not to laugh.

Quinn raised an eyebrow and refused to drop the act. "Did you think I didn't see you? Did you think I didn't notice the way you hike your skirt a little higher when I walk by? Or last week when you showed up bra-less and wore that sweet, little, pink shirt?"

An image of the made-up scenario flooded Quinn's mind. Ginnie's creamy legs, barely covered in frayed denim, her ample breasts visible under a vibrantly hued T-shirt. A lust-filled groan built up in the back of Quinn's throat. He fought it off.

"You wanna lie and tell me that wasn't an invitation?" he asked.

"Is that why you came here tonight?" she asked. "Because you thought I might be easy?"

That, he could give her a real-world answer to. "Not in the slightest. I was hoping for a challenge, actually."

"Oh, really."

"Mm hmm. If I wanted easy, I would've snuck into Hailey's room instead of yours."

"Hailey. The one with the globs of eye makeup and the pink hooker heels? Or the one with the belly ring and the weird-smelling locker?"

Quinn bit back a chuckle. "The first one."

"Hmm."

"Hmm, what?"

"A transvestite."

Quinn pulled back. "What?"

"That Hailey. She has a little sumpin' sumpin' extra under *her* short skirt."

This time, Quinn couldn't hold in his laugh. "You *are* a troublemaker, aren't you?"

"Don't tell my parents," she replied with an impish smile.

"Ginnie?"

"Yes?" *All innocence.*

"There are quite a few things I'm going to *not* tell your parents about."

A flush crept up her throat and her eyes sparkled. "Like?"

Quinn dragged his hand to the back of her neck, put his fingers under her bound-up hair and massaged lightly. "Like how this hairstyle is begging to be messed up."

Ginnie arched into the massage a little and half-closed her eyes. "Messy hair? That's not terrible."

"It is when it happens because I've got you underneath me, sliding in and out of you. Or when it happens because I've got your hands tied to the bed post and my tongue between your legs."

"Quinn?" His name was almost a gasp.

"Yeah, baby?"

"You worked hard to sneak in here, right?"

"Climbed a trellis, lost a shoe, and got chased by a rabid cat," he teased.

"So…"

"So…What?"

She met his eyes, and it was impossible to tell how much of her was lost in the game, and how much of her remained separate.

"Are you all talk?" she wanted to know. "Or are you going to see if you can get past first base?"

They stared at each other, the temperature in the room rising to the point of blistering. Ginnie's lips were parted and moist, and Quinn felt his breath turn from rapid but controlled, to shallow and more than a little ragged.

The things I want to do to those lips, he thought. *The things I want them to do to me...*

A sudden thump from somewhere out in the hall broke the tension abruptly.

"Shit!" Ginnie whispered, her eyes darting to the door.

"Don't panic," Quinn said. "If it's your parents, we can just tell them I'm the cable repair guy."

"Very funny."

But there was no further noise from outside the room, and after a quiet minute with Ginnie staying tucked in his arms, Quinn whispered, "You know what? I'm not convinced that a nice girl like you even knows what anything past first base is."

Under the blanket, Ginnie's palm inched its way to his body, landed on his elbow, then worked up to his bicep, and came to rest on his shoulder.

It was the first time she'd touched him voluntarily, Quinn realized, and it filled him with an odd mix of intense satisfaction and incredible longing.

When she tilted her mouth up and brushed his lips lightly with her, the groan he'd been holding in rumbled deep down in his chest.

"Christ, Ginnie," he said against her mouth.

"Show me," she murmured, and her thumb traced a delicate circle over his back. "That's why I wore the short skirt and the little T-shirt and no bra. Because I heard you knew a thing or two about base work, and I wanted a lesson."

Quinn let her continue her exploration of his shoulder blades for a moment longer, wondering if he'd ever been so turned on by such a small gesture. Or how it was even possible.

But apparently...it is.

He was dying a second-by-second death, his body a torrent of need.

So Quinn pressed his hand to her hip and kissed her, driving that need into his mouth. Into her.

He took the exploration slowly this time around, though, tangling his tongue with hers, soft, then firm, then soft again. He tasted each part of her mouth, and made her gasp against the attention. He drew his tongue away and used his teeth on her lips, tugging and pulling, while he skated his fingers down the side of her legs, then to the back of her thigh, then paused them just below her ass and pulled away.

"First base," he told her.

She was trembling a little, and for a second, Quinn thought maybe she was scared, but when he looked into her eyes, he saw nothing but a desire that matched his own.

"That was...very educational," she said.

He caught the teasing, challenging tone in her statement, and he was fully ready to rise to it.

Ready to rise? You've already more *than risen.*

It was true. He was hard as hell and so far past wanting to move on to second base that it wasn't even funny. He forced himself to rein it in.

"I should probably resent that remark," he stated.

"Why's that?"

"Being lumped in with the teachers – especially the *good* ones – is a grave insult to a true badass like myself."

"Does a true badass proclaim himself like that?"

"A true badass says and does *many* unexpected things."

Quinn moved his hand up and squeezed her ass – and it was smooth and firm and just as perfect as he'd been anticipating – so he didn't care when she laughed.

"That was *not* exactly unexpected," she teased.

"I must be slipping then. Maybe next I'll be saying *please* every time I want to kiss you. Every time I want to touch you."

"And maybe I'd like that."

"You think you'd like having me beg?"

"I think I'd like having you be *polite*."

"Polite? You trying to ruin my rep?"

Ginnie batted her eyelashes. "You trying to ruin *mine*?"

"Absolutely."

Quinn tipped up his chin and sunk his teeth into throat. She yelped, and he let out a dark chuckle – that'd teach her to mock his bad-assery – then soothed the bite with a suck and a kiss. She mumbled something, but Quinn didn't hear what it was. He was too busy making his way to second base.

Seventeen

Quinn's hands were everywhere on her body at once.
His fingers skimmed the semi-important parts.
Face.
Shoulders.
Throat.
Back.
They caressed the sensitive ones.
Breasts.
Thighs.
Ass.
It's a game, Ginnie tried to remind herself. *Role play.*
Then his fingers slid deftly between her legs, brushing the cotton fabric of the pajamas against her waiting wetness, rubbing firmly before they slid out again.

And it was too little and too much at the same time and any pretense of role play was lost. She was on fire. She was in awe of the way he lit her up while they were both still clothed.

Maybe it's a superpower.

She opened her mouth – maybe to ask if it was – but Quinn chose that second to find the buttons on her borrowed sleepwear. In one fluid motion, he rolled her to her back with her top open and one nipple in his warm mouth. Both his tongue ring and his lip ring were flicking across it in a searing dance that rendered speech impossible. So instead of words, a low, animalistic sound that Ginnie couldn't even register as her own escaped her lips.

And Quinn spoke against her, his voice a rumble. "So sweet."

Ginnie wasn't sure why, but the tiny, two-word compliment sent her into a full-body blush. Maybe it was the way he sounded like he meant it. Maybe it was simply the fact that he *had* said it. Either way, she wanted more. And he seemed to sense it.

His mouth opened wider, drawing in more of her tender flesh. Then he switched to her other breast and kissed it with equal fervor while his thumb slipped to the first one and formed a slow, firm, repeated circle.

Holy...Oh. Dear. Keep... Ginnie's mind was a mess.

But her skin...Her body...It was all focused on the attention Quinn was giving her. Every rub, every suck, every shift, every move, all of it brought her to exquisite attention. Her hands sought to touch him in return, but he stopped her before she got even close. He grabbed her wrists and pinned them above her head, leaving her lying beneath his denim-clad thighs. Completely at his mercy.

Quinn looked her straight in the eyes, the unusual amber of his irises all but obscured by his wildly dilated pupils.

"Baby," he said gruffly. "Don't get me wrong, I *want* you to touch me. But the second you do, I'm going to forget about that other base. The one that comes between second and home."

She tried to meet his stare with confidence, tried to mask the flare in her chest and the penetrating heat between her legs.

"You want me *that* badly?"

She meant it to come out teasing, for the question to be a joke. Instead, it sounded small and insecure. Ginnie cursed her slip up and waited for him to pull away. But he didn't. He adjusted his grip so that her wrists were in one of his hands instead of both, then dragged his freed fingers from her cheek to her neck.

"Do those football boys you usually run with *not* want you this badly?"

Quinn's question made Ginnie go a little still. He was still in the game – the fantasy that had been her idea. The one she'd all but forgotten about the second his mouth met her skin.

"They don't say much," she replied with a swallow against the sudden lump in her throat.

"No?" He dragged his thumb along her collarbone.

"No. They just grunt a lot."

An irresistible grin lit up Quinn's face for just a second before he shot her a scowl instead. "Clearly, the football boys have been hit in the head too many times."

"Clearly."

Quinn leaned close and rubbed his cheek against hers, and Ginnie was sure she could feel every piece of his barely-there stubble. Rough, but somehow soothing and sexy at the same time.

Just like Quinn as a whole.

He placed a soft kiss on her lips, then eased away again so that he was looking down at her once more.

"*Anyone,*" he said emphatically, "Who says he doesn't want you that badly is either a liar or an idiot."

Right then, she realized he wasn't talking about the fantasy world after all.

"And Ginnie?" he added. "I'm neither of those things. And I want you very, *very* badly."

Her breath caught, and her chest rose, and Quinn's eyes moved away from her face and back to her body. Like he couldn't help it. Like he meant those words as much as he'd meant *so sweet.*

He rolled off of her then, and though Ginnie missed the contact immediately, Quinn didn't leave her wanting for long. Lying on his side, he cupped her cheek and tipped her face toward him. He gave her a long, lingering kiss. As his lips laid claim to hers, his palm slid down her body, stroking each bared breast. When he'd drawn both of her nipple into hard, aching points, he moved his fingers to her cleavage, then drew a searing line to her belly button.

Hot. So very hot.

The edge of his pinky pushed against the waistband of her pajamas and rubbed along it, back and forth, lowering it until it was just above her pubic bone.

The need she felt was everywhere. Consuming beyond words.

She wanted his mouth on her and his hands. She wanted to thrust her hips up and tear at the sheets.

"Oh, God," Ginnie moaned.

Quinn's teeth nibbled her earlobe and he whispered, "Shh, baby. Gotta keep it down or someone'll hear you and then we'll have to stop before I get to third."

She knew he was kidding.

He had *to be kidding.*

He wouldn't stop.

Would he?

Ginnie wasn't taking the chance. She bit her lip to keep from crying out again as Quinn's hand went *under* the pajamas and came to rest just above the most needy of all her parts. Very gently – *too* gently – one of his fingers stroked her. Just once.

Ginnie whimpered through her closed lips.

"A bit more?" Quinn asked, his voice thick.

Ginnie nodded, afraid to speak.

His hand slid lower, cupping her, then pressing into her, then drawing out.

Not enough.

He gave her another little push, just a bit deeper, once, twice, and on the third time, his thumb came up to circle her clitoris. Then stopped. It was torturous. Incredible. And this time when her body wanted to do it, Ginnie did thrust herself up. She couldn't help it.

Quinn let her push herself into his hand, keeping his fingers in just the right place and he growled, "More, Ginnie?"

"Yes!" she cried, careful to keep her voice as quiet as possible.

"Slow and steady?" He rocked his hand over her, and she moaned.

"Or fast and hard?" He plunged his fingers into her, pulled them out, then plunged them in again, and she bit down on her lip so forcefully that she tasted blood.

"Genevieve?" he prodded.

"Both! Slow. And hard," she gasped.

She was far too turned on to care if she sounded greedy or contradictory. All she cared about was getting more of Quinn.

Quinn.

She wanted to say it out loud. So she did.

"Quinn! Please!"

"Slow and hard," he agreed. "Since you asked so nicely."

And he stopped teasing her, stopped holding back. He tunneled into her, and Ginnie's insides pulsed in response. She could feel her muscles contract over his fingers as he explored her more intimately than she'd ever been explored before. Her need grew unfathomably strong.

How was it even possible, to want someone like this? To want to be so *consumed*?

Quinn's ministrations intensified.

She'd thought she wanted him on the plane. She'd known it was good. But maybe she'd believed the incredible, touch-less experience there to be a one-off, a release of pent-up need and frustration.

So wrong.

This was much more than that.

Oh, God.

Up, went her hips.

In, went his fingers.

Stroke, went his thumb.

His attention ruled her body.

A wild spiral of heat wound tight in her core. It grew hotter and hotter and tighter and tighter, making Ginnie shake.

"Quinn, I'm going to – *oh* – I – Quinn – "

"Yes," he replied. "Do. Now, Ginnie."

His mouth found hers, sealing his gentle command with a deep kiss.

And Ginnie *was* consumed.

The spiral exploded in flames that extended from where Quinn held her to every other part of her body. Her fingers and toes tingled with it. Her mind spun with it. And her heart bloomed with it. It let loose in a mad crescendo of release that left her panting. Her pulse thundered through her, and her chest rose and fell erratically, but the rest of her was a pool of molten liquid, unable to move, even if she wanted it to.

And she didn't want to.

She just wanted to lie there and forget about everything, to selfishly hold onto the glow that warmed her. The glow that Quinn brought her.

Quinn.

Her eyes dragged open slowly, seeking his face in the dark. And there he was, lying on his side, his dark-lashed eyes glinting at her and his mouth turned up at the corners in a pleased, sexy smile.

"Good, baby?" His voice was rough-edged velvet.

"Good?" Ginnie whispered back.

She didn't think a word had ever sounded so inadequate. And suddenly she wanted to show him just how much better than *good* she felt. She reached for him.

And without warning, the door swung open, bathing them in fluorescent light, and an embarrassed gasp and a stammered apology carried across the hotel room.

With her face flaming, Ginnie yanked the quilt up to her chin, and Quinn grinned at her before he jumped to his feet.

"Busted!" he announced a little too gleefully, then added, "Don't worry sir, I'm just here to change a light bulb."

"Uh."

Ginnie refused to look at whoever made the slightly strangled noise. It sounded like a man. And if she ran into him in the hall, or in the gift shop, or *any*where, She didn't want to recognize him. She didn't want to see his face and know that he'd gotten a full view her while she was practically topless. Post-orgasm. Her mind full of hedonistic debauchery.

God.

She squeezed her eyes shut, and she didn't open them again until she was sure Quinn had closed the door firmly behind the unfortunate delivery man.

Then she sat bolt upright, her hands holding her pajama shirt closed tightly, and she shot Quinn a glare.

"What the hell was that?"

He looked amused. And he was holding a sandwich.

"You said you wanted to know what it was like to be at risk for getting caught," he pointed out.

"Not like that!"

"I was trying to add some authenticity."

Ginnie did up her buttons. Not as swiftly as he'd undone them, but still quickly.

"Remind me to never ask *you* to do something with handcuffs," she muttered.

Quinn chuckled and leaned against the tiny table across the room. He lifted the sandwich.

"Want a bite?"

And Ginnie wanted to say no, just for spite. But as she glared at him, wondering just how he could sit there so casually after totally rocking her world and *not* having his rocked in return, her stomach rumbled. And the sandwich started to look almost as tasty as the man holding it.

Saturday
Eighteen

Quinn made his way back to the hotel room, coffee and cookies in hand.

Out of habit, he'd risen early, then headed downstairs to see if he could get some information about their flight to Vegas.

And the news was bad.

Or good, depending on how you look at it.

They were stuck in the bowels of Asscrack, Colorado for at least another twenty-four hours. And he kinda thought Ginnie wouldn't be too pleased, so he decided to soften the blow with a little caffeine and a little sugar. Now that he was almost back, though, he was doing his best to keep quiet.

If last night was any indication, Ginnie needed a good rest.

He grinned.

Minutes after offering to share his sandwich with her, Quinn had found himself prying the last piece of it from her limp hand as she nodded off, mid-chew.

He'd never been so ridiculously grateful for – and ridiculously resentful of – a food item before.

He'd seen the look in Ginnie's eyes right before that door flew open, and there was open invitation there in those wide green irises of hers. He thought it was probably a damned good thing that his prescheduled interruption came when it did. No way would he have been able to hold back.

The sandwich saved her.

Instead of ravaging her the way he wanted to, Quinn had tucked her into the bed. She hadn't even fought him as he did it. Hell, she hadn't even bothered with a clever retort when he teased her about wearing her out so easily.

Then he'd climbed in beside her, more for a need to torture himself than actual rest, because he'd thought there wasn't a chance he would fall asleep himself.

Except Quinn *did* fall asleep.

In fact, he'd had the best sleep he'd had in years. Maybe since the day before his senior training officer pulled him from a class and asked him if he'd ever considered the fact that he had no family and few friends a blessing. Less than twenty-four hours later, he'd been on the street, hocking his falsified experience as a low-level dealer to a recruiter for the Black Daggers. It was a successful sell.

And no. The eight years following that weren't restful at all.

"It's done now," Quinn muttered.

When he realized he'd almost walked past his own room he balanced the cups, one on top of the other, and opened the door. Then he froze in the frame.

When he'd left, the room has been swathed in darkness. Now the sun, still on its ascent, peeked through the curtains and hit the edge of the bed, lighting up Ginnie's hair. The tight bun had managed to come loose – this time all on its own – and fanned out across the cream-coloured pillow in a shiny array of gold and blonde. Her eyes were closed and her lips sealed and her whole body was peaceful.

That right there, he thought absently, *might be the best view in the world.*

As Quinn stared down at Ginnie, the big man – tattooed, pierced, and who considered himself pretty fucking clueless about every part of living a normal life – felt a little piece of his heart shift.

Was there a chance that this was *right*? That *he* might be right for her?

Ginnie exhaled in her sleep and rolled a little so that one foot stuck out from the blanket, and Quinn noticed that the nails had been painted a shimmery shade of pink.

Had she treated herself to a pedicure before leaving for her trip?

No nail polish. It was at the top of Jason's this-is-how-down-to-earth-my-sister-is list.

Maybe she kept her toes covered around him.

Quinn winced a little. He really owed his friend a call.

As if on cue, a buzz and a muffled bit of music drifted up from somewhere in the room.

Shit. Ginnie's phone.

Where the hell was it now?

It rang again, and Ginnie stirred.

It's under the bed.

Quinn set the cups on the table and dropped to the floor.

Under Ginnie's *side of the bed.*

"Of course," Quinn muttered.

He stuck his hand underneath, trying to keep his body from bumping the mattress. The sparkly case was just out of reach.

C'mon, Mcdavid. You used to be a cop. Cops retrieve guns from floors. They use gum attached to coat hangers to do it. They do it from inside closets. In rooms full of gangsters. You shouldn't have a problem getting a phone out from under a bed.

The phone rang a third time, and Quinn finally managed to get a hold of it. He dragged it out from under the bed, pressed the *off* button hard, then slid open the night stand drawer and dropped it inside.

"Quinn?"

He jerked his head up.

Ginnie was leaning on her elbow, her wide green eyes blinking at him sleepily.

He forced a grin. "Morning, baby."

"Quinn?" she said again.

"Yeah?"

"Are you on the floor?"

Quinn looked down, then up, then dropped her a cheeky wink. "Appears so."

"Why?"

"I wanted to let you have the upper hand for a minute."

She yawned. "I think you might be lying."

Shit.

"Lying?" he replied innocently.

"Mm hmm. You would *never* let me have the upper hand on purpose."

"Well," Quinn teased. "I wasn't going to *tell* you about it. But then you woke up."

"What *were* you going to do, then?"

"Kiss you."

"Kiss me?"

This time Quinn's grin was real. "If you insist."

He came up to his knees and grazed his lips over hers quickly, then pulled away.

"Quinn?" Ginnie murmured.

"Uh huh."

"You taste like coffee."

"Probably."

"I want coffee."

He chuckled. "You want coffee, do you?"

"Yes."

"More than you want another kiss?"

"It's a tough call."

"Let me see if I can sway your decision."

He grabbed the edge of the bed with the intention of pulling himself up and tackling her. Instead, he gripped the sheets a little too hard, and without warning, the blankets and Ginnie both came sliding forward. With a little shriek, she slammed into him. Quinn toppled over. The blankets twisted around their legs binding the two of them together.

Ginnie wriggled on top of him like she was trying to get away, but the harder she tried, the more they stuck together. And the more they stuck together, the harder *Quinn* got.

Christ.

He clearly had no control.

"Stop," he said with a groan.

"What?" She wriggled a little more.

"Stop," Quinn repeated.

"But we're stuck."

"And what you're doing is *un*sticking us?"

"Yes."

"No."

She put her hands to the ground and held herself up. If she was trying to put some space in between them, she failed. So badly. There were only a few inches between their faces. There were *no* inches between the rest of them. She moved up and….*Jesus*. There was also no chance she couldn't feel what she was doing to him.

"Ginnie…"

Her eyes widened and she finally stopped moving. "Oh."

"Yeah. Sure as hell *not* unsticking."

"What're we going to do?"

Quinn had a few ideas. "Is that a real question?"

"We can't stay like this all day."

"Actually…" he raised an eyebrow suggestively.

A blush crept up her cheeks. "We'll miss our plane."

"Right. About that."

"What about it?"

"You want the good news, or the bad news?"

"Bad," she replied immediately.

"The storm's picked back up and the planes are grounded. They figure we won't get out until tomorrow morning at the earliest."

"So we're *extra* stuck?"

"Mm hmm. No Vegas for us."

Her face fell. "And the good news?"

Quinn forced one of his arms out from the tangled mess of bedding and cupped her cheek with his palm. He ran his thumb along her lip, watching as the bottom one dropped open and she tried to cover her quick inhale and failed.

"The good news," he said softly. "Is that there are *no* extra rooms available in the whole hotel." He pulled her lips open a little more. "Or anywhere close by." He moved his thumb to the edge of her tongue, then used his fingers to close her mouth overtop of the digit. "So we're stuck *together*."

She sucked on his thumb gently and it was Quinn's turn to draw in a breath. He pulled his hand from her mouth, freed his arms, then planted both palms on her hips. He held her there for a long moment, revelling in just how good she felt, even fully covered.

"Ask me again what we're going to do, Ginnie," he suggested in a thick voice.

"What're we going to do, Quinn?" she whispered.

"We're going to make our *own* Vegas."

"We're going to…Oh."

Quinn chuckled at the poorly disguised disappointment on her face.

"What were *you* hoping for?" he teased.

"Nothing."

He moved swiftly, flipping them over so she was pinned underneath him. "Have you *been* to Vegas before?"

"No."

"Well I have. My old boss had a big, sore thumb of house out in the desert, so I got to spend plenty of time in the city. And it's full of naughtiness," he said. "Trust me when I say you're going to enjoy my version of it. It'll be right up your good-girl-gone-bad alley."

"Is that what you think I am?"

He bent down and closed his lips on hers, dragging her mouth open and flicking his tongue ring across the roof of her mouth. When he pulled away, she shivered.

"*Isn't* that what you are?" Quinn asked.

"No."

"Liar."

"I'm a self-improvement mission, not a self-destruction mission."

"And you're self-improving by making out with me on a hotel room floor?"

Her blush deepened. "Everything's a learning experience."

"Spoken like a true good-girl," Quinn joked.

"I'm not that good," she insisted.

"Is that right? Tell me then…What would you be doing right now if you were at home?"

"Drinking coffee and watching pornography."

Quinn burst out laughing, then rolled off Ginnie and pushed himself to his feet.

"Well. I can help you with the first thing right now. But the second thing may have to be worked into the fully customized, Huntingdon-Vegas experience I've created for you. Maybe between the poker and the strippers."

He picked up her coffee, waited for her to seat herself on a chair, then handed it over. She took a sip, and Quinn wondered abruptly if she would notice that it was made exactly the way she liked it. Another Jason-fact. Ginnie pretended to drink it black, but secretly added a package of raw sugar. Quinn had made it that way automatically, not thinking anything of it until right this second.

If she does notice, will she be suspicious?

Quinn watched her savor the mouthful of coffee.

It was another opportunity to tell her the truth. His tongue flicked to his lip ring nervously as he waited for her to say something about it.

Either she kills you now, or Jase kills you later, he reasoned.

But she just took another sip and shot him a thoughtful look. "You know what? We can easily fit in the pornography if we make a *tiny* adjustment."

"What's that?"

"Turn the poker and the strippers into *one* activity instead of two." Ginnie shot him a sweet smile that was perfectly – sexily – at odds with her suggestion. "So. Let's see this list of pseudo-Vegas activities."

Nineteen

Ginnie squirmed a little as Quinn reached into his pocket and withdrew a crumpled piece of paper scrawled with messy handwriting. She should've been disappointed that she was going to miss Vegas. She should've been gritting her teeth at the fact that she wasn't going to get to stick it to Lawrence by using the non-refundable ticket that *he* had paid for. Maybe she should've been wondering if she was being punished for making the decision to go, for deciding that hell yes, she was going to spend Lawrence's money – the little bit she'd managed to secure before he cleaned out their joint accounts – while she was there.

Instead, a little bubble of elation was growing inside her.

She was *excited.* Thrilled that rather than spending her Saturday surrounded by ka-chinging slot machines and girls in glitter and drunk newlyweds, she was going to spend it surrounded by Quinn.

Or he's going to be surrounded by you.

Her body tingled at the deliciously naughty thought.

They were going to share this hotel room again. A bed. And this time it was deliberate.

It was crazy. Far crazier than Vegas alone.

And last night had been…Was there a word for the way he'd made her body hum? For the way he'd swept away lucid thought? For the way he'd made her feel sexy and raw and powerful and wanted?

God, how she wanted it again. Wanted more.

So does he.

That little thought made her squirm almost as much as the jumble of excitement percolating just under her skin.

She made him…*Hard.*

She did. Genevieve Louise Silver.

This sex-in-a-tattooed-package man definitely wanted her. She'd felt it – literally – this morning when they'd been tangled in the sheets.

So why doesn't he just take you? she wondered, a tiny bit of insecurity slipping back in.

An answer was fast on the question's heels. And there was nothing shy about it.

Who cares about why*? Just seduce him. Make it impossible for him not to follow through. Make him take those big, messy-looking but oh so adept hands of his and put them all over you. And maybe his mouth, too. Or maybe his –*

"Ginnie?"

She flushed, and her head snapped up. "Yes?"

"Coffee's that good, huh?"

She realized a little belatedly that her breathing had sped up and that she was holding the paper cup in a death grip.

"It's perfect," she agreed quickly.

Which was true, anyway. Just the way she liked it. Black with a hint of sweetness. What were the odds?

Quinn is outside the odds, she reminded herself and forced her mind back to what he was saying.

"Tell me what you'd planned for Vegas. Besides copious amounts of pornography, I mean," he teased.

"I don't know," Ginnie said honestly.

"Okay. What's the first thing you think of when you think Vegas?"

"Slots."

Quinn tapped his paper. "Done. There's a miniature casino at the airport. What next?"

"A show?"

"Also done. This hotel has a resident entertainer on Saturday nights."

"Entertainer?" Ginnie repeated. "The vagueness of that makes me nervous."

He grinned. "This is Quinn-Vegas, baby. Ready to surprise and delight."

She narrowed her eyes at him. "You didn't even ask what kind of entertainer it was, did you?"

"Nope."

"It could be a ninety-year old Elvis Impersonator."

Quinn's eyes lit up. "I hope so."

"It could be a male stripper," Ginnie said. "With a bad case of plumber's crack."

"Doubtful." Quinn tapped the paper again. "A stripper here would create too much competition for the adult establishment just down the road."

"Huntingdon has a strip bar?"

"Huntingdon has a strip bar that we're going to," Quinn corrected.

Ginnie's pulse skittered, and she forced a laugh. "You're taking me to see strippers?"

"Yep. I took care of that particular Vegas stereotype, too. Unless you don't want to go."

Ginnie licked her lips nervously. She somehow doubted that Quinn was talking about a *male* revue show. Which meant pasties and G-strings. Bumping and grinding. T and A.

Would it get him all riled up? Was he the kind of man who liked that stuff?

Is there a man who doesn't?

"Ginnie? If you don't want to go, just tell me."

"No," she said. "I do want to."

And saying it somehow made it true. Really true. She wanted to sit beside him and watch him watch them. Her heart actually *raced* at the thought. It beat so loud in her chest that she could barely hear Quinn's voice, and she had to make herself pay attention.

"First things first," he told her as he pried the fully crushed coffee cup from her hand. "You think you can find something in that pile of not-yours underwear that'll work?"

"Work for what?"

Quinn shrugged. "To wear until we find you something else."

The all-over her body rush of blood stopped abruptly. "You want me to wear Lawrence's girlfriend's underwear?"

His hand slid across the table to squeeze hers. "I just meant some clothes to borrow. Unless you think you can pull off wearing my pajamas to the strip club?"

"Actually, when you put it like that, I think the other girl's underwear would probably help me fit in better."

He shot her a very serious, utterly scorching look. "Ginnie...I don't want you wear *any* underwear. Let alone someone else's."

Her heart started thumping at double time again. "Do I need to remind you that I'm *not* wearing any?"

"Trust me," Quinn said. "I am *very* aware of what you don't have – and what you *do* have – under those pajamas. And unless you have the world's biggest box of condoms hidden somewhere that I *don't* know about, you might want me to keep my mind elsewhere." He paused and bit his lip ring so hard that Ginnie thought it might break, then asked, "Do you have it hidden somewhere, Ginnie?"

She shook her head. Because if she answered him out loud, she was going to say the first thing that popped into her head. And she thought maybe *fuck the condoms* would have consequences she might regret later.

Quinn shrugged at her silent response.

"So," he said. "In t-minus ten minutes, we go onto Vegas time. Which means *no* time. No watches, no clocks, no – "

"Shit!" Ginnie interrupted as thoughts of timing invaded her oversexed mine.

"What?"

"My brother."

"Your brother?"

"I don't have a watch. I usually check my phone, and thinking about that reminded me that I should've called him. But I left the stupid thing at the airport as an act of rebellion."

"An act of rebellion?"

"I just – Never mind. My point is that now I *can't* call him now, which mean he'll freak out. When he freaks out he does dumb stuff," she explained.

"So...Shit." Quinn tapped his lip ring.

"Exactly."

"You don't think he'd freak out a little *more* when you tell him you're sleeping with me?"

Ginnie knew he'd dropped the double entendre deliberately, but she blushed anyway. "I wasn't planning on telling him about you."

"What *were* you going to tell him?"

She frowned, wondering why he sounded a little tense, then dismissed her worry. *He's just worried about keeping his own ass safe. Especially since you made it clear how protective Jase can be.*

"Just that I'm not dead," she said.

Quinn's face relaxed. "All right. T-minus *twenty* minutes then. Use the hotel phone to call your big, bad brother. And *don't* tell him about the big bad wolf in your room. Then we go onto Vegas-time. Champagne breakfast to start the day off with a buzz. Strippers at eleven. Tattoos at noon."

"Tattoos?" Ginnie repeated faintly.

Quinn ignored her. "A maybe-illegal poker game at two, followed by an all-you-can-eat buffet. Early bird special is at four-thirty. The ninety-year old Elvis stripper with the plumber-butt issue comes on at seven. Then some dancing. And after that, if we don't get arrested…" He gave her a lascivious onceover, leaned in, and whispered, "That pornography I promised."

Ginnie barely heard him. And she hardly noticed as he placed an order for room service. Even when he winked at her and told the person on the other line, "She said *yes*," in that smirk-y, self-satisfied way of his.

She knew she ought to move. Maybe pick her jaw up off her chest. Straighten her hair. Blink. Argue. Point out that she hadn't said *yes*. She hadn't said anything.

But she was too busy being one-part stunned, one-part overwhelmed, and one-part dizzy with anticipation.

Quinn had clearly spent the better part of his morning planning their weekend together. And there were so many things that went along with those last three words.

Ginnie couldn't help but break it down.

Their.

Weekend.

Together.

She didn't want to read more into that than she should. But how could she not?

Almost forty-eight more sinful hours with Quinn Mcdavid. Blissful, mind-boggling, nerve-wracking.

And oh. He wanted to get tattoos. Or in his case, *more* tattoos.

Ginnie's own skin was currently as bare as the day she was born. She didn't even have her ears pierced. Yet.

You are not *getting a tattoo. Or making porn,* she told herself firmly.

But the other stuff…

She watched Quinn as he moved around the room to the bed. He reached out and grabbed the sheets from the floor.

He's making *the bed,* she realized.

And Ginnie was pretty damned sure she'd never seen anything so sexy as the thickly muscled, ink-covered man performing the simple domestic task. Who knew something so basic could be so freaking hot?

Yes, of the emotions fighting for supremacy, it was definitely anticipation that was gaining momentum.

"Hey, baby?" Quinn said as he tucked in a final, near-perfect hospital corner.

"Mmph?"

Ginnie hoped it sounded more like an answer than like a bad attempt to cover the spike in her temperature. From his damned bed making.

"My stuff's in the bathroom, so I'm gonna get changed in there. If you want some privacy…" He gestured around the room at the still strewn-about clothes.

"Okay."

Quinn turned away, stripping off his T-shirt as he moved toward the bathroom, and Ginnie couldn't bury a sharp inhale as she caught sight of his back. A wide, star-shaped scar stood out starkly. The skin there was whiter and thicker than the rest of the surrounding area, and as he tossed his shirt to the bed, it rippled. Something about it drew Ginnie in. Cemented her attraction to him.

A perfect imperfection.

"Quinn?" she called, right before he closed the door.

"Yeah?"

"Can you add one more thing to the to-do list for the day?"

"Sure. What did you have in mind?"

Ginnie took a breath. "We really need to buy the world's biggest box of condoms."

Twenty

Quinn shut the door silently, and for a long second after it closed, his fingers stayed on the handle. Like they had a mind of their own.

He shot them an angry look.

Quit fucking lingering, he commanded.

It was hard to make them obey. Especially when he felt like he could suddenly relate so well to a word like *linger*.

"Christ," he muttered as he finally managed to pry his hand away. "Next thing you'll be doing is *swooning*."

He spun to the sink, turned on the cold tap as high as it would go, then ducked his head under the punishing stream of icy water. He refused to come up for air. He'd stay there until the cold became a burn and actual tears threatened to squeeze from his eyes.

Even crying was better than the weak-kneed feeling that had swept through him when Ginnie had added her little request to the end of his fake-Vegas list.

What the hell was it about that bold comment that made him want to drop and worship at her feet, anyway? The fact that she was owning her desire? The fact that saying *condom* made her blush?

As his head started to ache with cold, Quinn shut the water off, but continued to grip the edge of the faux marble sink, watching the water drip from his hair to the drain. It spiraled down, taking his mood with it.

"What the hell is wrong with you?" he asked himself out loud.

Quinn steeled himself to face his reflection in the mirror, half-expecting to see some simpering Bronte sister looking back at him instead of his usual grim exterior.

He took a breath, and when he looked up, he was almost disappointed to find his plain old self. His face was rough with a day of stubble, and his reflection glared back at him in the usual way.

He grabbed a towel from the rack, ran it over his hair in a half-assed drying effort, then draped it over his shoulders and pulled his shaving kit from his bag. He went through the motions, slashing at his own skin, still unable to figure out why he was angry. Why he was mad because he got his way.

You are not *going to have sex with Genevieve Silver.*

The answering thought came out of nowhere, and Quinn didn't know if it was a resolution, or simply a realization.

Whatever it is, it's ridiculous, he said to himself.

It was his *goal,* for God's sake. To make her see how sexy she could be. How sexy she already was. Which, judging from her request for condoms, he'd done.

If anything, his quick success should be making him gloat, not goddamned…linger. Not decide not to follow through.

God knew, he wanted her. Enough to be pissed off at himself for even *thinking* about not doing it. But somewhere not far below the surface…he was relieved, too. *Not* having sex with her absolved him of guilt.

Guilt? Or responsibility?

Quinn squeezed the sink harder.

Both.

He didn't want to take advantage of her, and he didn't want to become something she wished she hadn't done, either. The thought of doing that – of becoming his one and only friend's one and only sister's one and only regret – cut into him like a knife. A dull, rusty, tetanus-encrusted knife. That looked suspiciously like the one on his arm.

Ridiculous, he thought again, and finally released the sink so he could grab a pair of reasonably unwrinkled pants and a long-sleeved dress shirt from his suitcase.

But sliding into the clothes didn't give him the usual satisfaction of projecting the *Yeah, I should be dressed up, but this is as far as I'm willing to go* attitude. Instead, he kinda wished he'd packed a suit. Or that he even *owned* a suit.

Oh, good, he thought sarcastically as he rolled his sleeves up to his elbows and snapped a silver-studded belt into place. *Now I'm an* insecure, *lingering asshole.*

Enough.

No sex? Fine.

Moping? Hell, no.

He flicked his hair out of his eyes and shot himself a final, disgusted look.

Then he flung open the door and caught sight of Ginnie.

She was sitting on the bed, her back propped up by a pillow, the phone from the side table pressed to her ear.

She looked…different.

And delicious as hell.

Her eyes were closed, giving Quinn a good long minute to drink her in, head to toe.

She'd left her hair loose, and full, and it framed her face perfectly. She'd obviously dug out some makeup from somewhere, and she'd rimmed her eyes in a bruised shade of purple. Her lips, which were moving in hushed conversation, were silver with gloss.

If someone had asked Quinn ten minutes ago if he'd like to see Ginnie made up like that, he would've replied with a vehement *no.* He would've said it would wreck the clean beauty of her face. Now…Shit. She was a whole different kind of stunning. A whole different kind of entrancing.

Quinn's eyes slid reluctantly away from her face to take in the rest of her appearance.

She'd picked a pale pink top, feathery-looking from the waist to the chest, but with a see-through strip of some stretchy material that clung to her cleavage and crept all the way to her throat.

Like a fabric blush.

She wore a shiny black skirt – satin, maybe, or something like it, Quinn wasn't exactly up-to-date with women's sparkly fabrics – that barely came to mid-thigh, even when she tugged it down a little.

Below that, on her pink-painted toes, were a pair of leather-strapped, stone-studded shoes that even Quinn knew classified as hooker-heels.

Holy, bloody, goddamned hell. That *is something to linger over.*

"Yes!" she hissed into the phone irritably, then made a huffy adjustment that drove the skirt up even further.

Which reminded Quinn that there was a hell of a lot more he could with her than just have sex. Things that would fill her with satisfaction instead of regret.

Oh, hell yes, there are.

With a growl that made Ginnie's eyes fly open and fix their ultra-greenness on him, Quinn strode to the end of the bed.

She mouthed something at him – maybe, "What are you doing?"

He ignored it.

He grabbed each of her ankles, strappy heels and all, and pulled.

Ginnie skidded down the bed and let out a satisfying little yelp.

"No," she said into the phone. "I'm fine. I, uh, bumped my foot. Stubbed my toes." Pause. "Yes, all of them!"

She tried to kick away Quinn's hands. He ignored that, too, and pulled her down a little further. She was lying almost flat now, and even though Quinn couldn't see her face, he could picture it. Annoyed and nervous and excited, eyes wide, lips pursed.

He chuckled, and she said, "Shh." Then added, "No, not you. Who? No one. No!"

Quinn brought his mouth to one of her ankles and gave it a nip. She tried to squeeze her feet together, but he felt her shiver, so he moved his mouth and did the same thing with the other. A little harder. Her ankles loosened immediately.

Good.

Quinn dragged his teeth and his tongue up one calf, then down the other.

"Jase," Ginnie said pleadingly.

Quinn wondered if the tone was really directed toward her brother, or if it was for him.

This time on his exploration up her smooth legs, he opened his mouth a bit wider and took it slower, exploring every inch with a thorough suck.

"Oh!" Ginnie exclaimed, and Quinn knew *that* one was for him. "No, I'm fine," she added. "I would've called you last night if I hadn't – "

Her words cut off abruptly as Quinn put his hands on her knees, pushed them apart and slid himself up. He kissed each of her thighs, just below the skirt hem, then lifted his eyes and found her returning his gaze, her chin pressed to her chest, her expression flushed.

Quinn grinned a sideways grin and whispered, "Hi, baby."

"Hi," she replied faintly, then let her head fall back and groaned. "No, Jase. I just – I lost you there for a second. I think the snowstorm's affecting the phone or something."

Quinn muffled his chuckle in one of her lightly muscled thighs. He was ridiculously turned on. Ridiculously pent up. And he was having far too much fun to stop.

He trailed kisses from her knees to the bottom of the skirt, then back, then again.

Ginnie continued to talk. Vaguely, Quinn heard her try – and fail at – begging off the conversation.

Quinn just moved up even farther. He slid the skirt to what would've been underwear level. If she'd had any on. Which, of course, she didn't.

Thank you, God.

Quinn gave her thighs a gentle nudge with his palms and they fell obligingly open.

Thank you, God. Times two.

He used his thumb to trace a pattern over her waiting wetness, and her legs parted even more.

Quinn leaned in and took a tiny taste.

Sweet. Hot.

He wanted more.

So he ran his tongue – and its helpful little piercing – along the length of her, pausing at the top to draw her clit between his teeth. Very gently, oh-so-carefully, he moved his head back and forth, up and down, then side to side again.

Ginnie's hips rose to meet the attention, and Quinn could feel the way she quivered. From the inside out.

He released her swollen clit, used his fingers to spread her open, then let his tongue do the walking.

In and out, around in a tunneling circle. She writhed underneath him, and Quinn pushed harder. Deeper. He drew out the heat; he drew out the wetness.

He heard the phone clatter to the floor, and Ginnie let out a cry, and if Quinn had been thinking instead of doing, he might've hoped to heaven that her brother hung up before the sound tore from her.

She tightened against his tongue and he knew she was close.

Fuck, how he wanted her. But he wanted *this* even more.

In fact, he could definitely see the appeal of spending the whole weekend *not* having sex with Ginnie.

Just like this.

Quinn brought his mouth back to her clit, then drove his fingers into her as roughly as he dared and – oh sweet lord – he felt her convulse against the attention. Again. And again. And again.

Twenty-One

As the last viciously sweet orgasm rocked her body, then subsided and left Ginnie a panting, sweat-sheened glob of goo, she realized she'd been duped. Two years of dating – one precious year of *waiting* – then four years of marriage, all of it culminating in an end *she'd* taken the blame for. Lawrence thought *she* wasn't good enough in bed. And she knew that wasn't just insecurity talking. She'd seen the look on Lawrence's face when they were in that boardroom. He'd claimed "they" weren't compatible. But his smug expression said what he really meant was that *Ginnie* wasn't compatible.

Unfuckable.

But what just happened – what Quinn just did to her – nothing like that had *ever* happened between her and her former husband.

It wasn't me *who stunk in the bedroom. It was* him.

The realization was like a percolation of understanding. A dawning of self-reclamation.

The bedroom was one of the only places Ginnie felt lost, and she'd always counted on the fact that Lawrence was older and more experienced to guide her through it. And the man had been...What *was* the right word?

Predictable?

Formulaic?

Boring?

All of the above.

What *else* had the fake-tan, high horse doctor misled her about?

"Baby?"

Whoops.

Ginnie flushed. She'd been so lost in thought that she'd slipped away from the source of her revelation. Who was currently lying beside her, propped up on one elbow, his dark faux hawk flipping forward a bit and his eyes locked on Ginnie's face.

"Hi," she said softly.

"Hey."

Quinn.

Whose fingers and tongue had a line straight to her O-button. Whose sexy, knowing, but not know-it-all smile was making her warm again, even though she'd just been thoroughly sated.

Hmm.

The burgeoning bedroom-confidence made Ginnie want to know what the *rest* of him was capable of. No. Not just want to know. Want to find out, like, now.

Unconsciously, her gaze slipped down. The cream-colored dress shirt he wore had slipped up to expose a teasing glimpse of his muscular abdomen. A belt glinted at his waist, just begging to be undone. And below that, a distinctive bulge.

"Uh-uh," he said, like he could read her mind. "Any second, that champagne breakfast I ordered is gonna show up, and as delicious as *you* are…I'm still hungry."

Ginnie inhaled and replied, "I can *see* how hungry you are."

Quinn's face split into a grin. "Is that right?"

Her eyes dropped once more, and her hand sought to follow. But Quinn grabbed her wrist.

"Uh-uh," he said again.

Ginnie shot him her best approximation of a scowl, which made Quinn laugh.

God, why did even his laugh *have to be sexy?*

He didn't let go of her arm.

"You won't let me touch you?" she asked, barely managing to *not* blush.

"Nope."

"Why not?"

"I think we covered that during the box of condoms discussion." He brought her hand up to his face and ran the backs of her fingers along his freshly shaved cheek. "You can kiss me though."

"Anywhere I want?"

"No."

Ginnie watched as Quinn's Adam's apple bobbed up and down, betraying the answer he wanted to give.

Fine, she thought. *We'll just see how that goes.*

She tipped her head up and inched forward while he continued to hold her hand in place. It wasn't until her lips met his and she caught a taste of herself on his mouth that she recalled where those teeth and that tongue of his had been just a few minutes earlier. She wondered if she should be squeamish about it.

But she wasn't.

If anything, it sent a little thrill through, knowing that he'd laid claim to her so thoroughly.

And Quinn let her take her time, touching his lip ring with her own lips, then with her tongue. He let her suck on it for a few seconds, and when she tugged on it a little harder, his mouth dropped open so she could work her way inside. She skated *her* tongue over the warm, smooth ball in the center of *his* tongue. Quinn was almost still as Ginnie kissed him, responding but not taking it any further.

It was remarkably sensual to have him that pliable under her mouth. Nearly erotic.

He loosened his grip on her hand just enough that she could slide her fingers to his throat. And she could feel his pulse thudding unevenly there under his skin.

When she pulled away, Quinn let out a groan of protest.

Take that.

Ginnie wiggled her hand from his grasp and brought her fingers around to the first fastened button on his shirt. And she undid it. Not as adeptly as he'd undone her pajamas last night, but quick enough that she got to the next button before he slammed his bear-trap hold on her once more.

"Please, Quinn," she said.

"Bad idea," he replied.

She opened her mouth to make an argument in favor of letting her touch him. Or maybe to just outright beg him to let her – at least a little bit – but a sharp rap on the door stopped her.

"Lucky," she muttered as Quinn jumped to his feet and moved quickly across the room.

He sent her a scorching look as he closed his hand on the doorknob. "Hardly what I'd call *lucky*."

"You could ignore whoever that is," Ginnie pointed out.

"I never ignore breakfast."

Ginnie sat up and watched with narrowed eyes as Quinn took the wheeled tray from the uniformed, female hotel employee, who eyed him up and down with an open appreciation that made Ginnie want to throw her one of her stupid, rhinestone-studded shoes at her. And her irritation doubled when the girl lifted an arm to brush a loose strand of hair off her face and Ginnie caught a glimpse on some ink in her wrist. She had a sparkly stud in one nostril, too.

Self-doubt fought to make its way back in. *Maybe* that's *the kind of girl he'd let touch him.*

But as quickly as the discouraging thought came in, it went out again. Because even as Quinn exchanged a few meaningless pleasantries with the girl, his eyes kept straying to Ginnie. They rested on her face, or on her breasts, and even on her hands for a moment. And every time they found a spot on her body, their heat seared into her, leaving no doubt as to where his interest lay.

Ginnie crossed and uncrossed her legs, and yep, his gaze stayed locked on her knees for so long that the hotel girl had to tap him on the shoulder to tell him she was done.

As Quinn handed her a generous tip, the girl sighed and acknowledged Ginnie for the first time.

"You're a lucky woman," she said, which made Quinn laugh silently as he ushered her out.

Once the girl was gone, Ginnie half-expected – okay, *mostly* expected – him to pounce on her. Instead, he began to set up the breakfast at a leisurely pace. But she was sure food was the last thing on his mind.

So why is he working so hard at pretending it is?

Ginnie continued to sit in silence as Quinn popped the top on champagne. He filled two flutes almost to the brim, handed one to her and held up the other.

He winked. "To luck!"

"Very funny."

She clinked her glass to his, then gulped back half of it, and as the bubbly liquid slid down her throat, a thought occurred to her.

And before she could stop it, it popped out of her mouth. "You're trying to protect my virtue!"

Ginnie's face flamed, but surprisingly, Quinn didn't deny it. He didn't even laugh.

"Quinn," Ginnie said, her blush easing off a little. "You realize I was *married,* right?"

"Actually," he replied. "Since the marriage was annulled...You *weren't.*"

Ginnie rolled her eyes. "A technicality. And not my point."

Though until that second, it hadn't *really* occurred to Ginnie that the annulment denoted a total redo. She wasn't a divorcee. She wasn't a scorned woman. She was, quite simply...single. And she liked that. She wanted to *do* something with that singleness.

Ginnie met Quinn's eyes. "There are a few things the annulment didn't undo."

He topped up her glass, drank his own, then filled it again, too. He straddled a chair, popped a piece of toast into his mouth and chewed it slowly before speaking again.

"How many men have you slept with?"

"What?"

"You heard me."

"Why does it matter?"

"It doesn't."

"Then why are you asking?"

Quinn smiled. "Give some leeway here again, judge."

Ginnie shook her head, refusing to be sidetracked. "I just don't see why I should tell you."

He raised an eyebrow and out came the oh-so-skilled tongue of his to fiddle with his piercing. "Was that a serious statement?"

"Of course it was."

He slid the chair closer. So close that his knees brushed hers.

"When you said you want to touch me..." His voice dropped low. "Was it because you were thinking about having sex with me?"

Ginnie thought about lying, then thought better of it. "Yes."

"And *that* doesn't seem like a good enough reason to answer my question?"

"What if I asked you the same thing?" she countered.

His eyes twinkled, and when he leaned back, Ginnie knew what was coming before he even said it.

"I haven't slept with *any* men."

"Give yourself a chance. We haven't made it as far as Vegas yet."

He grinned. "I don't think I'm going to include that in *my* version of Sin City."

"Mine either, apparently," Ginnie muttered, then colored again.

Quinn chuckled. "If you're not going to answer me..."

"Then what? You'll force me to *not* touch you some more?"

"I'm just trying to make my *own* point."

"Which is?"

"Tell me how many, Ginnie, and I'll get to it."

His face still held mild amusement, but there was a stubborn set to his jaw, too.

All right. I'll play along then.

"One," Ginnie stated.

For a second, the big man had a comically startled look on his face, but he smoothed it out fast. "One?"

"Yes."

"Dr. Douchebag and one other?"

"No."

This time, Ginnie noted that Quinn couldn't cover his surprised expression quite as quickly. "One total? Just your former husband?"

"Yes."

At her fourth one-word answer, a frown creased his forehead, and Ginnie wished she'd kept her mouth shut.

She could feel her face growing pink again. "Do you interrogate all of your one night stands like this?"

She'd been half-kidding – maybe trying to deflect the attention away from herself – but Quinn's expression grew dark, and for a heartbeat, Ginnie thought he was going to throw his champagne glass across the room. Instead, he set it down slowly and stood up. He pushed the chair away from his body and stepped toward her. And unexpectedly, he dropped to his knees and looked up at her.

When he spoke, his tone was a fierce as his eyes. "Is that what you think you want from me?"

"Yes."

"And if I say no?"

Ginnie hesitated.

No reason to hold back.

"Then I guess I'll just have to seduce you, won't I?"

And just like that, she meant it. She'd do whatever she had to, to get Quinn in her bed. Even just for the weekend.

Twenty-Two

Quinn knew right away his attempt to make Ginnie reconsider, to make her think about herself, or put things in perspective, or whatever the hell might make her *not* want to jump into bed with him right that second, had failed. Now she was thinking about him as a goddamned...wild oat, or something.

He could tell from the thoughtfully devious look in her eye as she gave him a soft shove and stood up.

For a blissful, torturous second, his face was at level with the edge of her skirt, the sweet scent of her filling him. Then she moved away, leaving him feeling more than a bit empty.

She filled her wine glass again, and snagged a strawberry from the tray. Quinn watched her dip it in the bubbly liquid, knowing full well what her intention was.

"It's gonna take more than that," he said.

It was a lie, though.

As she sucked the champagne from the fruit, Quinn had to adjust his kneeling stance to accommodate the significant increase in blood flow between his legs.

"Give me a chance," Ginnie replied sweetly with another little lick. "I'm new at this."

Quinn actually felt himself *twitch.*

Christ.

"You realize that this is a mess, right?" he asked, aware that his voice was a little raw.

He wished absently that she'd showed up in his room ten minutes later. At least then, he would've had a chance to relieve him*self.*

She dipped the strawberry again, then licked it and took a delicate bite. "How is it a mess?"

"Yesterday, at the airport, I'm pretty sure you wanted to punch me for kissing you."

"That's not quite true."

"True *enough* that it makes you standing there, licking the hell out of a strawberry like that a big, giant *mess*."

"You want me to stop? Give me what I want."

"What, exactly, do you think you want?"

"You."

She made the statement with a red face and a hair toss, but she didn't back down or pull her eyes away from his.

Dammit.

Quinn wanted to point out that he was pretty damned sure they'd had this conversation – but in reverse – the night before. He kept his teeth together in an attempt to stop himself from saying it, but apparently, he didn't have to. She remembered, too.

"Are you saying *you* don't want *me* anymore?" Ginnie prodded. "Because last night…"

Quinn couldn't stand the hint of real insecurity under her teasing bravado.

"Of course I fucking want you," he growled.

"Then what's the problem?"

I don't want to be a wild oat.

That truth dug at him. And he couldn't admit it out loud. It wouldn't make sense to her, even if he did. He was supposed to be a complete stranger, to not know enough about her that he could say with certainty that this bit of wantonness now would likely haunt her forever.

Hell. The only man she'd ever had sex with was the asshole of a husband.

That, Quinn hadn't known. Though he guessed he shouldn't have been so startled to hear her say it. It was perfectly in line with everything else about her.

"The problem is that you don't know a thing about me," he said.

"Isn't that the way this is supposed to be?"

"No." Quinn ran a frustrated hand over his hair. "Could you please stop making me sound like a girl?"

"Nope."

With a self-satisfied smile, Ginnie lifted her champagne to her mouth and took a sip. As she pulled the glass away from her perfect, sexy-as-hell mouth, she didn't tip it up in time, and a significant amount of the sweet liquid poured down the front of her shirt. The pale pink material became see-through immediately, and so did the bra underneath it. Quinn fought a groan as the whole thing clung to her curves and her nipples came to full, taut view.

"Shit!" she exclaimed. "Now I've got to change."

"Do it quickly," Quinn suggested. "Fake-Vegas awaits."

He needed to get the hell out of the room before he lost it.

Ginnie shrugged. "All right."

She turned away and walked toward the loose pile of clothes in the suitcase that wasn't hers. It gave Quinn a brief reprieve. A *very* brief reprieve. Until she bent down to lift an item, and the skirt lifted to almost-ass level.

Quinn swallowed and forced his gaze away.

Do not *think about what else is under that skirt.*

"So…Are you going to tell me anything about yourself?" Ginnie asked, interrupting his attempt at making his mind go blank.

Quinn closed his eyes. "No."

Do not *listen to the way that fabric sounds as she pulls it off her body. Seriously. Do* not.

"Now you're just being obtuse."

It took him a second to realize she wasn't talking about his internal orders. "Hardly."

"Oh, please. You told me the problem is that I don't know anything about you. But you won't *tell* me anything about yourself, either? You're the very definition of obtuseness."

"Is that even a word?"

"Yes, it is, Mr. Semantics Smartypants."

In spite of himself, Quinn smiled. "If either one of us was going to get the title of Semantics Smartypants, it wouldn't be me."

There was a brief pause before Ginnie said, "You know what I think?"

"I have a feeling you're going to tell me."

"I think you like control just as much as I do. I think your too-cool-for-school act *is* an act, and that you use that to stay in charge. So you can toss your 'life has lots of grey' bullshit around all you want. Underneath it, you have just as many tidy, black and white boxes as I have."

At the end of her uncomfortably accurate speech, Quinn's eyes flew open. But whatever he'd been about to spout off in reply was lost as his tongue stuck to the roof of his mouth and every ounce of blood in his body made its way with a dart-like *zing* to his crotch.

Ginnie stood across from him, one hand on her hip, the other holding a strip of something shimmery. She was topless. Her luscious, perky breasts were on alert and demanding attention. The skirt looked shorter than ever and Quinn's eyes worked on autopilot, exploring every exposed inch of her.

Those lithe thighs. Shit. They'd feel good wrapped around him.

Those toned arms. Hell, how they belonged draped over his neck, fingers yanking on his hair.

Those pink, delicious nipples. They needed to be kissed. Sucked. Worshipped.

That half-smile on her face as she reached to cover herself. Barely. It was –

On purpose, Quinn realized.

The spill. The teasing. The speech.

Damn.

She might be new at seduction, but she was sure as hell giving it a good shot.

Right that second, all Quinn wanted to do was unbuckle his belt, drop his pants to his knees, and take her against the wall as hard and fast as he could.

"My bra got soaked, too." Ginnie's words sounded like an apology, but her face told Quinn she wasn't sorry in the least.

"Borrow one from the pile," he said gruffly and turned his attention to his wineglass.

He felt the narrowing of Ginnie's eyes, even though he couldn't see them. "Even if I was willing to consider it…Not an option. Lawrence's girlfriend happens to be slightly better endowed than I am."

Automatically, Quinn's gaze flicked to her chest, which she still held not-quite-covered with her arm, then to her face. "Not a chance in hell is she better endowed than you."

There was that blush. "Fine. *Bigger* endowed than I am, then. And either way, I can't wear one of her bras. Which is why I picked this." She held up the shimmery strip she'd been holding in her hand. "It doesn't need a bra."

"That doesn't need a bra because it's not a shirt."

"Are you going to tell me what to wear now?"

Quinn eyed the sparkly fabric skeptically. Tell her what to wear? No. He wanted to tell her what *not* to wear. Except he had a feeling if he tried, she'd suggest they stay in, and he honestly wasn't sure if he could handle it.

"I wouldn't *dream* of telling you what to do," he said.

If she was disappointed, she hid it well. "Good. Then you can help me do this up."

Ginnie dropped her arm, and Quinn forced himself – really, really forced himself – not to look down again as she slipped both hands into the shiny fabric and shimmied a little. Even when she had the so-called shirt over her chest, it left little to the imagination.

Quinn exhaled. "I don't even see a part that needs to be done up."

"On the back."

Ginnie turned around, flipped her hair away from her smooth shoulders, and stood still.

With an uncomfortable and markedly thick ache between his legs, Quinn stepped across the room to the spot where she waited. Two tiny strips of ribbon hung loose on the back of the shirt.

Hardly even worth the effort, he thought as he reached for them.

As if to prove his point – or maybe as if to defy it, it was hard to say – the first ribbon slipped from his fingers the moment Quinn grabbed it. When he made his second attempt, his hand glided across Ginnie's lower back, and she drew in a sharp breath.

Not that he could blame her for the inhale. Not if she felt anything like he did.

That one bit of contact sent a shock of heat through him, and it was searing enough that he was surprised to see that her skin stayed creamy rather than erupting in red.

Easy now, Quinn.

He gripped each piece of ribbon tightly, and drew them together, speaking as he did it.

"Less than five women," he said, feeling an unusual flicker of uncertainty.

"Less than wh – Oh."

He looped one ribbon under the other, then paused, pushing his finger to her back to hold them together. "Is that an 'oh, you thought it would be more' or an 'oh, you thought it would be less'?"

"More of an 'oh, I can't believe you actually told me'," she replied before admitting, "And probably…A bit of the first one, too."

"I'm twenty-nine." Quinn wasn't sure if he was defending the number by stating his age, or just adding it to the mix of things he was sharing. "I was an only child, and my parents died in a car accident when I was seventeen."

"I'm sorry."

It wasn't the automatic, somehow detached sympathy that Quinn was used to hearing, and when she paused for a beat, then added more, he knew it was because she understood.

"My mom died when I was young, too," she reminded him, then added, "And a week later, my dad decided he couldn't handle the pressure of being a single dad, and he walked away. I was on my own until I met the Silvers and my brother, Jason. I know how lonely it can be."

He finished making a bow, but left his hand pressed to the small of her back. "I'm sorry, too."

For a minute, an emotionally raw moment hung in the air. It was different than the sizzling chemistry that had been bouncing back and forth between then for the last twenty-four hours. It was deeper. And it scared the shit out of Quinn.

"I like pizza, but hate melted cheese on anything else," he announced with a forced chuckle, and ran his finger up her spine. "I've never been to Europe or South America or Africa or anywhere off the continent, actually. But I've been arrested in two countries, though. I've never been married. You?"

He could hear the smile in her voice as she leaned into his caress and answered. "I'm twenty-four and I've never been married, either. Cheese can pretty much go on anything and I love hockey. Europe's a dream, and I've only been arrested in *one* country. You *done* back there?"

Quinn released her reluctantly. "Done."

Her last admission was a true surprise. Something Jase sure as hell had never mentioned. Or more likely…that he didn't know about.

What the hell had she been arrested for?

Ginnie flicked her hair over her shoulder, sending a cascade of curls down her exposed back, then spun to face him.

"How do I look?"

Quinn's eyes raked over her. "In-fucking-credible."

"Really?"

"Yes."

Yeah, and the second *I find a store, you're getting something to cover up,* he added silently.

The top was purple and silver and he could tell that each time she moved, it was going to bare her midriff. The fabric didn't just cling to her curves – it was like a second skin. He wanted to pant like a cartoon dog. And so would every other man who caught sight of her.

"In-fucking-credible enough for a one night stand?" she asked teasingly.

She did a little spin, flinging the skirt up to an unacceptable height, and Quinn couldn't answer her smile.

He grabbed her arm and dragged her close.

"My last relationship lasted *six years*," he told her. "And I'm not even sure I liked the girl. You, Ginnie…I like *you*. And you're worth a hell of a lot more than a one night stand."

Her mouth dropped open like she couldn't quite believe what he'd said – and maybe Quinn couldn't believe it himself, but he wasn't going to take it back.

It was true. The girl in question had been his by virtue of his rank in the gang, but never once had he thought of her as his by virtue of desire. The moment he'd been jumped out was the same moment she walked away. Quinn had barely blinked.

Ginnie, on the other hand, was the kind of girl who would never – should never – be a trophy.

He bent down and planted a soft kiss on her forehead, aware that it was more sweet than sexy, then pulled away.

It was *clearly* time to get out of the room.

Before he could change his mind, Quinn grabbed her hand, slipped his jacket over her shoulders, and yanked her to the door.

Twenty-Three

Ginnie wasn't sure if the things Quinn had just said to her were supposed to dampen her desire – or even if they weren't intended to, ought to anyways. Either way, they hadn't.

As they walked through the almost-silent hotel hallway, Ginnie felt a little like the bubbles from the wine had migrated from her stomach to cover every inch of her skin.

Quinn's coat smelled like him. Muted cologne and leather and something musky that screamed of masculinity.

Screamed? No, not screamed. Whispered something low and sexy and naughty in her ear.

His strong hand was wrapped around her smaller one, and his words had wrapped around some other, squishy part inside of her that she didn't want to say was her heart. Because that was a bit ridiculous.

But something that was close to that nonetheless.

So no. She didn't want him any less.

And her mind was bubbling, too.

It had never even occurred to Ginnie that Quinn might be a relationship-man. In fact, if she'd had to make an assumption, it would've been that he was the *anti*-relationship type. The rebound type. That was how he'd described himself, wasn't it?

But…

Six years, Quinn had said.

The same length of time she and Lawrence had been together.

Not that the two could be compared. Or even should be.

And you're not going to think about what a relationship with Quinn *would be like,* she told herself.

Six years, though. That was long enough to build a life with someone. To get married. To buy a house, or maybe two, and to talk about having kids, or not having kids.

Ginnie cast a sideways glance at Quinn. *Did* he have kids? She bit back an urge to ask. She was the one who'd insisted that they didn't really need to know anything about each other.

No matter what his past was – no matter what her *own* past was – this was a live-in-the-moment weekend. Just like she'd planned. Like she'd told Jase.

But Quinn liked her. And she had to admit that made her feel good. Almost as good as knowing that he thought she looked *in-fucking-credible.*

Ginnie savored the way the curse-modified word felt. The way his voice made it sound so damned sexy. The way it slipped around her body, even tighter than her outfit, even more intoxicating than the wine.

And even though she was trying hard to believe that their history didn't matter, she couldn't help but wonder...What if they had a week together instead of three days? Would she want to know even more about him? And would every detail make her plunge even deeper in lust?

She was so busy musing things over that she almost didn't notice when they bypassed the elevator. And when she did pause, two feet past it, Quinn caught her puzzled glance at the sliding doors right away.

"No way," he said.

"No way what?"

"No way am I getting into a tiny, enclosed space with you."

And of course, as soon as he said it, there was nothing she wanted *more* than to get into the elevator with him. She pulled on his hand.

"You're safe," she promised. "There's probably a camera."

"This from the girl who wants to make pornography."

Ginnie flushed. "I said *watch* it, not make it."

"I don't think you specified."

"I didn't think I had to."

Now he tugged on *her* hand. "I forgive you for your lack of attention to detail."

Ginnie snorted. If there was anything about herself she knew to be absolutely true, it was that she paid attention – too much of it probably – to details. Like right then. Quinn's brow was furrowed like he wanted to keep saying no, but she saw his eyes flick to the elevator, noted the dilation of his pupils, and she was damned sure he'd rather be saying yes. So she refused to be pulled along. She dug her spiked heels into the hotel corridor carpet.

"You realize at some point you're going to *have* to get into that elevator with me," she said.

"Not unless you break a leg while we're out."

She let out an exaggerated sigh. "When we're coming *back*, you'll be walking behind me up those stairs."

"And?"

"And what do you think's riskier? Getting in the elevator, or getting a full view of my ass?"

Without warning, Quinn let go of her hand, and the tug-of-war ended, sending Ginnie stumbling backwards. She caught herself on the wall behind her, but barely managed to get her footing before he was on her, his heated gaze pinning her to the spot.

"What do *you* think's riskier?" he asked. "Teasing a man like me, or being *taken* by a man like me?"

Ginnie felt her lower lip drop. He did look dangerous then, with his gaze grinding into her and the full size of his six foot plus height standing over her. One bare arm flexed, just a little, drawing her attention to the dancing ink.

Shit. You forgot.

It only took a moment for Ginnie to make sense of the thought.

In the closed quarters of the hotel room, with his confessions and his refusal to jump into bed, and his role play as the naughty school boy, he'd seemed softer. A milder version of the tattoo-covered man who'd kissed her when she wasn't just a stranger but a *complete* stranger, who'd given her an orgasm with words, who was now staring at her like he might devour her.

"Quinn – "

He cut her off. "Threaten me again."

"I – What?"

"Threaten to show me that sweet little ass of yours."

Right.

Her body told her to do it. Dared her *not* to. But her mind was kind of whimpering in the background, reminding her about fire and burning and being careful what you wished for.

Quinn took a tiny step forward. And he was twice as big. Twice as intimidating. And a hundred times as appealing.

Ginnie lifted her chin. "I can't help it if the sight of my ass is more than you can handle."

His hand shot out, dove under the far-too-big coat she wore, and slammed into the small of her back. He forced them into the wall and crushed her to his chest, and Ginnie tipped her head up expectantly. His lips were already close enough to warm her own. But instead of kissing her, he spoke to her.

"What you said earlier about control? It's true. A hundred percent. I like control. Live it. Use it. Wield it like a fucking sword if I have to. But I can adapt, and I can handle most curves that are thrown my way." His voice was the very measure of that control – burning desire carefully bridled. "The curve of your ass, though, is a different story. Could I handle it? In a way you can't even imagine. But control? With you? Not a fucking chance." With each sentence, his fingers found a different spot to rub. To caress. To bring to life. The swell of her hip. The dip between her shoulders. The length of her thigh. And with each familiar stroke, Ginnie's breathing quickened a little more. Her chest rose and fell at a distinctly not-fit-for-public rate, her breasts slamming into Quinn's chest, her nipples aching and hard. Quinn's hand crept across her knee.

"Is that what you want, baby? For me to lose control?"

Yes. Yes, please.

Because Ginnie definitely wanted this side of him, too. She wanted that edge, that ride with danger. The man under the tattoos *and* the man showcasing them.

She just couldn't form the words to articulate it. And the more he touched her, the more he refused to lean down and let their lips meet, the less coherent her mind became, and the more it refused to make her mouth work properly. Thankfully, as his palm skimmed over once again, her body spoke for her.

Her arms lifted and her hands clasped the back of his neck. She stood on her tiptoes, trying to drive them closer. When that wasn't quite enough, she lifted one knee and hooked her leg over his hip.

She was aware that she was more than a little exposed. Any second, someone could walk by. Ginnie didn't care.

She could feel every hard inch of him through his pants, and she could feel his heart hammering against her own chest.

He could strip those pants down, just enough to free himself, and he could take me here and now, and I still wouldn't care, Ginnie realized.

"Quinn," she breathed.

Then the elevator dinged, and someone cleared his throat loudly, and the big man pulled away as a young father with two kids gripping his hands slid past shaking his head.

"Well," Quinn said, his voice betraying his raw want. "Looks like we can take the elevator after all."

"We can?" Ginnie replied hopefully.

"Mm hmm."

He pulled her – still panting and still full of heightened anticipation – into the elevator.

Which was disappointingly full.

An elderly couple and a young family crowded the space between her and Quinn. They couldn't even touch each other without jostling someone else. And by the time they reached the lobby floor, it was clear that Quinn had regained that control he'd been lauding minutes earlier. His face was a carefully schooled mask of respectability, and even though he reached for Ginnie's hand as they exited, it was a strictly PG, palm-to-palm deal.

Two more seconds, she thought irritably. *All I needed was two more damned seconds and he would've been dragging me back to the bedroom, caveman style.*

Instead, he was pausing, pulling back, and giving her appearance a critical onceover.

"First things first," he said. "Let's get you a coat that fits properly."

"A coat?"

"I don't mind sharing, but when you're wearing mine, it looks like you've got nothing underneath."

Ginnie was going to argue, but when she glanced down, she saw that he was right. The jacket dwarfed her. It fully covered the short skirt and her legs stuck out from the bottom, and the jewelled high heels on her feet drew even more attention to the flasher look.

Oops.

She moved to shrug out of it, but Quinn's hand clamped down on her shoulder immediately.

"Leave it on. At least for now."

Ginnie frowned. "But you just said – "

"I know what I said. And what you've got underneath there is *worse* than nothing," Quinn told her.

She was still going to protest, but he spoke again, and his voice was rough.

"Please, baby."

And Ginnie could tell that in spite of his expression, the lid on his passion was still close to snapping off.

"All right," she said sweetly. "I'll let you buy me something pretty."

Quinn grabbed her hand again and grumbled, "I'm actually hoping to buy you something hideous."

Ginnie laughed, but two minutes later, she found herself standing in the boutiques shops adjacent to the hotel lobby, shaking her head vehemently at a hot pink parka. A very hideous choice.

Twenty-Four

Quinn lifted his hand to his mouth to cover his smile. He knew he didn't stand a chance in hell of convincing Ginnie to buy anything that came even close to resembling the ski jacket in front of them, but he figured if he started with the worst possible suggestion, she might be willing to go with something reasonably conservative instead of something as provocative as her current outfit. Which was clearly designed to kill him, bit by bit.

He had to admit he was also enjoying the horrified look on her face as she ran her fingers along the silver-stranded fur collar.

"You can't be serious," she said.

"There's a snow storm out there," Quinn reminded her.

"And you think *this* is appropriate snow storm attire?"

Quinn picked up the tag. "I think it's a waterproof, down-lined jacket, good up to twenty degrees below zero. With a five-year warranty."

"It's *pink*."

"So were your underwear." He raised an eyebrow. "And now, so is your face."

"Shut up."

Ginnie lifted the jacket off the rack like she was actually considering it, and Quinn bit back another smile as she held it up to her body.

"You actually think *this* is going to make me look less like I'm naked underneath?" she asked.

"It will once you put on the matching pants."

"That is *not* happening."

She slammed the hanger back onto the rack and strode away from the ski jackets toward the back of the store.

Quinn watched her go, admiring the way her swift, irritated pace made his jacket ride up. His admiration disappeared quickly, though, when he noticed another man giving her legs the same appreciative stare. Quinn's mood darkened immediately. He shot the man a glare, and the ogler jumped and hurried away.

Just to be sure, Quinn followed the man's flight until he was out of the store and had disappeared around a corner.

Yeah, that's right, buddy. Find some other girl to mentally undress.

Then he turned back to Ginnie, who was standing on her tiptoes, trying to grab a coat hanging just above her head. Her ass was practically hanging out. Again.

With an exasperated exhale, Quinn crossed the length of the store in four strides, positioned himself behind her, and placed his hands on her hips. He forced her to flatten her feet to the floor.

"Are you completely unaware of your general effect on every warm-blooded man in a ten-foot radius?" he said into her ear as he reached around her to pull the jacket down. "Or are you deliberately tormenting all of us?"

She leaned into him for a second, then snapped the coat from his hands and pulled away. "You could very easily end the destructive path I'm on. Just take me back to our room."

"Or you could let me buy you the hot-pink parka."

She shot him a dirty look. "Buy one for yourself. It's not as though *you're* hard on the eyes, either."

"Every woman that walks by isn't thinking about what *I'm* wearing under my jacket."

"Because you're not *wearing* a jacket. Speaking of which…Hold this?"

Ginnie slid his coat from her shoulders, and just the beginning of bare skin was enough to remind Quinn that he was thinking about what was under the coat himself. His hands shot out to stop her from undressing any further.

"You're half-naked under there for real," he said. "So let's just leave it on."

Ginnie rolled her eyes. "I can't exactly try on the other jacket if you won't let me take off this one."

"I'll buy you one in every size and you can put on the one that fits when we get somewhere…darker."

The suggestion was ludicrous, and the moment it was out of his mouth, Quinn knew it. He still meant it. He waited for Ginnie's responding sarcasm, but she just took a step forward, which loosened his hold on the jacket. It fell to her elbows, and she tipped those oh-so-green eyes up at him.

"What is it, exactly, that you're scared of?" she asked teasingly.

Scared?

Quinn opened his mouth to scoff it off, but the briefest hesitation gave him enough time to consider that it might be true.

No.

That it *was* true.

He was scared shitless. Afraid that the draw he felt to her had more meaning that it should. Or worse...That it had *less* meaning that he thought it did. Scared of hurting her. Scared that a day ago, they hadn't even met, but today, it made him crazy just thinking about some stranger checking her out. Scared that he wanted to share personal things with her, things that were true instead of some façade created to keep the undercover operation in play. Hell, he was even worried that he wasn't capable of being that real.

"Genevieve..." He trailed off as he realized she wasn't even looking at him anymore; her eyes were trained to his left, and her expression was pained.

Quinn turned sideways, already knowing what he'd find.

Dr. Douchebag. And his groupie girlfriend was nowhere to be seen.

"Shit," he muttered.

The fake-tanned asshole was swaying a little on his feet, and Quinn knew the man was drunk. Not in a nice, shared a bottle of sparkling wine with a pretty girl tipsy way, but wasted as hell. He tripped and bumped into a woman, and the man beside her righted the jerk and shook his head before moving on again. The doctor stumbled and took two steps nearer to Quinn and Ginnie.

Fight or flight.

Quinn wasn't entirely against the first, but he knew there was sometimes a need for the second, too.

"We should go," he said quickly.

"Too late."

Ginnie was right. Her ex had spotted them and was weaving in their direction. He was already close enough that Quinn could smell the liquor.

Fight it is.

As he got even closer, a sales clerk – the first one Quinn had seen since they came in – darted her nervous gaze from one man to the other, then took a miniature step toward them. Quinn shot her a quick headshake, then turned himself all the way around, making a wall between him and Ginnie just as the doctor stopped directly in front of them.

The other man's hand sought a clothing rack for stability, missed it once, then twice, then managed to grab it on the third attempt.

"Can I help you?" Quinn asked coolly.

"You have something that's mine," came the slurred reply.

Quinn's temper flared. *Like hell she's yours.*

Except a heartbeat-long assessment told him that the doctor wasn't referring to Ginnie at all. He was talking directly *to* her, his glassy-eyed glare sliding right past Quinn.

"Give them back," he ordered. "You're fucking with my *life*."

He made a stumbling lunge past Quinn, but Quinn's hand shot out and closed on his arm.

"Hey!"

Quinn ignored both his cry and the way he cringed under his grip.

"Lawrence, is it?" he asked.

His voice was calm, but on the inside, his blood was moving through his veins at a slow boil.

Seriously. How had Ginnie ever been married to this guy?

"What's it fucking to you?"

"Second time you've caused a problem for Ginnie. I just want to make sure I've got your name right when your girlfriend comes crying to me and I have to apologize to her for kicking the shit out of you. Speaking of which…Shouldn't you be attending to her instead of hassling us?"

Dr. Douchebag didn't take the not too subtle hint. He tried to shake off Quinn, and when it didn't work, he glared up sullenly.

"I need to talk to my w – to Ginnie. Alone."

"Not happening."

"She's got stuff that belongs to me."

"Still not happening."

"Shouldn't *she* have a say?"

Quinn's preference would've been to flatten Lawrence outright, but the man had a tiny point. Ginnie was an extremely capable woman. She could tell him to go fuck himself on her own.

And if she doesn't?

Quinn gritted his teeth at the idea. Then he'd find a different excuse to knock the other man on his ass.

He stepped back, just enough that both of them had a view of Ginnie, who'd pulled Quinn's coat tight around her body. Whose face was more emotionless than Quinn had seen it.

"I don't want to talk to you, Lawrence," she stated, her voice a match to her expression.

"There you go," Quinn said, his own tone full of satisfaction. "Go back your girl and leave mine alone."

"Ginnie isn't your goddamned girl," the other man growled.

It was all Quinn could take.

Fight or flight.

Own or be owned.

Kiss or kill.

He spun toward Ginnie, slid his arm around her waist, and pulled her close. He didn't give her a chance to react. He just slammed his mouth into hers. He dug his palm into the small of her back and forced her lips open with his tongue. Very quickly, he forgot why he was doing it, forgot that he'd stolen the kiss to show up the man who'd once been married to the woman in his arms.

Ginnie melted into him, her fingers creeping up the back of his neck and finding purchase in his hair.

She was so damned sweet-tasting. So damned sweet-feeling. She moaned a little against his mouth.

Quinn pulled back, turning the kiss tender. He ran his fingers under her coat, up her spine, then back down again. He dragged his mouth from her lips to her chin, then along her throat.

My goddamned girl.

That's what he wanted. Even if it was just for the rest of the weekend.

And he needed her to know.

He brought his hands up to her face and poured that need into their contact. When he finally eased away, they were both breathing heavily.

"I'll take you back upstairs," he offered softly. "If you still want me to."

"We can go out," she replied, her words just as low. "If that's what *you* want."

"We can go back upstairs, *then* go out."

"Compromise. I like it. But it might mean we have to miss out on a little fake-Vegas action."

"For fuck sake!" Lawrence snapped, temporarily breaking the spell.

Quinn reined in another urge to send the other man to the ground.

He let out a thick breath and said instead, "Their bag *is* up in our room."

"So I guess we *have* to go up there anyway then? Fake-Vegas or not…"

"I guess we do."

"Compromise *and* sacrifice. We should hurry."

Quinn turned and shot Lawrence a smirk. "I'd say I hope you can keep up, but what I'm really hoping is that you'll fall flat on your face, break your nose, and spend the rest of your weekend in whatever passes for a hospital here in Asscrack, Colorado."

Then he slid his fingers between Ginnie's, pulled her from store, and didn't bother to look and see if Lawrence was behind them or not.

Twenty-Five

Even though Ginnie could feel Lawrence slugging along behind them, she didn't care. In a few minutes, she'd have shoved the suitcase into her former husband's hands, slammed the door, and she'd be in Quinn's arms.

A delicious shiver crept up her spine.

She wasn't gloating. She didn't quite feel like she'd gotten her way. This wasn't seduction. It was something more. Or at the very least, a lead-up to something more. And it might be even better.

Ginnie was practically bouncing in her near-stilettos as they waited for the elevator. It was funny to her how little it bothered her that Lawrence stood to one side of them. It didn't matter to her what he thought of the fact that she was sharing a room with the hard-edged man who currently held her hand tightly. In fact, the only real thought she had about Lawrence was that she'd never been so glad to not be married to him.

It was funny – really funny – to her that just a few months ago, the man had been her husband and she'd been satisfied with that. When now she felt like he was a stranger. And Quinn, who *was* a stranger, felt so much more an intimate part of her life.

It scared her a little.

More than a little.

But she wouldn't trade in the last thirty hours. Not even if it meant going back to never knowing what she was missing.

That shiver of anticipation swept over her again, and Quinn kissed the top of her head.

"Almost there," he murmured.

And like his words prompted it, the elevator doors slid open.

Quinn put his hand on the door and said, "Ladies first," and Ginnie stepped forward.

But so did Lawrence.

And as he did, all hell broke loose.

Lawrence lunged at Quinn, and for all the other man's size and strength, her former husband had surprise and drunken stupidity on his side. Quinn lost his footing, just for a minute. It was enough. Lawrence lifted a loafer-clad foot and drove it into Quinn's knee. And before Ginnie could react, before Quinn could recover…Lawrence was in the elevator beside her, one hand slamming on the button labelled *Close Door* and the other on Ginnie's arm.

And then they were alone, Ginnie cowering against one corner of the elevator while Lawrence stood in front of her. He glared down at her, more intoxicated than she'd seen him in all their years together. With his bloodshot eyes and clenched, unsteady hands, he looked far more dangerous than Ginnie had ever considered him to be. Certainly scarier than Quinn.

"Why are you doing this to me?" he demanded.

"What do you think I'm doing to you?" she said.

"Fucking following me!"

Ginnie stared him, worry and fear charging through her. He sounded nothing like the man she married. Her doctor husband rarely swore, rarely drank, and never raised his voice.

Breathe. Keep him talking.

"I'm *not* following you," she corrected as calmly as she could manage. "We booked this vacation months ago. When I called the airline, they told me a refund would go to you. So I came anyway."

"And the fucking thug? What's your excuse there? *He* wouldn't give you a refund either?"

The elevator lurched to a start, and began a far too slow ascent. Ginnie inhaled, picturing Quinn and his furious, protective self on the other side of the door waiting. He'd have taken the stairs three at a time to beat them. She hoped to God he was feeling *particularly* thuggish.

"Quinn is just…" She swallowed. *Just what?*

Just a fling? Just some guy she'd started out using to make Lawrence jealous? Just some guy who'd had his tongue between her thighs?

No. The thing about Quinn was, he wasn't *just* anything.

"Quinn has nothing to do with you," she managed to get out.

Lawrence didn't seem to notice Ginnie's slip. "So it's just a coincidence that you...*hook up* with a criminal and my shit goes missing?"

"A criminal?"

"Oh, c'mon. What else could he be? Even you aren't that naïve. You guys stole my bag and I want it back."

I was that naïve, Ginnie thought. *When I married you. But not anymore.*

Out loud she said, "Are you talking about the suitcase that looks *exactly like mine?*"

"What other one would I be talking about?"

"I didn't steal it. It was just a mix up at the airport. And I thought I was giving it back. At least I did until you decided to take me hostage."

"Did you go through it?"

Ginnie thought of the explosion if underwear in the hotel room and winced. "Not exactly."

"What the hell does that mean?"

The elevator came to a halt, and Lawrence swayed a little, nearly lost his hold on the button, then righted himself and pushed it down even harder.

How long until it sets off an alarm? Ginnie wondered. *And how will he react if it does?*

She didn't want to find out.

"No, I didn't go through it, Lawrence," she said evenly. "What you and your new girlfriend do is your business."

He rolled his eyes. "Just like what you and your new boyfriend do is *your* business. Or it was until you took my stuff."

Ginnie refused to take the bait. "I still don't know what it is you want."

"What I want is the same thing you and that overgrown monkey of yours want. The whole reason you took the bag in the first place."

"I didn't – God, Lawrence. What do you think I stole? Your stupid dildo and your stupid handcuffs? Sorry, but second hand sex toys aren't my thing."

"I know exactly what is and what isn't your thing, sweetheart."

"You don't know me at all."

He leaned forward, breathing an alcohol-infused breath her way but still holding the *Close Door* button.

Could Ginnie shove him away? Would it give her time to get out, or make things worse?

"You shared my bed for *years*," Lawrence reminded her. "And quite frankly, most of what makes up the list falls under the *isn't-your-thing* category."

Ginnie bit the inside of her cheek and snapped, "Fuck you."

"Already did." He was smug.

And disgusting.

If Ginnie hadn't been so indifferent to him, she might've hated him. But as it was, all she wanted to do was get out of the damned elevator. And her patience was nearing the end.

"Let me go," she said.

"I will. If you tell me that you have my prescriptions and you're going to hand them over."

"What?"

"White sheets of paper. My name, office address – "

"I know what a prescription is," she interrupted. "But if you're talking about that huge stack of them in your bag, then no, I don't have them. Airport security took them."

Lawrence sagged back and closed his eyes. "Fuck."

Ginnie had all but forgotten about the confiscated items. But by the devastated look on his face, they were important. She fought back the automatic sympathy. Her former husband didn't deserve it.

"What the hell is going on, Lawrence?" she asked.

He opened his eyes and examined her face. "Holy shit. You really are this naïve, aren't you? Of course, that's one of the things I always liked about you. Even when you were acting like a tough bitch, I knew underneath that, you were all innocence."

Ginnie didn't like the sudden change in his tone. Not that she had liked the other one, either, but now…He was almost leering at her.

"You're drunk," she said softly, hoping to diffuse whatever nefarious thoughts were forming in his head.

She failed.

"Must be why you look so pretty," he told her.

She inched a bit farther away. "Is that supposed to be a compliment? I'm pretty because you're drunk?"

"You were *always* pretty," he amended. "Not much more than that. But definitely pretty."

Lawrence's gaze found her bare legs.

Shit.

Hadn't the man dissolved their marriage because he found her sexually unappealing?

But there was no mistaking the way his bloodshot eyes moved up her body, and for the first time since putting on the revealing outfit, Ginnie wished she hadn't.

Stop it, she chastised herself. *Wearing something sexy doesn't invite perverts to check you out.*

And just like that, the fact that she felt so comfortable with Quinn, but completely unconnected to her former husband – that she simply thought of him as a creep she didn't want to be stuck in an elevator with – was as far removed from funny as it could possibly be.

She steeled herself and straightened her shoulders. "I'm smart and resourceful, too. And I've taken a few self-defence classes."

Lawrence smiled. "Since when do you need to defend yourself against me?"

Since when, indeed?

His smile widened, and he took a step toward her.

Ginnie refused to give in to the panic building in her chest.

He's closer, but his hand is almost off the button.

Ginnie moved back, and Lawrence followed.

Now!

She dove sideways, and when he put up an arm, she ducked underneath it. Her hand grazed the panel and a half a dozen buttons lit up before Lawrence pulled her back. As the elevator started up again, he spun her around, slammed her to the wall, and suddenly his sour-tasting tongue was between her lips, his once-familiar arms crushing her in an unwanted embrace.

No. This isn't happening. It's not going to happen.

Ginnie bit down on the intrusion in her mouth, and when Lawrence pulled back with a yell, she brought her knee up and drove it straight between his legs. He dropped to the ground, and for good measure, she gave him another kick.

The elevator jerked to a stop, and tears blinded Ginnie as she sought the *Open Door* button.

C'mon, c'mon, Ginnie urged silently.

On the floor, Lawrence muttered something unintelligible about tattoos and knives.

"Shut up," she snapped, and refused to look his way.

"Ginnie," he wheezed.

"I said – "

He cut her off. "Ask him about the ink. Then ask what he really wants."

In spite of her resolve not to, Ginnie looked down at him. "What?"

"Ask yourself why a guy like that is so interested in a girl like you. Or better yet, ask *him*. You're too *good* for him. And I don't mean that nicely."

And at last, the doors slid open.

Ignoring the way her former husband called after her, Ginnie threw herself into the hallway and stumbled toward the stairwell.

One floor down. Just one floor to Quinn.

She flung open the heavy door below the exit sign, and she collided with something solid. She drew back a fist.

"Baby."

Quinn's voice, gruff and familiar, cut through the anger and the fear.

Thank God.

And she tossed herself into his arms hard enough that he had to catch himself on the railing and hold them both back from tumbling down the concrete stairs.

Twenty-Six

Quinn sat across from Ginnie, watching her down another shot. Her fourth since they made their way into the corner booth of the strip bar.

Scantily clad servers worked around them, smiling and spilling drinks.

Even *more* scantily clad women gyrated on raised mini-stages placed strategically throughout the club.

A thumping beat boomed out above them, and the dollar bills were flying.

Quinn was pretty sure that Ginnie didn't notice any of it. She hadn't spoken a word in the two-minute, SUV-style cab ride over, hadn't commented when asked to hand over her I.D. to the bouncer and he'd called her Mrs. Michaels.

Now, her focus was taken up by the clear liquid in the little glass. That, and whatever thoughts were going on inside her head. Which Quinn would've given his *own* last dollar to hear.

And he was near explosion.

His fury at the other man for jumping him and dragging Ginnie into the elevator was surpassed only by his fury at himself for letting it happen. He should've anticipated what was going to happen. In all his years undercover, no one had *ever* got the better of him. Not in a fight. Not in a surprise attack like the one that just happened. Never. He could read situations and he could read other men, and he was sure he'd pegged Dr. Lawrence Michaels.

High and mighty, shit-don't-stink weasel.

No way in hell had he expected the man to have the balls to do what he'd just done.

Quinn had been so stunned that his reaction had been delayed. He'd sprung to his feet a second too late and been forced to watched as the elevator doors slid shut.

Then the light above the door lit up, indicating which floor it was stopping at, and Quinn had finally come to his senses. He bolted up the stairs, not quitting until he reached the correct floor.

When the elevator lights sprung up – a dozen goddamned floors in a row – he'd all but panicked. The sense of helplessness – *where the fuck was the asshole taking her and for the love of God what was he doing to her* – had been overwhelming.

He'd run to each floor indicated by the lit-up elevator sign, glad that at least the old fashioned piece of technology offered minimal guidance.

On the last floor, when Ginnie came flying through that door and just about knocked them both over, Quinn's relief was as thick as his anger.

He'd wrapped his arms tightly around her and pulled her close.

She was shaking. Crying. And the bastard who'd grabbed her was nowhere to be seen.

"You're okay, baby." He wasn't sure if it had been a question or a statement.

Her reply – "Take me out drinking. Now." – was what had brought them here. And it hadn't satisfied Quinn in the least.

He'd opened his mouth a half a dozen times since they took their seats, unsure what to say. What to ask. What to do to get that mask on her face to fall away so she could work through whatever had happened in the elevator.

What the fuck did Dr. Douchebag do to her? If he – no. Fuck. Just no.

"Drink with me."

At the soft request, Quinn's eyes flew to Ginnie's.

"Drink with me," she said again.

"One of us should stay sober."

"I can feel you sitting there, *brooding*."

"If I'm brooding, what are you doing?"

"Wallowing." She pushed her newly replaced shot glass toward him.

Quinn exhaled and pushed it back. "Sobriety is the only thing keeping me from breaking something. Or someone."

"Do you want to know what happened in the elevator?"

"Yes."

"Then drink with me."

He met her level stare with one of his own, shot back the burning liquid, then flagged down the waitress for another round of shots. And a beer, just for good measure.

Ginnie didn't speak again until they'd clinked their shot glasses together and slammed away the vodka inside. When she did open her mouth, it wasn't to offer an explanation.

"Talk to me," she commanded.

"Ginnie..."

"Just for a minute, Quinn. I need a distraction."

The waitress came by again, dropped down two more shots, and Quinn drank them both quickly so that Ginnie couldn't help herself to another. He had to admit that the liquor was going to his head a bit, too, and that he didn't mind the sensation at all.

"What would you like me to talk about?" he asked.

"I don't know. Yourself?"

"Myself?"

"Is that a problem?"

He met her gaze. "No."

She swept her hand through the air drunkenly. "Good. Because I don't see another hot, melted-cheese hater at my table."

He forced a grin. "You think I'm hot?"

"Only in a tattooed Sasquatch kind of way."

In spite of himself, Quinn's smile turned genuine. "What do you want me to tell you?"

"Besides about cheese? I dunno." Her gaze travelled around the bar, then came back to his face. "Have you been in a lot of strip bars?"

His grin slipped. Girls and drugs were the bread and butter of the Black Daggers.

"Quinn?" Ginnie prodded.

He sighed, wondering again what it was about her that compelled him to tell the truth when he knew he should do the opposite.

"Yes, I've been in a lot of strip bars."

"So this is what does it for you?"

It was it his turn to take a perusal of the club. When he was younger – first on the job and green as hell – he'd considered the chosen business venue something of a perk. Naked flesh and pretty girls. Hard for a twenty-one year old man to dislike it.

Pun intended.

As time went by, though, he got to know the women – mothers and students and moonlighters and addicts, there was no one set of rules for what brought them to the stages. And as much as he hated to admit it, once their stories were in his head, he found it that much more difficult to enjoy himself.

Quinn took a generous pull of his beer. "No. This isn't what does it for me."

"What *does* do it for you?"

"It's not obvious?" he asked.

"No."

"You."

"I was being serious."

"So was I. A dozen naked girls around and all I see is you."

It was tough to tell if the pink in her cheeks was from the alcohol or from a blush. "I bet that line's worked for you a few times before."

"If I was a betting man – which I'm not – I'd give you pretty shitty odds on that." He leaned across the table. "Mostly because I've never used it."

This time, it was definitely a blush. "So if you're not into strippers, and you're not into betting…Why you were going to Vegas? The all-you-can-eat buffets?"

"Isn't that obvious, too?" Quinn deflected. "I was going to a hot, tattooed Sasquatch convention."

"You're sooooo funny." She tapped his hand drunkenly.

Quinn tried to thread his fingers through hers and suppressed disappointment when she jerked away immediately.

"Maybe I was going to Vegas to do the same thing that you wanted to do…" he said lightly. "Sully my reputation a bit."

"You just admitted that you spend an inordinate amount of time in strip clubs. I think it might be hard to *sully* your reputation."

"You make it sound so dirty."

"Isn't it?"

"Not if it's work."

"Work?"

Quinn realized he'd slipped up and he covered it with another smile. "You don't think work happens in strip bars?"

"I guess it depends on what line of work you're in."

"I guess it does."

He felt her scrutiny as she examined his face.

Too smart for her own good, her brother had once told Quinn.

"You're not going to tell me what you do for work, are you?" she asked.

"Do you want to know about me?" he deflected. "Or my job?"

"Aren't they kind of the same thing?"

"Related, maybe. But definitely not the same thing."

"I don't understand the difference."

"What do *you* do for a living?" he asked, fully aware of the answer already.

Ginnie's responding smile was best described as sardonic. "At the moment…Very little. I went to school to become a medical office assistant. But my – but *Lawrence* always said I didn't need to work."

"And is that what defines you?" Quinn wanted to know. "Your lack of a job?"

She narrowed her eyes. "Are you avoiding my question?"

He shrugged, took a sip of his beer and said, "Definitely."

"Why?"

"Why aren't you telling me what just happened between you and your former husband?"

A pained looked crossed her face before she looked down at the table. Quinn knew he was being given yet another opportunity to tell the truth. He knew also, that this was the worst possible time. Ginnie's body language told a story that her easy, tipsy tone didn't match. Her hands were tense, her mouth pinched, and the only sparkle in her eyes was a result of the vodka in her system.

That. Or you're using it as convenient excuse to avoid being completely honest.

Quinn shoved aside the voice in his head guiltily. "Ask me anything else, Ginnie."

"All right. What's the going rate for a lap dance?"

The unexpected question startled him. "What the hell are you talking about?"

"I want one of those girls..." She pointed toward the closest mini-stage. "To give me a lap dance. Shimmy shimmy shake herself all over me."

"That is *not* happening."

"I'm pretty sure it's not up to you."

"You're drunk, and – " he cut himself off, sure he was just going to dig a hole he couldn't readily climb out of.

"And what?"

Quinn ran a hand over his hair. "And something obviously happened in that elevator that's affected your judgement."

"You don't know a damned thing. And being unreasonable is my prerogative."

"You're right. I *don't* know a damned thing because you won't *tell* me a damned thing. But taking you out of here before you do something you regret is *my* prerogative."

"You're not exactly being forthcoming, either. And you don't get to make decisions for me."

"Clearly, someone has to," Quinn muttered.

"Why do you care what I do with my lap?"

Because your brother is paying *me to care.*

Quinn clamped down his jaw – hard – to stop the furious, barely true statement from slipping out.

Now isn't the time.

He leaned back on his chair.

"I *don't* care," he lied. "If you want a damned lap dance, get a damned lap dance."

For a second, he was sure he saw hurt mingled with surprise in her eyes, and then it was gone. "Fine."

"Hell, I'll pay for it myself."

He dragged his wallet from his back pocket, peeled out two fifties, and held them up until the waitress bounced over.

"Tell her what you want," he ordered.

Ginnie's eyes widened nervously, and her voice had a distinct tremor in it. "A lap dance."

The waitress shrugged. "For you or him, sugar?"

Quinn watched Ginnie inhale and smooth her hands over her very short skirt, visibly steeling herself. "For me."

"Private room?"

"Yes, pl – yes," Ginnie said firmly.

The server's eyes flicked back to Quinn. "It's an extra twenty if you want to watch."

He opened his mouth to tell her how little interest he had in seeing someone grind all over Ginnie, but when he actually spoke, what he said instead was, "I wouldn't miss it for the fucking world."

Twenty-Seven

On shaking legs, Ginnie followed the waitress across the bar.
You should stop this before it goes too far, ordered a voice in
her head.

But she couldn't.

She didn't even know what *too far* was. And she
needed…something. She didn't know what that was, either. The
liquor hadn't washed away the sickening memory of Lawrence's
mouth pressed to hers, nor had it cleared what he'd said about
Quinn not possibly wanting her just for *her*. And his ink…Who
cared about its why? But all of that created a nagging doubt that
even the cloud of alcohol couldn't cover.

And still Ginnie wished she had another shot of vodka.

The waitress stopped in front of a small, curtained-off area in
the corner of the club, then turned and faced them.

"You probably know the drill," she said to Quinn. "But in
case *she* doesn't – " A nod toward Ginnie. "Or in case you
conveniently forget…I'll go over the rules. You do *not* touch the
girl. You do *not* touch the girl. And you do *not* touch the girl. Got
it?"

"Yes." Ginnie's voice was an embarrassing – and humiliated
– whisper.

The fact that this girl recognized Quinn for the strip club
type…Ginnie hated it.

"You?" the server prodded.

"Yeah, I got it," Quinn confirmed.

"Good. The rooms back onto a one-way mirror. Break the
rules and you can bet your ass you'll wind up with a broken
arm." The waitress smiled sweetly. "Get comfortable. Your
dancer will be with you shortly."

As she flounced away, Quinn reached around Ginnie to grab
the curtain and pull it aside. For one, blissful second, the scent of
him filled her nostrils. And she felt okay. Drunk. But all right.

Then Quinn stepped back and the feeling was lost, and Ginnie
was drowning again.

"You heard the girl," Quinn said gruffly. "Get comfortable."

Ginnie took a cautious step into the so-called private room. It was small. Barely big enough to fit her and Quinn, let alone have enough space to fit another girl.

Not a lot of room needed for a dry-hump, I guess.

The thought might've made her laugh if it hadn't been so true.

A wide backed chair – wooden with a green plush seat – sat in the center, and some kind of filtered light hung above it, casting a weird spotlight.

Is it supposed to be sexy?

If it was, Ginnie was going to have to rethink her own definition of the word. To her, it looked like an interrogation room. In fact, if she thought about it, the setup kind of *did* remind her of the interrogation room at the airport.

One-way mirror? Check.

Solitary chair, bolted to the floor? Check.

Distinct feeling of discomfort? Double check.

"You're going to have to sit down," Quinn told her.

"*You* sit down," she retorted childishly.

"You don't have to prove anything, Ginnie. Not to me."

"I'm not trying to prove anything! Not to you. Not to Lawrence." She snapped her mouth shut as Quinn's face clouded.

"What did he do to you in that elevator?"

Sickness rose in Ginnie's stomach and she fought it off. "Nothing. All I want is a lap dance."

"All *I* want is to know what the fuck happened. What changed?"

"Changed? We met a day and a half ago," she said. "That's barely long enough for a first impression let alone long enough to decide that I've *changed.*"

"You know damned well that's not what I mean." He tapped on his lip ring. "You're smart and sexy and sweet and too good for this girls-gone-wild bullshit."

Too good.

The phrase was too damned close to what Lawrence had said in the elevator. Nausea hit Ginnie again.

She shook her head. "I've spent the last twelve years – half my life in case you're counting – trying to be the best *me* I can be. I've always thought that being on the straight and narrow would lead me somewhere good instead of – "

Quinn cut her off, his face darkening even more. "Instead of what? Hanging out in a strip bar with a man like *me*?"

Ginnie swallowed against the lump in her throat. "Instead of dead like my mother. Or overwhelmed and then just *gone* like my father."

"Jesus, baby."

"I don't want your pity, Quinn."

"I'm not offering you *pity*. Is that what you think this is? All I want is to help you."

"I don't need your help, either."

"Tell me what you *do* want from me," he said, almost pleading.

"I want you to tell me why."

"Why what?"

"Why *me*?" Ginnie was surprised at the amount of bitterness in her own tone. "Is it because I'm *nice*? Because you think I'm sweet? Naïve? You want to put me up on a pedestal? Or would you prefer to tear me down?"

She was driving a wedge between them. She could feel herself doing it, and she couldn't make herself stop, even though all she really wanted to do was throw herself into his arms and let it all out.

And for the life of her, she couldn't figure out why Quinn was putting up with it, why he was sticking around when he could be running in the other direction. *Should* be running.

He paced the tiny room, once, then twice, then a third time, then ran his fingers through his faux-hawk and slumped into the chair. He looked from Ginnie's face to his rough fingers, then back again. His expression was haggard enough that her heart lurched.

Weak, she chastised herself.

But she still wished she had the courage to reach for him.

"Baby – " he started, then stopped abruptly as the curtain behind them slid open.

Ginnie spun to face the dancer and sucked in a gulp of air at the girl's appearance.

No wonder Quinn's suddenly tongue tied.

The girl was leggy and exotic, with full, pouty lips, and kohl-rimmed eyes a color that Ginnie couldn't quite pinpoint. Her skirt made Ginnie's look like a burka, and her sheer blouse left nothing to the imagination.

Until that moment, Ginnie had never thought of herself as plain – not that she was high on her own looks, but she wasn't oblivious to her appearance, either. But in comparison to the dancer, she felt like a troll.

Are those jewels *on her nipples?*

Yes. Yes, they were.

As a low, rhythmic beat filled the room, the girl shook, and the jewels caught the spotlight and sent little shimmers bouncing along the black curtains. Ginnie guessed that might be the very reason for the light's existence.

With a red face, she realized she was staring, and she jerked her eyes away from the dancer's ample chest. But the only other place to look was at Quinn, and the last thing she wanted was to see his attention on *her*.

You can't just stand here with your eyes closed.

Reluctantly, her gaze sought the big, tattooed man.

The other girl had taken another, shimmying step toward him, and too late, Ginnie clued in to what was about to happen. *He* was in the chair. *He* was going to have the girl gyrating on his lap.

Jealousy hit her like a semi-truck.

Oh no.

But he wasn't looking at the dancer at all. Not even when she reached his knee and spread her thighs overtop of it and thrust her hips forward in time with the music. Instead, his eyes were fixed on Ginnie, burning with intensity.

"I don't want to do either of those things you mentioned. Not tear you down from a pedestal or hold you up on one." His voice was just barely louder than the music, and thick with emotion. "You want to know if I like you because you're *sweet* and naïve and good? Yes. Plus a hundred other reasons that are going to take me a lot longer than a three-minute bump and grind to explore. But saying I like you because you're sweet is like saying I'm attracted to you because you have pretty eyes. It's so much more than that. It's more than a fucking strip bar and a fight about a lap dance and a weekend in Vegas. *You're* so much more than that, baby. From the second I laid eyes on you at that airport bar, you've been the only thing I think about. The only thing in my head. And you know what? I don't want to get you out. I don't even want to try. That's why – the biggest reason anyway – that I didn't just jump into bed with you and why I'm trying to stop you from going ass-crazy and doing something you'll regret and why I need to make sure you're okay. Can't you see that I care about you this much and it's only been a couple of days and – *fuck*. Not even a couple. Whatever this connection is between us, Ginnie, I don't want to lose it. I don't want to make it less than it is by saying it's just about your goodness or my badness or ideals or those tidy boxes you like so much. What I *do* want is to take it and see how much further it can go."

When he finished his speech, the room felt still, and Ginnie was surprised to see that the dancer was still going, moving as though he hadn't said a word.

Maybe she doesn't care. Or maybe she's used to it.

Quinn didn't seem fazed by the other girl's attention, either. His gaze continued to hold Ginnie.

"There's no way in hell you don't feel it, too."

She couldn't deny it, even if she wanted to. But her mouth was too dry to speak. And her heart was pounding unevenly in her chest, and she didn't know whether it was from fear of Quinn's declaration, or from the rapidly waning effects of the alcohol, or whether it was because she was still hung up on what happened in the elevator with Lawrence.

All three, probably.

The way Quinn pulled at her, made her heart beat fast and ache at the same time…it terrified her. The liquor made her worry that she couldn't control it. And Lawrence. She felt like the six years she'd spent with the man was a blank. A black out. Two thousand, one hundred and ninety-one days of nothing. He didn't know her. He probably never had.

"He kissed me," she finally managed to choke out.

"What?"

"Lawrence kissed me," Ginnie repeated. "And in my head, I know it doesn't make sense for me to be so horrified. I didn't kiss anyone *but* Lawrence for six years. But how dare he call me pretty and think that I'm going to kiss him back? How dare he make me not good enough, and then make me the other woman and make me doubt myself and *kiss* me?"

"Ginnie – "

She cut him off. "I can still taste him. I thought the vodka might help wash it away. But he tasted like booze and now I taste like booze and I think I might've made it worse. I don't *want* to taste him, Quinn."

And for the first time, Quinn acknowledged the dancer.

"Off," he commanded roughly.

But the girl didn't move. Not quick enough, anyway. He shoved his chair back, put a hand on her arm, and moved toward Ginnie.

And he only made it two steps before a three-hundred pound bouncer shoved his way into the room and slammed a meaty fist onto Quinn's neck.

Twenty-Eight

The bouncer shoved Quinn along, his grip tight.

Quinn balked against the aggressive contact, but he knew better than to start a fight with a man who outweighed him by eighty pounds or more. Sure, he might be able to win. Speed, agility. Quinn had both. What the big man behind him had, though, was friends. Probably eight or nine of them back in the club, just waiting for an excuse to jump in and help.

Self-control.

He prided himself on that, didn't he?

Maybe not with Ginnie. Maybe not with anything that had something to do with protecting her.

And not just physically, either.

No.

Quinn wanted to protect her heart, too.

And that sonofabitch former husband of hers was making it harder.

He watched Ginnie's defeated form move along in front of him, shoulders slumped as they moved to the back of the bar and through the service exit into a dimly lit corridor.

Her ex isn't the only one making it hard.

Quinn swallowed guiltily.

The bouncer gave him another, rougher shove, and Quinn gritted his teeth.

Self-control.

He needed to get a hold of some. Right now.

No. Not now.

Five minutes ago. Or forty hours ago.

He felt torn in a dozen directions, all of which needed freedom. His emotions were tumbling over themselves for supremacy.

He wanted to toss off the bouncer's firm grip and throw himself down to beg Ginnie to forgive him for not being more patient and understanding.

He wanted to maim that douchebag, Lawrence Michaels, with a blunt object.

He wanted to take Ginnie in his arms and kiss away the fucking *taste* of her ex.

Then maim the asshole.

The taste. Jesus.

He'd kissed her. Kissed the mouth that Quinn had laid claim to.

It could've been worse.

So much worse.

So why does this feel so fucking bad?

He was near-blind with the feeling of wrongness. Even more so with the feeling of needing to make it right.

Self. Fucking. Control.

Quinn opened and closed his fists, trying to hold on.

You're okay, he told himself. *We'll get out of here and go upstairs and sort everything out.*

His eyes focused on Ginnie's silhouette. He would make her forget Lawrence for good, make her see herself the way he saw her.

Then, without warning, the lights above flickered and the already dark hall grew momentarily darker, and Ginnie stopped moving.

"Keep going," the bouncer growled.

Ginnie took a step. In the dark, Quinn saw her stumble, saw her reach for something to steady herself, saw her fail. She landed on the ground with a stifled cry.

Goddamn.

Quinn went for her, tearing away from the rough hold on the back of his neck. For a second, he was free. His fingers even grazed Ginnie's soft, bare shoulder. Then the bouncer was on him, dragging him back with one hand.

Automatically, Quinn fought against him. He writhed away and moved toward Ginnie again. The bouncer took a wide step in between them, and Quinn's temper flared.

And then it happened.

Ginnie righted herself.

The bouncer threw back his arm while yelling something angrily at Quinn.

And the other man's fist smacked Ginnie hard enough in the jaw that she reeled backwards.

The bouncer spun to face her – maybe even to apologize – but it was too late.

Red.

It was all Quinn could see.

Any pretence of self-control went out the window as he jumped at the big man. His hands closed around the bouncer's waist and he pushed with all his might, trying to get the other man to fall.

He's too damned big.

He was a tank.

An angry tank.

The bouncer shook like a wet dog, trying to dislodge Quinn, but he held fast.

"Keep your hands off my girl," he breathed.

The bouncer grunted. "You don't like it when I put my hands on your girl? Well, guess what? My boss doesn't like it when you put *your* hands on *his* girl, either. One goddamned rule and ninety percent of you feel the need to break it. I should break *you* in return."

With a snarl, the other man backed up and slammed Quinn into the wall, and he couldn't hold on no matter how badly he wanted to. His arms released and he sank to the ground.

Shit.

Quinn tried to get back up, but the bouncer smacked a fist into his shoulder, sending him straight down again. With a groan, he rolled over to avoid being hit again, then sprung to his feet, ignoring the shooting pain in his side. He squared off against the bouncer, hands up defensively.

"What the hell are you doing?" the bigger man demanded.

What the hell was *he doing? One job. One* fucking *job. Keep Genevieve Silver out of harm's way. And he was incapable.*

His self-control wasn't just a pretence. It was a joke.

He drew back a fist and he dove forward and drove it into the man's solar plexus. A soft grunt was the only reaction. Quinn tried again, twisting viciously and throwing another punch.

The bouncer's palm came up to meet his hand. It closed around it, crushing Quinn's fingers under his grip.

Then the other man's gaze landed on Quinn's wrist, on the tattooed dagger. He dropped his hold immediately, and Quinn could see the sudden caution there. He seized on it, shoving down the self-loathing he felt at using the gang association for his own benefit. He lifted his arm and shook it at the bouncer.

"You recognize this?"

"I do," the bigger man admitted reluctantly.

"Think your boss would recognize it, too?"

"Likely."

"Then you both know better than to fuck with me."

There was a long, drawn out silence, and Quinn could read the other man perfectly. He'd seen it before in his time undercover. That weighing of odds.

"Risk it," Quinn dared.

The bouncer stepped back. "The exit's five feet to your left. If you go now…"

Quinn smiled a dark, practiced smile. One he'd used hundreds of times. A threat under the thin guise of pleasantry.

"Then what?" he asked. "You won't try to stop me?"

He watched the Adam's apple in the other man's throat bob up and down. He almost wanted the man to make the wrong choice. To give him an excuse to embrace the identity attached to that tattoo and everything that went along with it.

"Quinn?" Ginnie's soft, worried voice drew his attention back to reality.

His eyes flicked in her direction, and his heart squeezed. She had one hand at her lip and the other pressed to the wall.

"Can we leave?" she asked.

Quinn shot the bouncer a look, half questioning, half-mocking. "Can we?"

The other man gave him a short nod, and it was all Quinn needed. He pushed past the man to grab Ginnie's hand. Without looking back, he yanked her along, focusing on the flickering red exit sign. When they reached the door, he forced it open with his hip and pulled Ginnie out into the alley behind the club.

Quinn didn't give himself time to feel the cold, or to acknowledge the snow falling from the cloudy sky. He grabbed Ginnie and pressed one hand to the nape of her neck and the other into the small of her back. For one moment, he stared into her eyes. Their temporarily midnight shade of green was even deeper than usual, and they were full of hurt.

"One job," Quinn muttered.

"What?"

In reply, he slammed his mouth into hers. He could taste the rusty flavor of her split lip, and it infuriated him. He kissed her harder. The force of his onslaught drove them backward into the exterior, brick wall of the bar. Quinn's knuckles smashed against the clay, scraping and burning.

He didn't care.

He slid his hand to her soft, thick hair, and pulled. She yelped, but it didn't stop him.

Quinn wasn't sure he *could* stop.

He brought his mouth to her deliciously exposed throat, nipping and sucking, and none of his attention was the least bit gentle.

He moved to her collarbone. Then her cleavage. Then along the curve of one breast, his teeth paying no mind to the thin fabric covering her. His mouth closed on her nipple, sucking it to a firm, hard point, rolling it with his tongue until she gasped. Then he moved on to the next and did the same. Hot. Fast. Sweet.

Quinn wanted more.

He dragged his hands to her waist, then down to her ass, and he lifted her from the ground. He drove his hips forward, thrusting his hard, needy self between her thighs. He rocked back and forth, enjoying the exquisite torture of being against her but not being inside her.

Inside her.

Just like that, a part of him had to be. It didn't even matter *which* part. He wanted to feel her surrounding him. Needed to.

He pulled away and ran a hand along her thigh, slipped it up her skirt and pressed it between them. Then paused as his fingers immediately found her waiting wetness and nothing else.

Wasn't she wearing underwear?

No, he remembered. *She couldn't be. She doesn't have any.*

Quinn wasn't going to let the opportunity go to waste. He pushed his fingers into her. Deep. Wet. Pulsing already.

Oh, God.

Ginnie pushed against him, her knees tight on his hips, and with her thrusts, his fingers went deeper. Soon, he was moving with her, his erection driving into the back of his hand. He ached to take her.

No time.

It was true. He was far too close.

Fuck it.

He circled harder, tighter, faster, pleasuring both of them at the same time.

"Come, baby," he ordered.

She *had* to.

Because *he* was going to.

With a deep, throat-tearing moan, he pressed the top of his palm to her clit, pushed his rock hard self to his knuckles, and as he thrust against her a final, satisfying time, she contracted around his fingers and cried out as he let go too.

For several moments, Quinn held her there against the wall, her thighs shaking and her chest rising and falling. He didn't release her until she spoke in a tremor into his ear.

"Quinn... What w-w-was that? Back there? And th-th-this – "

He cut her off. "That was me. *This* is me. The dark parts. The bad parts."

"Bad?"

"The part of me that uses everything I know to get what I want."

"You said there was no black and white. Only grey."

"I was wrong, Ginnie. There *are* parts of me that are black. And broken." He moved back, letting her legs drop to the ground, his heart like a stone in his chest. "If you can't handle that…If you don't want it…"

"I do."

He closed his eyes as her hand came to rest on his wrist and traced the dagger there.

"I want to know every part of you, Quinn," she whispered.

Her words brought his heart to life once again, and in spite of his very recent release, he wanted her once more. Right away. Properly this time.

Twenty-Nine

Ginnie let Quinn pull her through the freezing air, barely
noticing that the snow had now turned to a drenching rain, not
paying the slightest bit of attention to the goose bumps that rose
all over her body. She was on fire. The ache between her thighs
hadn't lessened with her release. If anything, it had increased.

And Quinn didn't speak. Not when they climbed into the cab,
not when they walked into the hotel again, or when they got in
the elevator.

The silence between them was thick. With tension. With
need. With anticipation.

And maybe a little bit of fear? a little voice nudged, and
Ginnie acknowledged it grudgingly. *A little, yes.*

But she'd wanted to see this side of Quinn. She'd been
craving that undercurrent of danger that ran beneath – or was it
alongside? – his rough charm and his sex appeal. Maybe she was
even the one who brought it out with her little stunt with the lap
dance. Had she done it on purpose? She wasn't sure. But she
did know that if she *didn't* get to know this side of Quinn, she
would never really know him at all. And the thought of that
made her throat tighten up.

She wouldn't let herself *not* know him.

Please let me know him.

Like he could sense her longing, like he could feel the
constriction in her chest, Quinn tightened his grip on her hand
and pulled her close. She inhaled his scent as his wide, strong
arms encircled her protectively. And Ginnie needed it. Needed
him.

She'd never needed something – or some*one* – so badly.

And even if there was nothing else, no other glaringly obvious
difference between Quinn and Lawrence, there it was. The
intense *need.* Ginnie had never needed her former husband.
Even when she'd been the dutiful, stay-at-home wife, dependant
on him financially, she hadn't thought of herself as needing him.

When he'd walked away from their life together, she didn't experience a loss. She experienced a failure.

Oh my God, Ginnie thought. *Did I even* love *Lawrence?*

Love? She shouldn't be thinking about love.

Her heart thundered so hard in her chest that she was sure Quinn had to be able to hear it.

So, yes. Fear. But perhaps not the way that little voice of hers believed.

The elevator doors slid open, his hand slid down her body to clasp hers.

"Come," he said, and the word – which echoed his earlier command – made her shiver with desire.

And she couldn't move her feet fast enough as they hurried from the elevator to their room. She forced herself to not jump in front of Quinn to drag him along faster. When they got to their door, he fumbled with the key and dropped it, and Ginnie almost leaped to grab it. She had to squeeze her hands at her sides to stop from doing it.

Hurry, hurry.

Quinn bent to grab the key, and finally jabbed it into the door with a loud *click,* and the solidity of the sound, the firm, undeniable fit of the shaft in the keyhole…It made Ginnie gasp. Loudly enough to draw a curious look from Quinn.

Oh, God.

She shook her head. "Just…Please," was all she could manage to say.

He eased the door open – why the hell was everything taking *so* long? – and pulled Ginnie into the room, then closed it behind them and turned to face her.

For an agonizingly long moment, they stood there in the pitch black, toe-to-toe.

Ginnie tipped her face up, waiting for him to take a hold of her. But except for his shallow breaths, Quinn was silent again. And as her eyes adjusted to the dark, she saw that his face had a guarded, cautious look to it. It wasn't the cocky mask she'd seen him use before when trying to cover some emotion; it was something else entirely.

"Am I your fantasy?" he asked softly.

Ginnie blinked in surprise. "What?"

"The bad boy. The one who throws rocks at your window, climbs up the trellis and sneaks in. Is that me?"

It was Ginnie's turn to be cautious. "Why?"

"I *can* be him. But if that's all I am, I want to know. Now."

That staccato beat of her heart started up again as she made her admission. "No. That's not what I want you to be."

Quinn met her eyes. "I need to ask you something else, and it might piss you off."

She took a breath. "Okay."

"If he – if Lawrence – came back to you, if he said getting the annulment was a mistake, would you consider going back to him?"

For a second, Ginnie *was* pissed off. Too mad to even speak. *How dare he* – she cut herself off, mid-thought. *Oh.*

He wasn't making an accusation or an assumption. He wanted to know if he was going to get hurt. This big, indestructible-looking man was insecure. Because of *her*. Ginnie might've laughed if it hadn't been so damned achingly sweet.

"*Lawrence* was the fantasy," she said slowly. "And there's no chance in hell I'd take him back. When he kissed me, I wanted to bite off his damned tongue."

Quinn stiffened, then chuckled, finally looking a little more relaxed. "There's a sentence I never thought I'd hear, let alone find sexy."

Ginnie reached up to stroke his slightly stubbled cheek. "In a million years, I wouldn't trade this weekend with you for a lifetime with Lawrence."

He put his hand on top of hers and leaned into the caress. "And at the end of the weekend?"

"Whatever you want, Quinn. I'll do it. I won't ask for what you can't give."

"All I want is *you*, baby."

She swallowed, terrified of bursting the balloon of elation in her heart. "Me too."

He bent his head and kissed her. Far too gently. Then pulled away.

"That's it," he told her, his voice husky.

"That's it?"

He nodded, his nose brushing hers sweetly. "I want you to take the lead."

A blush crept up Ginnie's face. "Me?"

"You wanted to seduce me," he reminded her with little smile. "It worked. I'm under your spell."

"Oh."

She couldn't think of anything else to say, so she took a tiny step away and gave him a shy onceover. And as she examined him, her shyness dissipated into the dark.

The lead. Where should she start?

Clothes.

Yeah, those would have to go.

But first...

Ginnie stood on her tiptoes and ran all ten of her digits through Quinn's still-damp faux-hawk. It was surprisingly soft. Even the short sides were like silk. It felt so good against her skin that she did it again, this time more slowly. And just as slowly, Quinn's lids dropped closed, his dark lashes nearly brushing his face.

I want to touch those, too, Ginnie thought.

So she did. She dragged her thumbs down his forehead, over his eyelids, along his cheekbones, and down to his mouth. She hesitated. But only for a second. One hand slipped to the back of his neck while the other tripped lightly over his firm lips, circling the warm bit of metal there in a sensual dance. Her knees grew weak, and Ginnie wasn't sure if it was from her exploration of Quinn's features or if it was from holding herself up.

It doesn't matter.

She was ready to move on.

She dropped back to her heals, putting her eyes on level with the top button on Quinn's shirt.

Ginnie brought her hands up. They shook a little as she fought with the button, and it took her three tries to get it undone. Embarrassed, she glanced up at Quinn's face. His eyes were still closed, and just the ghost of a patient smile touched his lips.

All right.

She was determined to be more efficient with the next few buttons, but as she unfastened the second, then the third and fourth, she realized Quinn's skin was almost icy, and a new idea came to mind.

Ginnie dropped her hand to his and pulled him across the room to the bathroom, glad to see that the bathtub was as big as she remembered.

Quinn's eyes opened when she flicked on the soft light over the sink, and he shot her a curious look.

"You wanted a bath yesterday," she said, trying to sound firm instead of questioning.

"It wasn't the main thing on my mind," he replied.

"I know." Ginnie used the excuse of twisting on the taps to cover her blush.

But she couldn't keep her attention away from him for long. As the room filled with steam, and the tub filled with water, she turned his way again, and her breath caught. He was so damned sexy, leaned against the counter the way he was, with his shirt half-open and his muscles and ink on display. She couldn't decide what she wanted more – to stare at him like that for a while longer, or to help him take the rest of his clothes off.

There's a third option.

Ginnie smiled. And slowly, deliberately, she reached behind her own back and tugged on the tiny tie there. It came loose with surprising ease – so much ease that without even a nudge, the shimmery top slipped off and floated to the floor.

She watched Quinn's eyes follow the shirt, then rise up to her chest. For a moment, she was self-conscious, but when his gaze finally met hers again, it was hungry.

Her smile grew.

She kicked off her heels and shimmied out of her barely-there skirt, and Quinn swallowed.

Ginnie turned toward the tub, flipped off the taps, then stepped into the scalding water, and faced him again.

"Come here," she ordered softly.

And even though he'd *told* her she was in charge, his quick obedience startled her. One second he was beside the sink, the next he was standing so close that she could smell his intoxicatingly masculine scent. It was her turn to gulp.

"Take off your shirt," she managed to say.

Without moving his gaze from her face, he undid the last couple of buttons.

"And your pants," Ginnie added breathlessly, afraid if she didn't say it right away, she'd chicken out.

Blood rushed through her body, sending waves of heat through every part of her. Momentarily light-headed, she dropped her gaze and closed her eyes. And when she opened them just a few seconds later, Quinn's clothes were in a pile on the ground.

She knew was he was completely bare, and she'd seen him that way before. But last time it was unintentional. Embarrassing. Now…she could take her time, perusing his body at leisure.

Her gaze slid up, inch by inch, moving with the beat of her heart.

Solid feet.

Well-muscled calves with just the right amount of dark hair.

Knees, held a foot apart, one lightly scarred, the other unmarred.

His thighs.

Oh, God, his thighs.

Strong and thick with muscle, there was no hiding the power in those thighs. They made Ginnie tremble. They made her nipples grow taut and her breath catch. They made her wet – so slick with want that she was sure she was giving the bathwater a run for its money.

And between those thighs...

Oh, sweet lord.

He was the embodiment of male perfection.

Huge and hard, full-mast and waiting.

Ginnie wanted to put *so* many parts of her body on him. She wanted to stroke him, taste him, ride him. She'd never felt a desire so strong.

Patient. Please let me be patient.

Because she wanted to savor him, too.

She forced her eyes to move on.

Was that a six-pack? It had to be more than a six pack.

Her hands itched to run over those abs, to slide up and caress his chest.

As Ginnie's gaze followed the path in her mind, she gasped. The beginnings of a mottled bruise covered his un-tattooed shoulder, and she knew immediately it was from the blow he'd taken from the bouncer. Guilt hit her.

"Oh, Quinn." Her voice was as miserable as she felt.

His expression filled with concern. "What's wrong, baby?"

"You're hurt."

He glanced down at his shoulder and shrugged dismissively. "It's nothing."

"It's not nothing. You got that because of *me*."

"I got that because I can't control my temper," he corrected.

"All the time? Or just when I'm being ridiculously childish?" She couldn't meet his eyes, and she tipped her head down, full of shame.

Two swift steps put him at the edge of the tub, and a sweep of his hand brought her face back up. With her feet in the raised bath and his on the floor, they were almost on level. He fixed her with an intense, amber-eyed stare.

"Ginnie," his said. "You *do* make me lose control. But in a good way. I'm just not used to feeling like this and I'm trying to process it, trying to acclimate to it. It's not easy. But my temper is *not* your fault and it was stupid of me to let it get the better of me. All I wanted was to protect you."

She touched his injured shoulder gently. "Promise me you won't do it again."

"Protect you?"

"Get hurt on my behalf."

Quinn shook his head. "I can't make that promise, baby. I'm the kind of man who fights for the woman he l – for the people he cares about."

Ginnie heard the sudden adjustment in his statement and she knew what he'd been about to say.

He was the kind of man who fought for the woman he loved.

But it was too soon, both to say it and to feel it. A crazy leap.

That didn't stop every fiber of her being from wanting to hear it.

"Quinn…" she trailed off, unsure how a girl was supposed to ask a man she barely knew to tell her he loved her. And mean it. She chickened out. "Can you…umm…can you get in with me?"

Wordlessly, he stepped into the bath and draped his arms around her, and her careful examination of her emotions went out of her head as physicality took over.

Solid chest. Protective embrace. And his long, hard erection, pressed to her abdomen.

Yes. Oh, yes.

Ginnie drew her fingers along the corded muscles in his back and up the planes of shoulder blades, trying not to be as frantic as she felt. His skin was warm now, and covered in a light layer of steam. She liked the way her palms slid so easily over him as she brought them down again. His ass was as firm as the rest of him, and she couldn't stifle a moan as she slid her hands over it.

More. She needed more.

"Kiss me," she half-begged, half-demanded.

"Yes, ma'am."

And he didn't just kiss her. He slammed his lips to hers, tore her mouth open with his tongue, and plunged it into her. He *devoured* her. And it felt so good. So right to be tasted like that.

Ginnie pushed herself to him.

Still not close enough.

She lifted a knee and draped it over his hip, then dropped a hand between them. And touched him at last. She gripped his smooth, rock solid erection in her palm and stroked him. If she'd thought the kiss was hot, it had nothing on this. She quickened her attention, enjoying how he throbbed in her hand.

"Fuck," he growled against her mouth.

She knew it was an exclamation versus an invitation, but the word made her quake, and she couldn't help but moan back, "Yes."

Quinn scooped her from the tub and lifted her over the side effortlessly, and Ginnie marvelled at how natural it felt to be carried in his arms, even naked.

No. Especially *naked.*

He brought her to the edge of the bed, bent to pull back the covers, then laid her down gently and stood back. His face was alive with tenderness, but as his eyes raked over her body, it grew heated. Then scorching.

Was visual foreplay a thing?

If it wasn't before, it is now.

Each place his gaze landed lit up, then ached. From her toes to her head, she was on fire with longing.

Why wasn't he touching her already?

Oh. Right.

Because she was supposed to be in charge.

So be in charge.

"Now, Quinn," she stated.

He moved toward her, then paused. "Condom."

And fast as lightning, Quinn crossed the room, then returned, a little silver packet in his palm. Ginnie couldn't be bothered to stop and ask him where or when he'd grabbed it. She was just glad he had.

She watched him rip it open and unroll it, incredibly turned on by the way his strong hands smoothed the latex over his shaft. Her hips wanted to lift, and he wasn't even near her yet.

When he knelt at the bottom of the bed, sheathed and ready, Ginnie let out a little whimper. She couldn't help it. And her legs dropped open.

Quinn inhaled sharply, then moved forward to position himself over her.

"Baby?" he murmured.

"Please," she whispered back urgently.

He kept his eyes on her as he eased into her, filling her exquisitely, almost – but not quite – painfully.

"Genevieve," he said. "I've been waiting for you forever."

And then he began to move. He rocked, not in and out, but inside, pulsing.

Oh.

Oh. Wow.

Oh. Fuck.

Ginnie didn't know if she cried out the curse, or if it was in her head only. But holy hell, he felt amazing. He was way inside of her, his tip reaching a part of her that had never been touched before. One that wanted to be touched, again and again.

He picked up speed, and now he *was* moving in and out, and it was as good as the other. She could feel each thrust through her core, and soon she was lifting herself to meet him, perfectly in time.

Their rhythm was incredible. Unsurpassed.

Ginnie was sure it couldn't be topped.

But Quinn reached down, drew one of her feet up to his shoulder, and just like that, it was even better. Because now each forward movement brought him to *that* spot, the one that was created just for him. Again and again, he drove himself into her.

Then, without warning, he released her leg and flipped them over and he was *so very deep* inside of her. Impossibly so. And his hands were on her hips, guiding her up and down.

Holy...Oh wow...Holy...

She couldn't find a word that fit. It was just –

"Quinn!"

Yes, that was the one. It was just *Quinn*.

His name left her lips again as the momentum inside her built to an almost unbearable level. "Quinn!"

"Yes." His reply was a barely audible, desire-filled groaned. "Oh, yes."

She moved forward and back and up and down and the heat spiralled inside of her spinning into a tight spring. And with a shuddering, gasping cry, Ginnie came on top of him, releasing the insurmountable pressure he'd wound inside of her, pulsing against him. He held her in place, and he was throbbing too, his breath labored as he climaxed with her.

Never, ever in her life had Ginnie imagined sex could be like that.

And if she'd been able to think of anything other than Quinn, she might've noted that it turned out that Lawrence was right. They *hadn't* had any chemistry in the bedroom.

And now she knew exactly what she'd been missing. It was this sweet perfection.

It was Quinn.

Thirty

Quinn held her above him, enjoying the last, drawn-out pulses of their mutual orgasm, staring into her incredible eyes, feeling her incredible body. He'd never in his life experienced something so singularly heart-pounding-ly satisfying.

Why did we wait so long?

Then he remembered. They *hadn't* waited. Two days ago, Ginnie was a stranger.

Incredible.

Quinn couldn't wrap his head around the idea of not knowing her.

He slid his hands up her bare thighs, along her hips, then cupped her face tenderly before he finally released her so she could roll off. She settled beside him, her fast breaths evening out until Quinn thought she was sleeping.

Then she spoke, stopping and starting with an endearing awkwardness. "Was that – Is it always like that for – I mean – with you – You know what? Never mind."

"I can honestly say it has *never* been like that *for* me." Quinn chuckled and trailed a finger down her bare shoulder. "As far as *with* me…"

She smacked his stomach lightly. "Shut up."

"You *asked*," he teased.

She sighed resignedly. "I guess I did."

Quinn leaned back just enough that he could steal another look at the girl who'd so quickly and thoroughly invaded his heart in so short a time.

"Ginnie…"

"Mm hmm?"

Quinn paused, unsure what he wanted to say and finally settling on, "You're extraordinarily beautiful."

She colored. "Be careful or your sappiness is going to damage your bad boy rep."

"Oh you think so, do you?"

"Yes."

He kissed her forehead. "Well. If it helps any…I stole the condoms."

"You what?"

"Stole them."

Her eyes widened. "From where? When?"

"The store with the coats. I grabbed them with the intention of paying, but everything went south and they were still in my pocket, so…" He did a horizontal shrug. "I stole them."

"Great. Now I'm an *accessory*."

Quinn cocked an eyebrow. "As I recall, you were a perpetrator. But if you'd rather, I could go back and pay for them. Is that what you want?"

"Yes!"

He ran a finger along her elbow. "What if it was *only* that good because of the stolen condoms?"

"Then I guess we'll have to settle for a one-time thing."

Quinn knew she was kidding, but it made his heart squeeze anyway. He slid his hand down to her wrist, lifted her arm over her head and pinned it there. She wiggled, and he grabbed her other wrist and raised it up, too.

"Hey!" she protested.

"Take it back," he ordered.

"Or what? You'll shower me with compliments on my beauty?"

"Take. It. Back."

She stared up at him like she was trying to figure out if the warning tone in his voice was a joke or not. Quinn wasn't sure himself.

"I take it back," she finally said softly, and the pressure in Quinn's heart released.

He leaned down and kissed her, pouring every ounce of tenderness he had into the contact. When he pulled away, Ginnie's sheet-covered chest was rising and falling rapidly, her bottom lip was damp, and Quinn already felt the next stirrings of desire.

"You *are* beautiful," he told her. "And hell if I'm going to let this be a one-time thing. We're going to use the *entire* box of stolen condoms before we even get close to that store again. Then *you* can tell the clerk why we're paying for three more boxes when we're only buying two at that moment."

She narrowed her eyes. "Quinn?"

"Yes, baby?"

"I might be extraordinarily beautiful, but you...I think you're the sexiest fucking thing *ever*."

Quinn's mouth dropped open in surprise, and she shot him a triumphant grin that made him pull her close and chuckle.

"I've ruined you completely," he stated.

"Definitely."

She put her head back onto his chest and Quinn traced the line of her spine. It felt good and right to have her curled against him, making jokes and teasing and kissing and taking as much damned time as he liked to touch her. It filled his mind with things he'd never thought about. Ever. A future with lazy Sunday mornings and white picket fences and stupidly fluffy dogs. And – God help him – a blonde-haired, amber-eyed kid with Ginnie's smile.

Are you fucking nuts?

He thought he must be, because she wriggled a little closer, and her fingers made a slow circle up his stomach and the one kid became *three* kids and the dog became a dog *and* a cat.

But when Ginnie's had reached the puckered scar on his chest, Quinn's little daydream cut off as he stiffened automatically.

"Can I ask?" she wanted to know. "Or no?"

Quinn forced himself to relax. Then forced himself to tell her the truth. And to say the words he'd stumbled over before.

"As it happens, I'm not only the kind of man who's reckless on behalf of the woman he loves. I'm also the kind of man who'll take a bullet for a guy who doesn't quite deserve it."

He waited for her to comment. To call him out on the insanity of mentioning the L-word. Instead, Ginnie just went still. So still that Quinn almost leaned down to check her breathing. Then she inhaled deeply and circled the scar again.

"This is that grey area, isn't it?" she asked.

"Very grey," Quinn agreed, wondering if she was deliberately deflecting and wondering also if that's what he preferred anyway.

"Do you want to talk about it?"

He opened his mouth to tell her no, but what came out instead was a story he'd only spoken aloud once – in his official police statement, and then only because he *had* to – since it happened.

"It was supposed to be a routine drop," he told her. "Meet up with the client, trade the goods for the cash, get home. The guy above me got sick at the last second. Pinkeye or something ridiculous like that. No one else was around, so my boss – PJ – decided to run the stuff himself. I warned him I thought going without protection was a bad idea, but he laughed and asked why I didn't think I was capable of watching out for us on my own. I shouldn't have let it get to me, but I did. Pride, maybe. So we went, just the two of us. Me and PJ."

Quinn closed his eyes, remembering it. Walking into the rundown house, seeing the guarded looks on their contacts' faces and knowing, without a doubt, that they'd been set up.

He'd managed to excuse himself momentarily, even gone so far as to dial his undercover contact. Then he'd frozen, the code word sticking in his throat. Eight full years undercover and it felt so unnatural to ask for help. Like admitting defeat. That hesitation gave just enough time for the shit to hit the fan.

The screaming and the glass shattering.

In the time it took Quinn to drop his phone and make his way back to the living room, the place was exploding with cops. Rife with tension. Unbearable with back and forth hollering.

The rest had played out in slow motion.

PJ, reaching into his coat.

The officer across the room, going for his weapon.

The split second where Quinn knew he had to choose between blowing his cover and saving the other man's life.

And the latter winning out.

"Quinn?"

His eyes whipped open, and he realized a little belatedly that he was squeezing Ginnie's hand too hard. He eased his grip and tried to smile. The sight of her caring eyes almost let him succeed.

"It was instinct, I guess," he said, his voice a little rawer than he liked. "I dove between my boss and the bullet, and I woke up three days later in the hospital."

The semi-heroic, mostly-stupid act was what earned him his retirement. From both the Black Daggers and the police force. It was an odd situation. A unique one, by all accounts on both sides. The bullet went in perfectly, then made its way cleanly out the other side. No nicked arteries, amazingly little penetrating trauma. Three months of recovery. PJ James was eternally grateful for his life, and happy to cut him loose, and the police department felt it would serve no purpose to reveal Quinn's identity. Unbelievably…no strings.

"I'm a lucky sonofabitch," Quinn added.

Ginnie ran her hand over the scar. "Someone really should explain to you what *luck* means."

"I distinctly recall telling you the same thing just this morning," he teased.

"Yeah. Well. That was before. Clearly, your definition can't be trusted."

He started to argue, but her fingers had moved on, landing on the knife tattoo on his wrist. Quinn braced himself. If she pressed for details, he knew he'd feel compelled to tell her the rest of the truth, right then and there.

Which is dangerous for both of us.

When she spoke, though, it was a statement, not an inquiry. "It was a gang, and you were running drugs."

"Yes." He caught her hand in his and pressed them to the ink together, tracing the curved blade.

"They put the outline in when you pledge." He moved their fingers to the hilt. "Each of the lines represents a complete job. Three lines means you've finished your pledge." Back to the blade. "The shading is for full members." To the jagged tip. "The tiny break here signifies that I've been jumped out."

"But?"

Quinn inhaled, wondering again how she could so easily read his feelings. "I saved PJ's life and almost died in the process. As a result, I'm in the unique position of not owing the Black Daggers anything. PJ's a bastard, but he's got a thing about trust and a thing about loyalty and a weird sense of honor. He swore to me that he'd never ask me for a thing, so he won't."

"You sound like you admire that," Ginnie said.

"I do," he admitted. "PJ always knows where he stands. Kind of like *you*. Black and white."

Ginnie smiled. "Did you just compare me to your *gang* boss and make it sound like a compliment?"

Quinn touched her lips and smiled back. "I think I did."

She reached up and slid her hand beneath his fingers. "So you admired your boss, who was a bad man. But you left that life behind, and I don't think that's what's bothering you."

"No," he agreed softly. "Ginnie…Even when you leave the life behind, it never really leaves *you* behind. I can't remove the tattoo or what it means. I'll have that association forever, no matter what I did before, or why I joined them, or what I do after. I can't get rid of the way being in the gang changed me. It's hard for me to even feel *normal*."

The words hung in the air, the truth of them hitting him again. It didn't matter than the gang involvement was undercover work. The things he'd seen. And done…

Ginnie's palm landed on his cheek, drawing him back to the moment in that way that only she could.

"You know, Quinn. Every normal moment I've had has been a fraud," she said. "My mom, pretending to be healthy, right up to the end. My dad, smiling as he walked out the door on the last day before he turned me over to social services. And Lawrence, getting up every day, going to work, being married to me…" Her face got funny then, and she went on barely audible and sounding like she was in awe of her own words. "And me, being married to him. All a fraud." She cleared her throat. "I've been searching for normal since I was a kid. Trying to make up for the things that were less than average in my own life. No mom, no dad, no chance. It's taken me this long to realize I've been doing it wrong. I don't *want* normal. I want *you*."

Quinn lips turned up. "I know I compared you to a gang leader, but...*Ouch*."

She didn't smile back. "My point is, we grow and change and have scars and we forgive and we love. I'm not going to let you go just because everything in your past isn't perfect. That wouldn't just be hypocritical, it would be downright stupid."

His own smile faded, not because what she said made him unhappy, but because he felt it so acutely. The sentiment behind them, the passion they exuded – they matched his own so well, and he'd never been so damned serious about something.

Neither of them might be able to say the words directly, but he knew they shared them anyway.

We love.

The phrase echoed in his mind as he drew her face to his and did his best to turn what was in his heart into a kiss. He touched her with the leisure of someone who had time to do it again and again, and with the thoroughness of someone who knew just how privileged he was to be *allowed* to do it. Then, for the first time in the nearly thirty years of life he had behind him, Quinn made love to a woman he never wanted to lose. Hard and fast, then sweet and steady.

All-consuming desire. Just the way it should be.

And he forgot everything but her.

Sunday
Thirty-One

Ginnie woke slowly, an all-over body ache making her smile.
Smile? Since when does hurting *make me feel good?*
Then she remembered.
Since Quinn.
And a silly, sleepy grin turned up her mouth as she reached
across the bed.
Empty.
For a second, a deep sense of unease crept through Ginnie's
mind. And her heart thumped nervously in response before she
remembered he'd been gone the previous morning as well.
For coffee.
God, how Ginnie needed one now. A hot, caffeinated
beverage would soothe away some of the soreness, and to help
clear the fog in her brain.
Though if she was being honest, if the choice was between
coffee and Quinn…There was no contest. Quinn and his sexy
smile took that cake on what fuelled her, and she blushed again at
how badly she suddenly wanted him. Was it normal to feel so
much desire after already having been so thoroughly satiated?
Because she had *definitely* be satiated. Repeatedly. In many
ways. Last night had been a breath-stealing, pulse-pounding,
contortionist-worthy workout.
Her smile widened at the memory, and she winced as even her
cheek muscles screamed. She was going to have to hire a
damned physical therapist for sex recovery if it was like this
every time.
Every time.
She shivered pleasantly at the possibility of his hands on her
body, night after night. Of his voice, rumbling in her ear as he
replied to the thoughts and feelings she shared with him, and he
shared a few of his own.

The last thing Ginnie remembered before drifting off, her arms and legs wrapped around him, was a question that held a delicious promise.

"Where would you like to wake up Monday morning, baby? Your place, or mine?"

And Ginnie had told him that she didn't care. As long as it was with him.

It was so *easy* to say things like that to him. To be honest and not worry if it was the right thing or the wrong thing because all that mattered was that it was the *true* thing.

Until that second, she'd never thought about how her crazy obsession with doing things perfectly also affected her ability to do them authentically. Of course, she'd never considered it *crazy* before, either. But right then, it seemed far more insane than lying in a hotel room bed picturing a long-term life with a man she'd just met and was already halfway in love with.

Only halfway *in love?*

And even though there was no one around to see, Ginnie colored. If she thought anything was crazy, it should be that nudging voice was crazy. But even the logical part of her brain was jumping up and down with agreement, offering its totally typical, totally reasonable list as evidence.

Palpitating heart? Check.

Can't think about anything else? Check.

Unreasonable wish that he was there right that second? Check.

"Stupid logical brain," she muttered.

With a self-directed eye roll, she decided she'd better get out of bed before she had a whole wedding planned. She flung the sheets back, swung her aching legs from the bed and placed her feet on the toe-curling carpet. Then went still.

What the...

She forced her hand to reach for the partially open nightstand drawer. She slid it wider, her heart in her throat.

Her phone sat in the bottom of the drawer.

Very slowly, Ginnie scooped it up. It felt like a lead weight in her hand. And the weight was somehow connected to her stomach, dragging it down to her knees.

What was the phone doing there? Quinn had to have put it inside the night stand, which meant he had to have grabbed it from the bar where Ginnie had given it its ice bath. But why had he held onto it until now? And why had he hidden it?

The door squeaked open, and Ginnie's eyes jerked up as Quinn shouldered his way into the room. For a second, his face split into a goofy smile. A no-holds-barred, heartbreakingly sweet grin that was at odds with his tough-guy looks and that made Ginnie's chest want to burst with joy. Then his eyes landed on the cell phone and his face changed. A whole range of emotions played across it, and none of them made sense. Fear. Guilt. Pain.

The feelings were so obvious and so strong that Ginnie had to look at her own hand to see if she held something far worse. But no…

It's just a phone.

Except for some reason, she knew it wasn't. Not with the way he'd looked at it. Not with the way he was now looking at *her* as he set down the coffee and cookies on the table.

The perfect coffee from the perfect man.

And Ginnie's mind flipped through the last forty or so hours of memory. Some of them were clear as day, some were muddled with alcohol. All of them centered around Quinn. And all of them meant something. Though she wasn't sure what.

Just…something.

Quinn, at the airport bar, zeroing in on her as she mentally stripped him.

Quinn, so insistent that he accompany her and protect her and help her.

Quinn, asking so few questions and refusing to answer any of her own.

One question and its lack of answer, in particular, stood out.

"Why were you going to Vegas?" she asked slowly.

She watched as Quinn tongue darted out and poked at his lip ring, giving away his state of mind.

Definitely something more, then. Something you're missing.

"You said it was for work," she reminded him. "I don't think you *meant* to tell me that." She closed her eyes, remembering the way he'd covered it by turning the question back on her, and how she'd been too drunk to care. "But you *did* mean it when you told me you weren't in the gang. So if you're not in the gang...and you had my phone, and..." Her eyes flew open as she made a sudden mental leap. "It's *me*."

"Ginnie..."

He took a step toward her, and she put up a hand. He stopped immediately. Like he'd hit a force field. Or a brick wall. Which Ginnie felt, too. Slamming between them, piece by piece, the mortar setting as soon as it landed.

"I'm the job," she stated, disappointed at how small her voice sounded.

"I can – "

"Please don't say *explain*." *Yes, better. Firmer.* "It's far too cliché for a man like you."

"I can – "

She cut him off again. "Can what?"

"I don't know."

Why did the big, tattooed man have to look so vulnerable? So broken. So much like he needed her. And how could the quick tap of his tongue on his lip ring and the sharp tug of his hair make her want to tear down the just-built wall?

No.

Ginnie wasn't going to give in. She wasn't going to be weak again.

She looked down at her hands so she wouldn't have to look at him anymore. "I should just go."

"Please, baby. Just hear me out."

The endearment snaked into Ginnie's chest and squeezed at her heart and she had to force aside how bad it hurt to know that he could get to her with just a word. When she'd been nothing but a *job* to him.

And his next words slammed it home.

"Jase just thought you needed someone to protect you."

Ginnie's gaze snapped back up. What the hell did her brother have to do with this? With Quinn's work? And – *Oh.* One plus one definitely added up to two.

She swallowed. "He hired you to *protect* me."

"Yes."

"He told you about me, and how I like my coffee."

"Yes."

"And he gave you money."

"Yes."

Which meant…She'd slept with a man who was *paid* to do it.

A wave of nausea hit her, and her stomach dropped down to her knees as she stared at Quinn, trying figure out how she could have been so easily duped. She watched his mouth work.

He's still talking. Why is he still talking? Why are we still in the same room?

She needed to get out. But when she stood, she felt like she was moving underwater. Slow and clumsy and unable to breathe. Unable to get to the door with any kind of speed. And that gave Quinn just enough to push through that invisible shield between them and press a hand into her elbow. His touch seared into her skin, and she jumped away, half-expecting to find a brand where his fingers had been. Instead, there was just…nothing. Her arm and her aches. No other evidence that Quinn had touched her in any way.

The cold tendrils of sickness that took up residence in Ginnie's gut fanned out through her body. They became brittle and threatened to crack. And oh, god, how they hurt. Threatened to knock her breathless.

She had to get past it.

Strength. Please.

She inhaled. "You can go, or I can go. Either way, one of us is leaving."

"I didn't know what was going to happen between us, Genevieve. I couldn't have known."

She shook her head. "*Nothing* happened."

"Nothing? How can you say that? It's bullshit."

"What do you *want* me to say? You *manipulated* me. You and Jase both. And I'm just the stupid girl who fell for it."

"It wasn't supposed to be manipulation."

"No? What was is supposed to be?"

"A job. And – Christ, Ginnie." Pause. Click of the ring. "Can we just start this conversation over?"

"I don't think so, Quinn."

He flinched liked he'd been struck, but still shot her a pleading look. "Please."

Another deep inhale. And an equally forceful exhale.

"Why?" she said coolly. "So you can tell me how you didn't *mean* to sleep with me? That it was just a bonus? An expected side effect? Sorry, no. The why and the how don't even matter. This weekend has been great. But we need to be honest with each other and with ourselves." The words sounded like a lie, even to Ginnie's own ears, but she pushed on, certain of what would dislodge the stubborn set to Quinn's jaw. "I would have had sex with you, either way." *That,* at least, was true. "I was looking to get wild, looking for an excuse to live outside of my tidy boxes. Desperate, I guess. So if you'd just walked up and *told* me Jase hired you, I would probably have been so mad that I would've jumped into bed with you right that second. You didn't have to hold my phone hostage or keep it a secret or anything like that." Also true, or close to it. "You know what's good though?"

"There's something good about this?" His voice was so very rough, so full of pain.

Ginnie forced a tiny laugh. "Okay, maybe not good. If we're getting into semantics again."

"Fuck your semantics," he snapped.

She ignored him. "Maybe it's just a relief."

"What does that mean?"

She shrugged. "It means that it's over. And *both* of us got the job done."

Quinn stepped back, hurt making his big body fold in on itself. Ginnie steeled herself against it. She had no reason to feel guilty about her word-spinning. After all, *he* was the real liar. He was the one who'd *chosen* to keep the deception alive.

And now it's time for the nails in the coffin.

She went on. "Now we can get on that plane and head home. I'll go back to being the girl who used to be married to a doctor. And you'll go back to being the guy covered in tattoos who once got shot protecting a drug dealer. We could never be anything more than what we already are. There's no point in prolonging the inevitable. This ending couldn't be more perfect, right?"

His mouth opened, but just barely. Then he ground it shut so hard that Ginnie could practically hear his teeth smacking against each other, smashed his hands into his pockets, and spun.

Ginnie waited.

For him to turn back and get the last word.

For him to plead one more time for her to listen.

For him to sweep her up and kiss her with brutal need before storming out again.

But he didn't. He didn't slam the door; he didn't look back.

He's gone.

And without his presence to buffer her against the torrent of emotional pain, Ginnie fell to the bed and let a wracking sob take her.

Thirty-Two

Quinn eased his back away from the hallway wall of the hotel room he'd shared with Ginnie for the last two days. Some of the best hours of his life. He'd been standing there for a good ten minutes, furious as hell, fighting the underlying hurt.

The pain in his chest was overwhelming, the crush of everything under his ribcage threatening to suffocate him. He tried to latch onto the anger, tried to hold it and use it as a shield against the burn of rejection, tried to use it as fuel for the fire of hatred.

But he couldn't hate her. Her words, the sting they left, his own insecurity brought to life…those he could hate. But Ginnie? Hell, no. He was man enough to know that if he hated her, he wouldn't care so fucking much about what she thought of him. And apparently, what she thought of him was so very little.

She has to be lying. Has to be.

Unless she wasn't.

Because wasn't he the one who'd told himself that *not* sharing his connection with Jase was a bad idea, one that would piss her off and hurt her and jeopardize everything? And hadn't he also been the one who'd said he wasn't good enough? The one who'd pointed out that his past would shape him, haunt him, not just right then, but always? All Ginnie had done was realize it, too. Or maybe she'd simply known all along and just needed an opportune moment to throw it in his face.

So why can't I move away from this wall?

He realized he'd pressed himself back into it, his hands flat against the wallpaper, wondering desperately what she was doing on the other side. He closed his eyes and let himself imagine her soft cheek pressed to the door, her thoughts on him, too.

No.

Even if she *was* lying…it didn't matter. In fact, it was worse. It meant she took what would hurt him most and used it anyway. He didn't need that kind of bullshit in his life. He didn't need *any* kind of bullshit.

Quinn pushed himself away again, this time a little more forcefully. As he did, the familiar cock of a gun made him freeze. And he found himself staring into the crazed eyes of Dr. Lawrence Michaels.

Calm. Keep it calm.

Quinn repeated the mantra to himself and held very still.

The man across from him was clearly unstable. Possibly still drunk.

Or maybe drunk again.

Most importantly, he had the weapon trained on the hotel door, right where Quinn had pictured Ginnie just moments earlier, his finger on the trigger. Any tiny move, any tiny slip…No. Quinn wouldn't let himself consider it. No matter how badly he was itching to flatten the other man. Because he'd recognized the look on the doctor's face for what it was.

Desperation.

Reason and hope had been pushed aside, and the man might not be crazy, but he clearly believed he had nothing to lose. Quinn had underestimated the man once before. Now that he knew why, he wasn't going to do it again.

Calm. Keep it calm.

But try as he might, his words – spoken low enough to not be accidentally overheard by anyone behind any door – betrayed his true feelings. "Give me one good reason why I shouldn't jump you, take that gun, and shoot you with it right now."

Lawrence smiled. "Just because you *look* stupid doesn't mean I believe you *are* stupid. We both know you won't jump me. I'm one little bump away from firing. Do you know where she is in the room?"

Both of Quinn's hands balled up into fists. The idea of the other man lying in bed with Ginnie made him sick to his stomach. And the thought of him accidentally firing at her…There weren't words for that particular emotion.

He forced himself to keep an even tone. "Let's move this conversation out of the hall. Have a discussion where an accident is less likely."

"And lose my one bit of leverage? *I'm* not stupid either."

Quinn gritted his teeth. *Leverage? She's a fucking person.*

"Dr. Michaels," he said stiffly. "I give you my word that I won't lay a finger on you. My only condition is Ginnie's safety."

Lawrence gave him a considering look, then – very, very slowly – he moved the barrel of the gun to Quinn, who never thought he'd be so relieved to have a pistol pointed at his chest.

Thank god.

"What is it you want, Dr. Michaels?" Quinn asked, and he braced himself for the answer.

Don't let him say Ginnie. If he says he wants her back, I'll – What? Risk her life just to keep her? No. Hand her over like a commodity? She's not even mine to –

His thoughts cut off as the other man spoke. "Relax, Mr. Mcdavid. All I need from you is a favor."

Quinn tapped his lip ring and narrowed his eyes. Favors came with a price. Always.

"What kind of favor?" he replied cautiously.

"You have to come with me to Las Vegas."

"What the hell for?"

"I want you to help me broker a business deal."

"I don't know if you've noticed, Dr. Michaels, but the very last thing I am is a businessman."

Lawrence smiled. "Quinn Mcdavid, former member of the Black Daggers. Small-time drug dealer for a mid-level gang. Up close and personal with that gang's number one man. You're the exact kind of businessman I'm looking for."

"What kind of – " Quinn cut himself off mid-sentence as his mind – one-part experienced criminal, one-part trained cop – made the only logical jump. "*You're* selling drugs."

"I prefer to think of it as repaying a debt. Creatively." The other man paused, then added. "PJ James."

Quinn saw no point in denying his association with his former boss. Dr. Douchebag obviously had that part of his past locked down already. For all Quinn knew, PJ himself had shared the information.

"What about him?" he asked.

"A while back, I ran into some trouble. Gambling debt. An associate of PJ's, as it happens. And PJ, well, he's the one with the creativity."

Debts and collections. Yeah, those made the man creative all right.

"What are you asking me to do?"

The asshole doctor shrugged. "Simple. Intervene on my behalf. Explain to your former boss that I didn't intentionally lose his prescription pads. Then ask him to forgive the debt."

Quinn resisted an urge to roll his eyes. PJ was a lot of things. Being forgiving sure as hell wasn't one of them.

"You seem to have missed the significance of the word *former*," he said. "I severed my ties to PJ and the Black Daggers a long time ago."

"Un-sever them."

"It doesn't work like that. Jumped out is jumped out."

"My understanding is that you took a bullet to get out. Is it going to take another to convince you to get back in?"

Something in Quinn's gut twisted. How the hell did the man know the specifics of his circumstances? He opened his mouth to ask, but another guest ambled past with an ice bucket and a friendly wave, forcing a temporary silence. Lawrence shoved the gun into his coat pocket, but Quinn could still see the outline, see that it was still trained on him. Would the other man fire with an innocent stranger in the hall?

Probably.

Quinn wasn't going to chance it, either way. He waited until the sleepy-eyed man had filled the bucket and strolled away before he brought his attention back to Lawrence, who drew the weapon out and started talking again.

"I did the math," the other man said. "Conservatively speaking, those prescriptions Ginnie lost were worth a half a million dollars."

Quinn worked to keep his face impassive. Inside, he was cursing the doctor's sheer stupidity. Repeatedly and loudly. A half a million dollars wasn't something PJ James would walk away from.

He barely managed to keep the growl from his voice as he replied. "You're still a licensed physician, right? Make some more money, or get some more prescriptions."

"Not a chance of the latter. I reported those prescription pads stolen. Five of them. That's five *hundred* fucking sheets. Nothing puts a doctor on police radar faster. If I reported *more* missing…" He shrugged. "And as far as the former is concerned, the bastard will just keep extorting me, won't he?"

Quinn couldn't deny it. "Pick option C then. Jail time sounds a hell of a lot safer than whatever *creative* punishment PJ's gonna hand out for not paying him or for refusing to go along with his plan."

"You think he couldn't get to me in there anyway?" Lawrence shook his head. "I'm not going to jail and I'm not paying him back, either. Because you *are* going to help me."

"And if I don't agree, you'll do what? Go to jail for murder instead?"

"No. If you don't help me, I'm going to turn you in."

Quinn gave the other man an incredulous stare. "For *what?*"

"You should be more concerned with *to whom*."

Quinn's eyes flicked to the hotel room door. "She already knows who I was."

"I don't mean to *her*," Lawrence said. "I mean to PJ."

Quinn's blood went cold, but he maintained his steely mask. "I don't know what you're talking about."

"I'm talking about your real job, Mr. Mcdavid."

"I still don't know what – "

"Cut the bullshit."

The doctor reached into his pocket, and what he pulled out was far worse than the gun.

My retirement badge. Oh, Christ.

The leather wallet dropped open mockingly, its gold sending an accusing, invisible shot straight to Quinn's stomach.

"Where the hell did you get that?" he demanded.

Lawrence gave another of his irritatingly nonchalant shrugs. "Your coat pocket. Saw it sticking out while I was with Ginnie in the elevator yesterday, so I grabbed it."

The goddamned elevator. The kiss. Motherfucker.

Quinn drew back a fist and launched it halfway at Lawrence before he stopped himself, shouting internally that the man in front of him held his life in the balance. His. And Ginnie's.

Dr. Douchebag smiled like he knew it too. "Took me a bit to figure all this out, so bear with me here. A couple of weeks back, my benefactor – PJ James – casually mentions a man who saved his life – Quinn Mcdavid – and it strikes me as familiar, but I can't place why. I don't even bother to try, if I'm being honest. I've got a lot of shit on my plate. A recent split from my wife. An insatiable girlfriend. And the doctor stuff." He chuckled. "Believe it or not, that takes up some time, too. So, I let it go. Fast forward to Friday when you say your name on the plane and again, it rings a bell, but I'm with my girl and your face isn't familiar. Then I found the badge and it *hits* me. I was *at* the hospital that day they brought you in, Mcdavid. Hell of a situation. Cops made a big show of locking you to the bed even though you were unconscious and lucky to be alive. I remember it well because I was sweating bullets with all that blue around. I'd just done a few not-entirely-legal things in the name of online poker and well, that doesn't matter. Because it was *you*. No doubt about it."

"It's a stretch," Quinn lied, his voice strained.

Lawrence shook his head. "Tell yourself what you have to. But I guarantee you this. PJ's not going think it's a stretch. Not enough of one that he doesn't look into it anyway. And when he finds out it's true, he's going to get creative again. Probably with Ginnie."

Quinn's nails dug so hard into his palms that he was sure he was drawing blood. No part of him wanted to admit the other man was right.

Except he is.

Quinn took a steadying breath and forced his fist to uncurl. PJ was a ruthless bastard. He'd want to make Quinn suffer for the betrayal. But he owed him his life, too, and wouldn't straight up kill him. That kind of twisted logic was what made PJ tick. But hurting Ginnie – the one person Quinn cared about – was the gangster-logical thing to do, and he knew it.

So just kill Lawrence.

Quinn shoved down the dark suggestion. He might have a lot of gray parts in his soul, and more than his share of black ones too, but he wasn't a coldblooded killer.

"Vegas," he agreed gruffly. "On two conditions."

"Are you really in a place to ask for conditions?"

Quinn ignored the other man's smug reply.

"One, I want my badge back," he said. "And two, after this is done, you walk away and you stay the hell away from Ginnie. No calling in later favors, no showing up at the door looking for help, no telling her I helped you out of your fuck-up. Or I promise you, I'll show you how creative *I* can be."

"You get your badge when it's done," the asshole replied, sticking the wallet back in his pocket. "And you don't get to tell her anything either."

"I hadn't planned on it," Quinn said – not because the joke-of-a-doctor told him he couldn't, and not because Ginnie very likely wouldn't let him in, even if he begged her, but because he couldn't bear the idea of trying to explain.

And even worse…he couldn't stand the thought of saying goodbye all over again.

Lawrence blinked at him, and for a second, Quinn thought he might not agree to his terms. Then he stuck out his unarmed hand, and with bile in his throat, Quinn shook on the deal, quick to pull away his fingers as soon as he could.

"Let's move then," the other man said. "The gun'll be in my pocket. If you break your word…"

"I won't." *Not until I'm sure she's out of harm's way anyway.*

"Stairs," Lawrence ordered. "You stay in front of me. And just in case you *are* thinking about changing your mind…Liv –

my girlfriend – is going to come looking. She knows just as much about you as I do, and I left PJ as speed dial number one in her phone."

Fuck.

He didn't know if the doctor was bluffing or not, but once again, he couldn't take a chance. Quinn had no choice but to let the other man usher him down the near-silent corridor of doors.

As he pushed open the door to the stairwell, he wished he'd taken more time to *linger*. To stare at the gentle rise and fall of Ginnie's chest as she slept. To kiss her breathless one last time. To linger. And to beg.

His throat constricted; he was dangerously, humiliatingly close to tears.

But her former fucking husband had his gun bumping against his shoulder blades. So he kept moving.

Sacrifice and resolution and strength.

So this is what love feels like, Quinn thought. *Kinda hurts.*

Thirty-Three

He's not coming back.

Ginnie tried to tell herself that didn't dig. Didn't hurt. That it was what she wanted.

But she was alone, and that made it harder to maintain the lie.

She did another slow circle of the room. She wasn't sure how many times she'd walked around it already. Touching the furniture, imagining Quinn's big body taking up space in the bed, wishing she was stronger.

Instead, all she ached to do was to crawl back into the bed. To wrap the blankets around her, to inhale the residual scent of him. Or better yet...To close her eyes and pretend that his arms were around her.

If you want him so badly, asked a small voice, *then why did you chase him away?*

She shoved aside the question and wondered why she couldn't just walk away. Like, literally. Not just turn her back on the last two days and pretend they hadn't happened, but actually step out of the room. After all, nothing in it was hers.

Some of it was *Quinn's*. His suitcase and his toothbrush were still in the bathroom. A pair of his jeans were draped across the chair in the corner.

And there were a lot of things that didn't belong to either of them, too. Like the pile of underwear and skimpy clothes.

But nothing is mine.

Woodenly, Ginnie bent to pick up a few the discarded items. She folded them and tucked them into the suitcase that was hers (but not *actually* hers) and when she stood up and looked around again, she felt no better. In fact, she spotted a pair of silky undies snagged under the dresser.

"It's like the damned things are multiplying," she muttered.

She wanted to laugh. But she couldn't. Because laughter would turn into tears. She was sure of it.

Get rid of the evidence completely. That will help.

She bent again. And again and again. Her clean up became frenzied. The little bits of fabric flew from the floor to her hands to the bag, landing in a frustratingly silent pile. Ginnie thought they should sound like shattering glass. Like a breaking heart.

She spun around in search of something solid. Something that would make the noise she so desperately needed to hear.

She snapped up her dead cell phone and hurled it at a wall. It thudded in a satisfying way. But the bejewelled case split, sending rhinestones bouncing through the room, minimizing Ginnie's momentary sense of fulfillment.

"Dammit!"

She grabbed Quinn's jeans and threw them as hard as she could at the suitcase. They sounded like an exhale. *Less* than an exhale. And they sent the panties flying all over again.

Ginnie bent to grab them, and this time, with each one she dropped into the bag, another tear fell. By the time she was on panty number twelve – *and dear God...who needed* twelve *pairs for* one *weekend?* – she had lost all semblance of control. Her face was soaked, her chest was burning, and she was scraping up as much carpet fiber as she did satin and lace and leather garments. And pretty quickly, it was *all* fiber.

Ginnie blinked back another round of tears as she looked around and realized she'd picked up everything and packed it back into the suitcase.

"Back in its tidy box," she murmured.

Just like she'd promised Quinn.

But *she* was still empty.

With lead fingers, she flipped the bag shut. And when she did, she spotted the one item that hadn't made it into the bag.

The big, purple dildo.

As she reached for it, Ginnie decided it was oddly symbolic. She could stuff everything she wanted into a suitcase, zip it closed, and push it out of sight. But some sexy part of her was going to be free forever.

The mark she'd expected to see that last time Quinn touched her – the one that had burned so harshly – wasn't on her skin, she realized. It was somewhere deep in her soul. And if she never spoke to him again, never saw his face anywhere but her dreams, she would *still* never be the same.

The irrefutable truth hit her so hard that she almost missed the insistent thump on the hotel room door.

Quinn.

He was probably just there to get his things.

But maybe not.

She battled against the elation in her heart and lost. There was no denying the thump-thump of hope drumming against her chest.

So why are you just sitting here, then? Let him in.

She didn't bother to compose herself. She knew it was useless. But when she flung open the door, it wasn't Quinn at all. Instead, a short, curvy brunette with a downturned mouth stood just outside. It only took Ginnie a second to place her – Lawrence's too-young, too-busty, arm-candy girlfriend. She was dressed in one of Ginnie's frill-necked blouses and a flouncy skirt, and the ensemble made her look like a kindergartener dressed up for school pictures.

Did I seriously pack that outfit? she wondered with cringe.

But of course she *had*. Pre-Quinn.

"Can I help you?" Ginnie asked, keeping her voice cool and collected.

"Yes. You can. I just have one question and it's – " she started, then stopped, mouth agape.

"Yes?" Ginnie prodded.

The girl blinked several times, then asked, "Is that my – is that what I – what are you *doing*?"

Ginnie's followed the girl's gaze to her hand, where her fingers had squeezed tightly around the purple monstrosity. For a brief moment, she debated throwing it behind her and pretending she had no idea what the girl was talking about. But what was the point?

"It's exactly what you think it is," Ginnie replied, still calm, though she knew her face must be flaming. "And as far as what

I'm doing, I'm packing it up. Along with your underwear." She paused and raised a deliberately sarcastic eyebrow. "But I'm guessing that neither of those were *actually* your one question?"

The girl's shoulders dropped again. "No."

And suddenly, Ginnie couldn't even muster up enough resentment to send her away. She stepped back, and pretended that it was totally normal to use the giant dildo to gesture that the pretty brunette should come in. She couldn't even be annoyed when Lawrence's girlfriend accepted, then sank down onto the bed like it was *her* room.

Ginnie stared at her for a second, then cleared her throat. "Are you going to tell me what your one question is?"

"Do you still love him?"

"What?"

"Lawrence. Do you still love him?"

"I – why are you even asking?"

The girl met her eyes. "He's been acting crazy. And I kept just thinking something was wrong. Actually, I thought something was *right*. Even after he apologized to me because he kissed you, I still assumed…But now he's just *gone* and I'm not sure *why*. This is so much more than cold feet. Something is wrong."

As she attempted to process the rambling statement, it was Ginnie's turn to blink. "Cold feet? And wait. Lawrence *told* you he kissed me?"

She couldn't imagine he'd disclosed the exact details of the assault in the elevator, but the girl was nodding her head.

"Of course," she said. "He tells me everything. Or mostly he does. When it matters. I assumed it was nerves and the alcohol that made him kiss you, but then I started thinking about it, and I realized something was really wrong. I mean, he's spontaneous and fun and he makes lots of mistakes, but this?"

"Spontaneous?"

"He was supposed to *propose!*"

"Propose?"

The brunette bit her lip. "You must hate me."

"Hate you?" Ginnie was really starting to feel like a parrot.

"I know he was your husband first."

"Actually...he wasn't."

"Um?"

"Never mind." Ginnie let out a breath. "What's your name?"

"Liv."

"Okay. Listen, Liv. No, I don't love Lawrence." *Damn, does it ever feel good to say that.* "So if that's all...?"

"Do you know where he is?"

Liv sounded a little desperate, and Ginnie realized that it was quite possible that the other woman *did* love him. And if Lawrence had run off on her...Well. It didn't matter how *Ginnie* felt about him because she knew what it was like to lose someone that mattered to her. So as much as it galled her, Ginnie couldn't ignore Liv's feelings...*After all, love is love, isn't it?*

"I'm sorry," she stated, her tone gentle. "I don't have any idea where he is."

"Oh." The girl's body sunk in on itself even more.

"I do know that even though you see him as spontaneous, with me, Lawrence was always a creature of habit," Ginnie added. "If he *was* freaking out – cold feet, or whatever – he'd go somewhere familiar. Home, maybe? Do you want me to – "

"I called already. I checked home and the office and even the hospitals. Local *and* the one he works at."

Ginnie suppressed a sigh. After all, it wasn't like she had anything more important to do. Except chase after Quinn. Which she *couldn't* do.

"How long has he been gone?" she asked.

More abject misery. "I don't know."

"How can you not know?" Because Ginnie was sure she could count the exact seconds since Quinn walked out.

Walked out? You mean after you kicked *him out. He's not your father.* Ginnie shook off the snide voice and focused on what Lawrence's girlfriend was saying.

"Lawrence came back to the room so late and we had the fight about you, and...I was asleep..." Liv trailed off, and it was obvious that she was trying to fight a sob.

Shit. Ginnie wished she was immune to the other girl's suffering. But she wasn't.

"Okay," she said, trying to sound patient. "Let's build a quick timeline. Even if Lawrence left right after you went to bed, and even if he managed to get a flight out the moment he got over to the airport, he'd still barely have had time to retrieve his bags and make it home. And if he just left this morning, it will be at least dinnertime before he strolls through the door, right?"

"You're so right." Liv's face brightened a fraction. "Lawrence always said you were smarter than he was."

"He said I was smarter than him?" Ginnie knew her question was full of surprise.

Liv nodded. "Smarter. Higher expectations. It drove me crazy at first, how much he talked about you. Then I decided it was a good thing. Like, a blueprint to what was in his head. A what-not-to-do guide."

Ginnie grimaced, wondering just why the hell she was letting this train wreck of a conversation go on, but somehow not being able to stop it. "So you're purposely being not *me*?"

"Actually…it turned out I didn't even have to try. I could just be me, and I'm what Lawrence wanted all along."

It felt like an insult. "What does *that* mean?"

Liv shot her a knowing look. "He wanted the trophy wife. You're more than that."

Weirdly, a blush crept up Ginnie's cheeks. "I'm sure you're more than that, too."

"I don't *want* to be. I don't *need* to be. All I want is Lawrence."

Ginnie stared at Liv, unsure if the sudden, single thud she felt in her heart was a door opening, or a door closing.

Both, maybe.

Lawrence had never been all Ginnie wanted. Because she *was* more than a trophy wife. If anything, Lawrence had been the trophy. The doctor-iffic icing on her cake of a life. And it turned out she wanted pie.

And Quinn was the pie.

All she wanted was Quinn.

And then – just like that – it hit her.

It didn't take true strength to stay mad or to hold on to despair. It took true strength to admit that she was wrong. And even more to face what she was actually feeling. Which wasn't anger at all.

Love.

Crazy. Impulsive. Unstoppable. Undoubtable. *Love.* All for Quinn.

Her heart bloomed for a moment, full of the realization.

She *loved* him.

Then it dropped again.

She *loved* him. And couldn't do a damned thing about it.

Crap. How could I be so damned stupidly stubborn? The answer came immediately. *Because you were scared.*

Afraid that she was going to make another mistake like she had with Lawrence. Afraid that Quinn might leave, like her dad had done. Or maybe even that he might die, like her mom.

She'd used that fear to get angry. Yes, he'd deceived her. But he'd done it to protect her and her heart. He'd apologized and she'd sloughed it off.

Which was wrong. And it was wrong to project her past onto Quinn, too. Wrong to use her own fear to drive him away. Especially since he'd been so transparent about his own past and how he carried it with him. And she'd tossed that in Quinn's face. Sent him away. Worse than sent him away. She'd made him think that she believed she was too good for him. A doctor's wife and a criminal. Ginnie had never felt so desperately sorry. *She* was the criminal. The destroyer of love.

Melodramatic much?

But melodrama didn't shake the truth of it all.

Could she chase him down? Push aside her pride and her past and ask for forgiveness, too?

Why would he even let you get close enough?

The answer was simple. No. Why would he? And even if there was the remotest possibility...but no. Ginnie didn't have his number, or know his address, and she was sure he wasn't the kind of guy who made himself easy to contact. No Quinn Mcdavid with a convenient listing in the phone directory.

Maybe she could ask Jase…

She shook her head, her chest hollow. It was a hopeless situation. She loved him, and she'd driven him away, and now she had to deal with the fallout.

"Maybe if I hadn't let him go," she mumbled.

"What?"

Ginnie's eyes flicked back to the girl on her bed, and she realized Liv thought she was talking about Lawrence. She couldn't even muster the energy to explain. She just shook her head, whispered, "I have to go," and dashed out of the hotel room.

She didn't stop to think about where she was going or what she should be doing. Not until she'd already fled the hotel, torn up the walkway outside that led from the hotel to the airport, been thoroughly soaked by the snow-turned-to-rain, and was standing in the throng of travellers.

Home.

She needed to go home.

Thirty-Four

By the time he'd downed his first cup of shitty, airport coffee, a hundred scenarios had run through Quinn's torrential mind.

They all started out fine.

Quinn, turning Lawrence in to airport security.

Quinn, demanding to speak to the TSA agent, Gilligan, then turning Lawrence over to him, specifically.

Quinn, coldcocking Lawrence and hightailing it back to the hotel to take Ginnie into his arms.

Somehow, though, no matter how hard he tried, he couldn't make the fantasized upsets work out in his favor.

Airport security turning on him.

Gilligan locking him up beside the doctor. Or releasing him, revealing his undercover status to the world, and exposing Ginnie to retaliation.

Ginnie not taking him back.

The last was the most often repeated result, and the most feared. A big deal, for a guy like Quinn who feared so little. Who'd never – by his own admission – had much to lose, and ergo little to be afraid of.

"Scared?"

Lawrence Michaels' smug voice, asking a question that so closely echoed Quinn's thought, made Quinn want to snarl. He kept his own voice even, though, as he answered without lifting his face to look at the other man.

"Scared? Hardly." *Not of what* he *thought, anyway.*

"Oh, really?" Lawrence countered.

Quinn shot him a glare, annoyed at how self-possessed the douchebag appeared.

That's what you get for ordering him to shape the hell up.

It was true that it had been Quinn's idea to pause at the busy café. Lawrence needed to sober up; there was no way in hell Quinn was taking him to PJ if the man was going to keep looking and acting like a deranged lunatic.

He just hadn't expected Dr. Douchebag to transform into someone so very...doctor-ly...in a matter of an hour.

Somehow, in between the furious exchange and threats that took place at hotel, and the hastily booked flights with the ticket attendant, who was filing people onto planes like a sheepherder...Somehow, Lawrence had managed to smooth over everything from his face to his hair to his clothes to his attitude. There was no evidence of the fact that he'd stashed a gun somewhere before getting onboard. No evidence that the man had threatened Quinn's life, or that he was working with a gang to peddle prescription drugs. Charming and collected. Tanned and relaxed. Arrogant and articulate. It was how he'd scored them two seats in business class on a near-full flight that would start boarding in an hour. He'd used his toothy smile that matched Leila's perfectly.

Is that the kind of man Ginnie prefers?

Of course it was. She'd married the fucker, hadn't she? Made it *clear* what she did and didn't want.

Quinn forced his eyes back to his plate of dry toast again, unable to deal with the reality of it.

Obviously, if Ginnie had found out about Lawrence's little gambling problem, the charm might've faded. Then again, who knew what people would do for love? No one understood better than Quinn how that particular, thunderous emotion affected rationality. Never in a million damned years would he have described himself as the kind of guy who would fly to Vegas with a man he despised to bargain with another man whom he'd vowed to never interact with again, all to protect a woman he loved.

Christ.

He clamped his jaw shut to keep from giving in to an urge to tap at his lip ring. His tell. That's what Ginnie had called it. When his nerves were on alert, or something pissed him off, or when he was thinking too hard. She was right, obviously. He had never felt so on edge.

Which is why, when a server came by a second later, smiled at the too-suave man across from him, and set down a distinctly alcohol-scented beverage in a paper cup in front of Lawrence, Quinn lost control for a heartbeat. He snapped up the cup, slammed back the drink – rum and coke – then crushed the paper, ice cubes and all.

And finally, Lawrence's placid façade slipped. His eye widened, revealing the still-bloodshot rims, his mouth worked silently, and his gaze darted nervously around the café before he leaned across the table.

"Are you fucking *crazy?*" the other man hissed.

The question made Quinn even angrier. His tongue inched toward his lip ring and he just barely managed to keep from biting down on it. The asshole sitting in front of him was the crazy one. The one who'd annulled his marriage to the most incredible woman in the world.

Breathe.

Quinn tore his mind from Ginnie and reminded himself that he needed to be far less emotional, far less soft, if he was going to accomplish what the not-so-good doctor wanted. What he needed to do was crush the man he'd become over the weekend and channel his inner criminal. A man who could look down the barrel of a gun and grin. Who wouldn't possibly become weak-kneed when he thought about a girl getting hurt.

Quinn steeled himself. No, not steeled. He coated himself in Kevlar, then met Lawrence's glare with a wide grin.

"I *might* be crazy," he said. "I mean, in all likelihood, one of us is."

"One of us?" Lawrence sputtered. "You think that cup-crushing was a display of normal behavior? Someone could've seen it. Your reckless – "

Quinn cut him off, grin still in place. "This is a business trip, Lawrence, so you shouldn't be drinking. You asked for my help and I'm giving it."

"By causing a scene?"

Quinn dropped the smile, signalled the server for another drink and waited for her to bring it. When she set it down, he picked it up immediately and repeated his overly aggressive move. It made the girl jump. It made Lawrence clench his teeth. And it made Quinn stretch out his legs and lean back as he slid more comfortably into both the seat and the role he wanted to play. He ignored the muttered outrage coming from his travelling companion and let his eyes linger on the server's ass as she hurried away. He even managed to shove aside the voice in his head that pointed out the woman's rear end wasn't near as fine as Ginnie's and that it did nothing for him.

"Listen, *doctor*," Quinn said, his tone a jagged edged knife. "Maybe you asked me to come with you because you were desperate. Maybe thought you had an understanding of what I'm capable of. Or maybe you believed that because I was a cop first and a crook second, that I'm good man, or a kind man, or a man with a greater sense of justice. But you don't have a fucking clue. Because I don't fit into a box." *Ginnie. Yet again.* He shoved it off. Also yet again. "A good, kind man wouldn't be going to Vegas to speak to PJ on your behalf. A good, kind man wouldn't have put himself in a position to know PJ in the first place. So if you're looking for something other than a quick, dirty deal, you've come to the wrong person. You can go back to day-drinking and telling yourself you're too good to pay off your own debts. Just let me know. I've wasted enough time on you already."

Lawrence looked taken aback for second, but recovered quickly, his face growing shrewd. "Say what you want. I know you're doing this to protect Ginnie. You told me as much."

Quinn's heart banged against his ribcage. He hated the other man saying her name. He hated *himself* for having shown the other man his vulnerability.

Calm down. No tell. No reaction. No goddamned vulnerability to speak of.

He tossed out a knowing smirk. "Let's just say I've never been the kind of guy who lets something beautiful be destroyed out of sheer stupidity."

"Oh, c'mon," the other man cajoled. "I saw your face back there. You're telling me Ginnie was a piece of meat to you? I call bullshit."

Douchebag, Quinn thought, but in response just raised an eyebrow. "*Art.* Not meat. And what you saw was a connoisseur of art protecting an asset that you already discarded. When you were done with Ginnie, you walked away. You broke a perfectly good thing. Shattered it. Such a waste." God, how he hated talking about her like a commodity. He pushed on anyway. "I picked up those pieces, and in one weekend I created a masterpiece. Now I'm done with Ginnie, too. But unlike you, I still see value in my creation. If I ever want to visit that work of art again, I can. If that's bullshit to you, then – " He paused, shook his head, and sneered. "Fuck it. Who am I kidding? I don't give a rat's ass *what* you think. I'm done talking. Another word and – Ginnie or no Ginnie – I'll suggest to PJ that the best way for him to get payment from you is to take one of your balls, got it?"

Lawrence opened his mouth, and Quinn raised a warning finger. The doctor slammed his lips shut.

Good.

Quinn leaned back again, then closed his eyes.

He didn't have Ginnie anymore. He was about to swallow his last bit of pride – his last bit of decency, too while he was at it – to ask a *favor* of a notoriously un*favor*able man.

He told himself it was the right thing to do, that there *was* a greater justice. But he felt like hell. Like he and the asshole beside him were a matching set on the inside. And it was almost more than he could bear.

Thirty-Five

You have got *to be kidding me.* The incredulous thought temporarily cut through Ginnie's heartbreak as she finally got close enough to see the check-in counter.

There stood Leila. Hair shining. Teeth shining. Stupid airline badge on her lapel…Shining.

What was she even doing there? Didn't ticket agents normally work a solitary desk in a solitary city?

The woman probably decided to come to Vegas just to piss me off, Ginnie thought. *Then she got stuck, too.*

And more importantly, how did the woman manage to look so perfect and perky, even after two days stranded in Asscrack, Colorado – *pause for a serious gut-punch because that was Quinn's name for the town* – and with a lineup of cranky, frazzled passengers at her desk?

Ginnie glanced down at herself. She was a train wreck. She wore one of Quinn's T-shirts – *another gut-punch because why the hell hadn't she changed out of it?* – and a pair of boxer-style pajama bottoms courtesy of an airport souvenir shop. Because as per security, flying completely pants-less wasn't an option. Or shoeless. As evidenced by the one-size-too-small flip-flops on her feet. Given to her by the pitying clerk in the same souvenir shop which sold her the PJs.

She shuffled forward a bit more in the line, careful to look anywhere but directly at Leila, and instead caught sight of her appearance in the too-reflective surface behind the too-shiny ticket agent.

I'm worse than a train wreck, she thought immediately.

Her hair was a mussed-up disaster. Her mouth had a crushed, kissed a whole hell of a lot look to it – *ouch, was that gut-punch going to lessen anytime soon?* – and her face was blotchy red from crying.

Ginnie took a breath and decided that this time, when sparkly Leila didn't recognize her, she might actually believe her. Because she looked nothing like herself. She didn't even fit into any of her own boxes. Unless she had a special one hidden somewhere. One that was just the right size and shape for a raccoon-eyed, heart-crushed idiot who used to disguise herself as a doctor's wife when she was really a girl in love with a tattooed, dangerous, gorilla of a man with a heart of something stronger than gold.

Who's fond of run-on sentences, apparently.

Grammar? Who cared? But grammar was close to semantics and that was another – this time somewhat ridiculous – gut-punch.

Oh, God.

Ginnie needed to go home so very badly. To surround herself with her things, to immerse herself in her own life – in her *new* life – so she could become whole again. She only wished that she wasn't so sure that Quinn Mcdavid was supposed to *be* that new life.

Gut-punch. Punch. Punch!

"Um, hello? Can I help you, Mrs. Michaels?"

Ginnie looked up, once again distracted by Leila. This time less by her shininess and more by the acknowledgement that the girl actually knew her by name. The *wrong* name, but by name nonetheless.

Leila gestured to the still-huge line behind Ginnie, teeth glinting. "It's your turn, Mrs. Michaels. I'm assuming you want to return home and not carry on to Vegas?"

"Yes."

Clack-clack. Pause. *Clack-clack.* Pause. *Clack-clack.*

"No. Wait."

Another pause as Leila looked up and smiled brilliantly. "Wait for…?"

Very briefly, Ginnie considered whether or not she should even bother asking. But she couldn't help it. Maybe because Leila's jazzy, put-on personality made her dizzy with irritation.

"Mrs. Michaels?" the girl pushed.

"Never mind. It's nothing."

Clack-clack.

"Just..." Ginnie trailed off with a frown.

"Yes?"

"Why would you assume I want to go home?"

"Because your doctor husband and cop boyfriend went to Vegas together, so I just guessed that you were out of the picture."

The near-to-smug tone made Ginnie color. "He's not my – they're not my – Okay – Wait. Quinn's not even a cop."

"Yes he is."

"No he's not."

"Yes. He is."

"No. He. Is. Not."

"Yes. He. Is."

Ginnie rolled her eyes. "What is this, third grade?"

Leila's only sign that the back-and-forth bothered her at all was the way her pink-painted lips pursed for a second before she said, "For man who's not a cop, he flashed an awfully big badge at me."

"A badge?"

"Yes."

Ginnie opened her mouth. Then closed it. It could be the truth. Leila had no reason to lie to her, and it actually kind of made sense when she factored Jase into the equation. Her brother wouldn't have hired a criminal to keep an eye on her. He was too stupidly protective. But hiring a cop *disguised* as a criminal? Now *that* sounded like Jase.

And if Quinn was a cop...And he went to Las Vegas with Lawrence...Whose new girlfriend was sure he was in some kind of trouble...

Ginnie's chest constricted with worry. *Why was Quinn getting involved in whatever Lawrence was doing?*

Then she connected the dots. Or some of them, anyway.

Prescription pads.

Vegas.

And the desert house that belonged to Quinn's drug peddling boss, PJ James.

They had to be going there to see him. And something in Ginnie's gut – something underneath the punches – told her that whatever deal was being brokered between the three men, Quinn was in danger.

Oh, no.

Should she call the Las Vegas police? No. That might make things worse. Her brother, maybe? To confirm the story? No. He'd flip out before she even got a chance to explain. What was the best solution?

Leila cleared her throat, interrupting her worried thoughts. "Um, Mrs. Michaels, there are thirty people behind you. If you could – "

Ginnie cut her off. "I need to go to Vegas."

"But I already booked you in for – "

"I need Las Vegas."

"Fine." *Clack. Clack. Clackity-clack.* "Three hundred and forty dollars."

"What?"

"There's a cost difference between the two flights and the flight change fee."

"The airline promised everyone a reimbursing flight!" Ginnie didn't *quite* stomp her foot.

Leila smiled brightly. "I gave you one. And now you want to change it so there's a charge."

Ginnie cast her eyes heavenward, praying for patience. What she found instead was a mirrored ceiling. And her dangerously disheveled self. The woman who'd engaged in a weekend of incredible sex with a stranger who had quickly become the man she loved. And that was definitely *not* a woman who would take "no" for an answer in the name of manners.

Right.

Ginnie placed her hands on the counter and leaned forward, close enough that she could see the beginnings of a pimple on the end of Leila's nose.

"I don't like you," she said.

Leila's smile *almost* faltered. "I'm sorry?"

"I don't like you. You're the cheeriest – but somehow least helpful – customer service person I've ever met."

"Oh." A slight tightening of the eyes. "I'm sorry you feel that way."

"No you're not. And since you won't be honest, I will. Right now, I'd far prefer it if you were an utterly awful, utterly painful – but very helpful – bitch. I still won't like you, but maybe I'll want to hurt you a little less."

"Are you threatening me?"

"Not yet."

Leila's face was smiling so hard it looked like it might crack. "Excuse me?"

"Look. My boyfriend is a cop." *Unstoppable gut-punch.*

"You just said that he wasn't – "

"I don't care what I said," Ginnie interrupted. "My boyfriend is a cop. Which means that I can get away with a lot. And my husband is a surgeon." *Cringe. Deep breath.* "So trust me when I say that whatever I can't get away with can be repaired in the operating room."

Ginnie figured she must've sounded more dangerous than she felt, because without a word, the ticket agent clack-clack-clacked, printed out a paper boarding pass, and handed it to Ginnie. Who smiled her own version of a too-shiny smile, and which – judging from the genuinely nervous look on Leila's face – must've been a little less orthodontist-to-the-stars and a little more feral-cat.

"Thank you," she said sweetly, not actually caring at all.

It was a means to an end.

Thirty-Six

Quinn took a large sip of his lemonade and pointedly kept his eyes off of the semi-automatic weapon which lay across PJ James' lap. He couldn't help but notice that Lawrence was having an enormous amount of trouble doing the same.

Since the second PJ had started his little passive-aggressive routine – cold drinks, loaded gun and small talk that revolved around who the man had punished this week and for what – Lawrence had been looking squirrelly enough to set Quinn's teeth on edge. Even now, in spite of the cranked up air conditioning, a sheen of sweat laced the other man's brow. Every few seconds he *did* manage to look away from the weapon. But it was no better – Lawrence would pause, lick his lips, then seek the hall which led to the door with his gaze. Then stare at the gun once more.

Quinn might've rolled his eyes at the display if he hadn't thought it would draw to much attention to the fact that he cared at all what the other man was up to.

He wished he *didn't* care.

But you do *care.*

Because Ginnie's life was riding on the asshole who kept himself disguised as a doctor.

And you need him to calm the hell down before he gives you away.

Hoping Lawrence would take the hint and do the same, Quinn kept his attention on PJ James.

The man didn't look much different than Quinn remembered him. A little gaunter, a little more worn. He was a wiry blond, fiftyish and maybe looking a bit closer to it. At the moment, he wore a robe and a scowl, and he bristled with the same intensity as he always had – the one that made the casual observer assume he was dipping into his own stash. Quinn knew better. PJ was as sober as they came. That energy he exuded was simply a result of the man having far too much deviant creativity and always searching an outlet. Which Quinn had no interest in providing.

He took a breath and started to speak. "PJ – "

His former boss put up his hand, silencing him. A bad sign.

"Tell me something, Quinn," PJ said slowly. "Why shouldn't I break my no-killing-on-a-Sunday rule?"

At the end of the question, Lawrence flinched, and this time Quinn did roll his eyes. When he spoke, though, he directed his statement to PJ directly.

"You and I both know you wouldn't dirty your hands."

PJ ran his fingers up the gun. "Fine. Then tell me why I'm wishing I hadn't given my guy a day off for church."

"There are *so* many things wrong with that statement," Quinn replied.

PJ leaned back in his chair. "Give me three."

"What?"

"Name three things wrong with the statement and I'll consider not ensuring that you two never leave the desert."

Quinn suppressed an overwhelming sense of defeat. He knew from experience that PJ was serious. The man liked his games.

"One. You don't give guys a day off. Two. Church? Actually, scratch off that thing about days off. Church counts as three by itself."

At last his old boss cracked a small smile.

Thank fucking God.

PJ nodded toward Lawrence. "Why are you hanging out with this asshole, Quinn?"

Quinn's eyes flicked in the doctor's direction. Then he shrugged.

"It's nice to make new friends."

"As I recall, you don't *have* friends."

"It's been two years. A man can change."

"There's not enough time in the world to turn you into a friend of *this* guy." PJ narrowed his eyes. "Why don't you tell me the truth? When you walked away from the Black Daggers, I never expected to see you again. And I would've bet my left testicle that you wouldn't show up here."

"To be fair, I didn't walk away," Quinn corrected. "I took a shot in the chest, got laid up in bed, forcibly jumped out of the Black Daggers, then got marked up by a tattoo artist whom *you* sneaked into the hospital. The walking happened a lot later."

PJ's next smile was a little bigger. "See? You haven't changed that much at all. Now. Tell me about the asshole."

"It's simple," Quinn lied. "He's doing me a favor and I'm doing one in return."

"You do favors even less than you do friends." PJ gave him a considering look. "Lawrence owes me money. I owe *you* my life. So I'm thinking…What the hell is so important to you that you'd be willing to trade on *that*?"

As if in answer to his former boss's thoughtful question, a chiming doorbell rang through the room.

PJ frowned, then stood up, gun in hand. "I'm starting to think that I *really* picked the wrong day to be here alone. Quinn…Keep an eye on the asshole while I answer the door."

The second the other man exited, Lawrence rounded on him.

"Don't even bother," Quinn said, voice low.

"Don't bother?" the doctor replied angrily. "You're sitting there drinking your lemonade and you haven't said a single fucking word about the prescriptions."

"I will." As he went on, Quinn spoke slowly, like he was talking to a child. "But I couldn't just lead in with, *Hey PJ…It's been two years, but I need you to forgive this guy's debt of a half mil…Thanks*. There's a little more finesse involved in re-establishing trust with man who trusts almost no one." He paused and smiled darkly. "And hey. It's working. He asked me to guard you, didn't he?"

"Very funny. I – " Lawrence snapped his mouth shut as PJ stepped back into the room.

"Do me a favor, Mcdavid?" the blond man asked.

Quinn gave him a quick nod. "Sure."

"Stand outside of the spare room while a pretty girl name Liv changes into something more appropriate for our negotiations." He made the statement keenly. Expectantly.

Was it supposed to mean something significant? Was he supposed to recognize the name?

Quinn wracked his brain.

Liv?

No. Not someone he knew. So he did a mental shrug, then stood.

He'd do whatever he had to, to get PJ to listen to him.

But as he came to his feet, he caught a glance of Lawrence's face, and the quick look told him that whoever Liv was, she sure as hell meant something to the other man. His sweaty visage had grown pale, and now his gun-hallway-lip-lick routine included an extra-long pause at the hallway. The bedrooms were down there.

Quinn forced himself to move without looking back, but he knew already that PJ noticed the change in Lawrence, too. It was evidenced in his slow, dangerous smile and the statement he made as Quinn ducked into the hall.

"All right, doctor. I'm setting my watch. You have exactly fifteen minutes to explain to me why Liv is so eager to discuss both your finances and your relationship with me."

Shit.

Liv had to be the brunette who'd been hanging off Lawrence on the plane.

He crossed his arms over his chest, leaned against the wall opposite the closed door, envy-tinged worry making him tap his lip ring furiously.

Envy? What the hell – Oh.

Liv, the overly made-up, sex toy wielding, lingerie toting Barbie doll cared enough about Lawrence to follow him to a drug dealer's house. To fight for him, even if it meant risking her own safety. While the woman *Quinn* loved sent him packing because of his own history with the very same drug dealer. Which made him not good enough.

So. Envy. Yeah, that made a stupid kind of sense.

Quinn growled, shoved himself off the wall again, and paced the hall. He itched to knock down the door and demand answers.

Why the hell had the girl followed them? What did that mean for Ginnie? Was she okay?

Seconds later, he got his excuse. A thump followed by a muffled curse carried from inside the room.

Perfect.

Without pausing to consider propriety, Quinn swung the door wide. And there she was. Ass on the floor, bare feet sticking out from under a bed sheet, hands holding that same bed sheet up in what should have been an amusingly aggressive way. Except it wasn't amusing. Because the girl wasn't Liv at all.

It was Ginnie.

Oh, fuck.

Christ. He'd *missed* her. Six hours had felt like a year.

Almost, he opened his mouth to tell her. Almost.

She sent you away.

He grabbed onto the mental reminder. Held it against his heart like a cattle brand. Used it to steel himself.

Thirty-Seven

Ginnie let out a little yelp, then struggled to scramble to her feet as she stared up at the intruder.

Quinn. Oh, god.

For a solitary second, he leaned forward as though he might help her up. And for that same second, desire – unwanted but utterly unstoppable – coursed through Ginnie. Then a half a dozen emotions flickered across Quinn's face. And he stopped. He stilled his movement and his expression, and he let Ginnie stand up on her own.

A crushed-in feeling hit her in the chest.

There was a new raggedness to his appearance, she thought. His eyes were tight, his lips pressed together in a controlled slash. The lightness he'd shown all weekend was gone. He looked…heavy.

My fault.

Guilt joined the ache in her heart, and she opened her mouth to say something – she wasn't sure what – but Quinn beat her to it.

"What are you going to do with that sheet, Genevieve?" he asked, his voice heartbreakingly cool. "Wrap me up to death?"

Working at *not* flinching, she pulled the offending sheet to her body, fixed him with a glare, and schooled her own tone to an aloofness that matched his.

"People have been suffocated by less," she informed him.

"I suppose that's true. Still. I would've pegged you for a poisoner."

"And I wouldn't have pegged *you* for a cop."

His face went deadly still. "How the fuck did – Never mind. Breathe a word of that again, and we're both as good as dead."

"So it's true?"

A short nod. "Doesn't make a difference, though, does it?"

Crap.

How did he manage to sound so…casual about his own life? It made her want to reach out and draw him into her arms.

But you can't, she reminded herself. *Because you did your best to make sure he wouldn't want you to.*

And there was no time for self-pity about it. She needed to forget her feelings about Quinn and focus on her feelings about *saving* him.

But it was hard to do. Especially when he strode across the room to the bed, bent his long legs and sat down. Like he belonged there.

Then he rested his elbows on his knees, and his shirt billowed out, exposing that unique tattoo of his, distracting Ginnie to the point of a dry mouth and weak knees. When he tipped his head to one side and tapped at his lip ring, Ginnie wanted to cry.

In three days, so many parts of him had become familiar to her, so many of his gestures and habits felt like coming home.

There was nothing she wanted to do more than climb into his arms and stay there. If his face hadn't been indifferent, she might've been unable to stop herself from doing it.

"So," he said. "You wanna tell me what the hell you're doing here and why you told PJ that your name is Liv?"

"For Lawrence," she lied.

Quinn stiffened, but relaxed again so quickly that Ginnie thought maybe she'd imagined it.

"Hmm," he said.

"Hmm what?"

"I know it's been a few hours, but from what I understand, you and Lawrence are no longer attached. At the hip, or otherwise. If I'm wrong, correct me."

Color crept up Ginnie's face – then down. "You're not wrong."

"So cut the bullshit. Why the hell are you here for him?"

Ginnie took a breath and told the one-word story she'd rehearsed ad nauseam on the plane from Huntingdon to Las Vegas. "Money."

"What?"

"I want my half of Lawrence's money. And I'm not leaving without it."

Quinn's mouth twisted. "Well. That's just fucking amazing."

Ginnie blinked as the tears threatened again, then forced herself to speak in a strong voice. "I need you to leave the room."

"Fat fucking chance."

"In case you haven't noticed, I'm a little underdressed. And I have to get changed. Your boss *ordered* me to."

Quinn looked at her for a long moment, then glanced around the room. Ginnie's gaze followed his. First, it landed on her T-shirt – *his* T-shirt really – and the pair of airplane-print boxers which she'd left in a crumpled pile on the floor. Next, it found the pale pink dress had been laid out on the armchair in the corner. Finally, it came back to rest on her.

And Ginnie realized he *hadn't* noticed.

She was standing in the middle of the room, the sheet pulled around her body like a shield, and he *hadn't noticed.*

For some reason, that was as upsetting as his meanness and his coldness combined.

"So if you could excuse me…" she prodded, trying not to sound as annoyed as she felt.

"No."

"No?"

"PJ told me to keep an eye on *Liv,* so I'm keeping my fucking eye on her. On you. And as it happens, I've seen you naked before. So again. Fat fucking chance."

At his blasé tone – so at odds with his angry-sounding words – Ginnie's temper flared. "You want to cut the bullshit? Fine. Lose the asshole act and quit dropping the F-bomb every five seconds!"

"This isn't an act. This is me, showing you just how perfectly I fit into one of those tidy boxes you like so much."

"Fuck the tidy boxes!" Ginnie cried, so loud that Quinn whipped his head toward the door.

Oops.

She watched him stride to the door, then close it gently. When he turned back toward her, his face was dark.

"I don't think you understand the gravity of this current situation," he growled, low and intense.

"Of course I do."

He took a step closer. "I somehow doubt it."

"Why do you think I – " She cut herself off quickly.

"Why do I think you *what*?"

"Nothing. I don't know what I was going to say."

He took another step closer. "That's a lie."

"No, it's not."

Another step. "I call more bullshit."

He was close enough to touch. Close enough that she could smell his soft, masculine scent. Warmth crept up under the thin sheet she held.

Oh, god.

She took a step backward so she could turn and snap up the borrowed dress from the chair. Pretending she didn't care, Ginnie dropped the sheet and slipped the pink cotton over her head, then yanked it down firmly.

"PJ's waiting," she stated, her tone even.

"PJ is a killer, Ginnie," Quinn replied bluntly.

"I know."

"Then you also know that you need to leave."

"You don't get to tell me what to do."

She spun again and moved to go past him. Instead, one of his hands shot out, grabbed her elbow, and pulled her directly in front of him.

"You're right. I don't get to tell you what to do," he said. "But if PJ hurts you, I don't know what *I'll* do. And quite frankly, I'm feeling a little unstable."

Ginnie lifted her face, prepared to tell him off. But the second she met his gaze, she couldn't do it. Because any pretence of indifference was gone. His features were pained, his amber eyes agonized. Yet somehow…still full of unfathomable longing.

He ran his free hand over his faux-hawk and choked out her name. "Ginnie…"

And him caring…him hurting like that…She couldn't take it. Instead of opening her mouth, she stood on her tiptoes and pressed it into his.

As she gave him the gentle kiss, Quinn stood stock still. So still that Ginnie pulled away, an ache in her heart and an apology on her lips. But the words never made their way out.

Quinn reached down, slipped a hand to the small of her back, and dragged her close again. He stared straight into her eyes with wordless emotion, asking a question that made Ginnie's throat tighten.

Don't cry, she ordered herself.

But when she nodded, the first tear slipped out. And by the time he leaned down, they were pouring freely down her face. Ginnie didn't know if they were happy tears, or relieved, or something else entirely. She just knew that she needed Quinn. So badly. She couldn't believe she'd ever thought she could live without him.

He ran a finger down her chin, tracing the trail of tears. His lips were so near to hers that she could feel their heat.

Please don't stop, she begged silently.

And he didn't.

Oh, thank god.

This time when their mouths met, his was animated. Alive. Warm. Perfect.

Home.

Ginnie slid her hands to his shoulders and dug her fingers into Quinn's hair.

And the kiss became urgent. Almost needy.

Quinn pressed into her, his body enveloping her.

Almost needy?

No. There was nothing almost about it.

The hard length of his erection jammed against her thigh, and Ginnie let out tiny gasp. She was hot. Ready.

And he's still not close enough.

She pulled away just enough to slide her fingers to the button of his jeans. She only fumbled for a second before it sprung open. The sound of the zipper dropping was somehow deafeningly sexy. It carried over their sharp breaths and had a decisiveness to it that sent Ginnie's already spiked heart rate even higher.

Quinn brought his hands to her thighs, lifted the bottom of her dress, then lifted *her*. He carried her across the room, and for a moment Ginnie assumed he would take her to the bed. But he didn't do anything so delicate. Instead, he slammed her to the wall, his wide palms both cushioning and silencing the impact. He held her in place tightly with one hand and she could feel him using the other to slide his jeans down.

She wished she could touch him. But she sensed that there was no time. And this wasn't a sweet and loving release anyway. It was a desperate meshing of two souls. Two bodies.

Hurry, hurry.

Like he could read her mind, and without preamble, Quinn thrust forward, penetrating her. For one second, there was pain. He drew back, then forward again, and fullness replaced the soreness. On the third thrust, Ginnie's body opened to him, wet and waiting.

Yes.

Quinn's hips worked quicker. Harder.

Yes again.

He gripped her with one hand and flattened the other to the wall above their heads, driving himself into her.

And impossible heat ripped through Ginnie.

Soon. Too soon.

But there was nothing she could do to slow it down.

With a silent cry, she tossed her head back and let herself go. And as she pulsed around every inch of him, she felt an answering throb, deep inside. Quinn moaned against her throat.

And then he ripped himself away, leaving her empty.

Thirty-Eight

Quinn was disgusted with himself. One tiny kiss, one small nod, a few pitying tears, and he'd turned into an animal. He was *still* panting, *still* half-turned on, even though he'd been sated and even though he'd disentangled himself from her embrace.

He slunk across the room and sank into the armchair there. He could feel her eyes on him, feel the hurt they exuded.

Fuck. What kind of person am I? He didn't like the answer. *The kind who'll take his fix any way he can get it.*

Forgetting that a dangerous as hell man was in the next room and satisfying his own need instead. Ravaging Ginnie because she was as addictive as any drug. Because he didn't know if he would ever get another chance. And quite simply…because she let him.

"Quinn?"

Her voice was wobbly. Small. Worried. It dug straight into Quinn's heart, and he couldn't lift his eyes to meet hers.

"I'm so sorry," he managed to get out.

"Sorry?" she repeated.

"I know I don't measure up. I can think of a hundred reasons why you were right about that. I lied by omission when I left out the stuff about knowing Jase, and I'm not rich or tied up in a pretty package. I know I'll always have my past – hell, right now it's even my present – making things darker, and I can't change that. So I *am* sorry. But if you let me try, I think I could make you happy. I was a good man. Every day, I'd work on it. Work on us. Make you feel worshipped. Needed. You'd never want for anything, I promise you."

He sounded pathetic, even to his own ears.

Christ. Any way he could get it, all right.

He hazarded a look at her face. She still stood across the room, leaning a little on the wall. Her green eyes were wide, her hair a wild mess, her lips swollen from his rough kisses and dropped open in surprise. She was stunning, as always.

God, he loved her. More than enough to warrant begging.

"Even if you're going to say no to *me*, say yes to letting me get you out of here. I need to know you're safe."

For another long second, she stared at him silently. Then her eyes flicked toward the door and Quinn remembered.

The money.

"However much it is...it's not worth dying for," he said softly.

"Quinn...What are you talking about?"

"Whatever you think he owes you financially."

Her eyes widened even more. "Is that what you think I want?"

"Isn't it what you *said* you wanted?"

She shook her head. "No. I mean, yes. I said that. But Quinn...I'm not here for Lawrence or his money."

"You're not?"

Hope buoyed Quinn's heart, but it came crashing down when she spoke again.

"But I can't say yes to you."

"Please, Ginnie, just – "

She cut him off. "I came here for you. Whatever mess Lawrence got you into when I overreacted and kicked you out...I've got to save you from it."

Quinn felt his eyebrows shoot up, and his tongue came out to give his lip ring a single, solid tap. "Save me?"

Her cheeks went a bit pink. "It's not as silly as it sounds."

"Silly?" Quinn shook his head. "It's not silly. It's crazy as hell. You risked your life to save *me*? Why would you do that? You were free and clear. *You* were safe."

"Isn't it obvious?" She took a deep, deep breath, squared her shoulders and set her beautiful eyes on his face. "I love you, Quinn. So I can't leave until I've done what I came to do. And don't try to fight me on it. You won't win."

"You..." He trailed off, stunned.

Saving him was preposterous. But she wanted to. Holy hell. Quinn felt like a ton had been lifted from his shoulders.

My knight in soft, pink cotton.

At the thought, a tiny smile played on his lips.

Ginnie's eyes narrowed. Her chin was lifted defiantly and her hands were on her hips...And she fucking *loved* him. In spite of it all.

"Baby," he said, but whatever else he'd been about to add was lost.

The bedroom door flew open and Doctor Lawrence Douchebag Michaels burst in, shotgun in hand. The desperate look was back on the other man's face. He glanced around the room wildly – looking for Liv, probably. When he didn't find her, his sights set on Ginnie, and he didn't look happy.

This time, when the familiar, run-on sentence hit Quinn – *letmeatthatmotherfuckersoIcanbreakhisface* – he didn't stop it from taking over his body. He leaped from the chair, moved forward, and followed the motion through with his fist.

It was a good, clean punch. A satisfyingly thorough shot. As Quinn's knuckles met Lawrence's chin, the man went flying. He crumpled to the floor in a stunned, barely conscious heap, and the gun slipped from his hands. Quinn didn't have time to relish taking the other man down, though. Just as he reached down and his fingers closed on the weapon, PJ came limping in. He had a black eye and a sour look on his face.

In one hand, he held a pistol. And in the other...he held Quinn's badge.

Shit. Maybe he doesn't know it's mine. Maybe he thought it was Lawrence's. Maybe –

PJ held the badge out, cutting off Quinn's uncharacteristically frantic thoughts.

"I believe this is yours," he said casually, then cocked the pistol, far too casually.

Quinn remained motionless. Expressionless, as PJ looked from Quinn to Ginnie to Lawrence's still form, then back to Quinn.

"*Now* it makes sense," the other man stated. "This thing isn't about favors at all. It's about a girl."

Quinn adjusted his position, putting his body between PJ and Ginnie. Between Ginnie and the gun.

"What's the story, PJ?" he asked cautiously.

His former boss offered the badge again, and when Quinn didn't take it, he shrugged and set the wallet on the dresser. Then he sat in the armchair Quinn had recently vacated and rubbed at his bruised face with his free hand. The other stayed gripped on the gun, and the gun stayed aimed at Quinn.

"Your 'friend' tried to rat you out." He glanced down at Lawrence. "Guess you took care of punishing him for that. By the way, you can drop the gun any time, Mcdavid. Fucking thing's not loaded anyway."

Quinn didn't let the claim affect him, and he made no move to let Ginnie out from behind him. PJ noticed immediately.

"Her name's Liv?" he asked.

Ginnie spoke up before he could stop her. "Genevieve Silver. Formerly Michaels."

"Aha," PJ said. "Married to the doctor who just tried to out your secret identity to me."

"Yes," Ginnie said.

"Hmm." PJ turned his attention to Quinn again. "Married to him. But *you* love her."

"More than my own life."

"Well. Holy shit. This whole time, I thought you were an even more heartless bastard than I am."

"Apparently not," Quinn replied, then waited for his former boss to get to the point.

PJ sighed. "I have a confession to make. I'm not alone out here for fun. I'm in mourning."

"All right," Quinn replied. "I'll bite. In mourning for…?"

"Myself. I've got six months. Fucking lung cancer. Never smoked a day in my life, but I guess my other vices more than made up for it." The other man let out a short, bitter laugh. "You're my one good thing, Quinn."

"How do you figure?"

"Eight years ago, you walked in here with the same look on your face that you had today. Something to prove. Something to win. I've known you were a cop since the second I laid eyes on you."

"If I *was* a cop – hypothetically," Quinn said. "And – also hypothetically – if you knew it, why would you let me work for you all that time? And why let me go so easily at the end of it?"

"Hypothetically – why would I even let you *live*?" PJ countered agreeably.

"Hypothetically."

"As far as letting you go…" PJ offered up a shrug. "I really *am* a self-centered bastard. My own life means that much to me. As far as the other stuff…You were different, Mcdavid. Most low level guys, they give off a desperate vibe when they're trying to climb up the ladder. The ones who come in from the cop shop, they're even worse. They all try to pretend like they've got nothing to lose and it's all bullshit. It's like I can smell it. Not you. No desperation. Like you really *did* have nothing to lose. At the beginning, I admit, I thought I could use you. Counter intelligence, maybe. Then I got to know you, and damn if I didn't actually like you. And you were fiercely loyal to me from the get-go. To the Black Daggers, too. I've thought about that a lot over the last few days. A good man, maybe a bit damaged. Was that an act?"

Quinn was careful not to glance behind him as he made the admission. "No. It wasn't an act."

PJ made a satisfied noise. "Why?"

Quinn hesitated.

Now or never.

This was the true reason he wasn't good enough for Ginnie. The true reason he knew he could never fit tidily into a box. But honesty was his only chance of getting them out alive. Quinn could feel it.

And she loves you.

He latched onto the sincerity in her voice, the certainty in her face when she'd said it. He used it to shove aside his self-doubt.

Then he closed his eyes and spoke slowly. "I was alone. Lonely. My parents were dead. The drunk driver who killed them got off on a technicality. I couldn't connect with anyone at the academy. Even my training officers knew I didn't fit the mold. When I went undercover... The guys inside the Black Daggers didn't care if I was hurting. They didn't pity me or worry that I might snap. I was accepted. For the first time in forever. I still did the police work. I still reported when I had to and had guys arrested. But..."

"Things weren't black and white."

"Exactly."

"We gave you a fucking purpose. Something to lose. And that, my friend, is why you're my good thing. And the less self-centered reason I had for letting you go. Thought maybe you'd put a little good into the world."

PJ focused his gaze just to Quinn's right, his eyes on Ginnie, who'd come around and placed a hand on Quinn's elbow.

"So now you know it all," PJ said. "And do you still love him?"

"I do." There was zero hesitation in Ginnie's reply. "It might even be *why* I love him."

"The doctor's wife on the outside," PJ commented thoughtfully. "But not on the inside." PJ shot a decisive look Quinn's way. "*Now* we're close to square."

For a second, relief flooded Quinn's body. Then Lawrence groaned from his spot on the floor, and Quinn remembered that the doctor had an outstanding debt to pay, too.

Ginnie spoke again, and it was obvious that she remembered as well. "Do you like the Bahamas, PJ?"

"I don't hate them," PJ replied.

Ginnie smiled. "Because I know a guy whose got a house there. And I know a guy who can make it yours."

PJ smiled. Then he picked up Quinn's badge again and held it out. When Quinn took it, PJ flipped the gun around and offered that to him, too, butt-end first. After just a moment, he took the weapon. It was a sign of trust. And a perfect representation of Quinn himself.

One unregistered gun and one symbol of justice.

He had a feeling that PJ knew it, too.

His former boss offered him a nod, then turned back to Ginnie, his smile widening.

"Keep talking. And don't scrimp on the white sand."

And Quinn finally felt like he could breathe again.

Thirty-Nine

The Humvee rode smoothly along the desert highway, the light of Vegas beckoning closer and closer. Quinn was quiet, and the only noise came from the backseat, where a very bruised and very sullen Doctor Lawrence Michaels muttered the occasional semi-conscious curse.

It was Ginnie who spoke first.

"Did that really just happen?"

"Did what really just happen?" Quinn's reply was far too innocent.

"Did we really just uses my brother's illegal hacking skills to steal my former husband's house, then trade it to a terminally ill drug dealer for our lives and a big, ugly truck?"

"Oh. Well." He kept his eyes on the windshield, but Ginnie spied a little smile. "The truck isn't *that* ugly."

Ginnie rolled her eyes. "What are we going to do with Lawrence?"

Quinn's smile grew dark. "What are my options?"

"You already gave him a black eye," Ginnie pointed out. "And I did steal his house, so…"

"We can drop him in a hotel then. Maybe even a three-star."

"And call the real Liv?"

"If you think she *wants* to be called."

"I think she does."

"You think so?"

"She loves him."

"And love makes you crazy?"

"Definitely."

***

She sounded so damned sure that Quinn knew she meant it. Not just for Dr. Douchebag and Liv, either.

That's it.

He yanked on the wheel, hard.

Ginnie let out a surprised shriek that made him grin as he turned toward her.

"Marry me," he said.

"What?"

"Marry me."

She blinked, those green eyes sweetly puzzled, sweetly overwhelmed. "Quinn..."

"Now."

"Right this second?"

"Yes. You've got the white dress and we're a mile in any direction from an Elvis impersonator. Hopefully one without visible butt crack."

"Ew. And the dress is *pink,* not white."

"Semantics."

"Colors aren't sem – "

"Marry me."

"You're crazy."

Quinn grinned. "Just like you said. That's what love does. Makes people crazy. And quite honestly, Genevieve, I don't want to hear Leila the ticket agent call you *Mrs. Michaels* one more time."

Ginnie smiled back. "That makes two of us."

"So…"

She offered him an exaggerated sigh. "And I guess eloping would be better than hearing Jase tell the story of how we met during his best man speech."

"Is that a yes?"

Ginnie's face grew serious. "Are you sure about this?"

"More sure than I've ever been about anything. I love you, Genevieve."

He saw her little shiver, and he knew he had her.

Epilogue

Six months later…

The doorbell of Quinn and Ginnie's partially renovated, three-bedroom rancher rang out loudly.

"Third time in ten seconds," Quinn groaned, pulling himself away from what had been shaping up to be a very passionate kiss.

Ginnie brushed her mouth over his. "Might as well answer it then. Could be important."

"As important as this?"

He slid his tongue along her lips, then slid it inside, exploring her mouth as though it wasn't something he did every day. By the time he was done, Ginnie was breathless.

The doorbell rang a fourth time.

"Dammit," Quinn growled.

He stood, and Ginnie followed him to the door, her hand in his back pocket. As he opened the door, he grabbed her fingers and threaded them with his own. The simple, gold bands that decorated their ring fingers clinked together lightly.

Before they even got the door halfway open, a blur of rock-concert T-shirt and ripped jeans came barrelling in.

Ginnie jumped back as her brother shoved two envelopes into her hands.

"You have *got* to forward your damned mail!"

"Did you *open* my mail, Jase?" Ginnie replied.

"I thought the 'G' was a 'J'."

"Did you notice the last name said Mcdavid?"

"I chose to ignore it."

"Nice to see you, Jase," Quinn greeted dryly.

"I'm still not talking to you," the younger man gave him a narrow-eyed glare.

"It's been six months. And we're family," Quinn reminded him.

"I'll believe it when I've heard the vows myself."

Quinn rolled his eyes and took the envelopes from Ginnie's hands.

"The first one's a wedding invitation. A proper one. You know. The kind people get *invited* to?" Jase told them.

Ginnie rolled her eyes, too, then slid out the ivory card. She turned it over slowly.

"Liv and Lawrence."

Quinn's gaze sought hers. "You okay with that?"

"Yes." Ginnie said, then smiled. "Better her than me."

"I already sent the decline," Jase stated.

"Jase!" Quinn and Ginnie said together.

"You won't be able to go, anyway," he told them. "You'll be too busy vacationing in the Bahamas.

Ginnie blinked. "What?"

Quinn took the other envelope from her, flipped it open, and scanned the top.

"PJ died," he stated softly.

Ginnie placed her hand over his and echoed his earlier question. "Are you okay with that?"

"I have to be, right?" He offered her a small smile. "I *won't* say better him than me, but I made my peace already."

"Tell her the other thing," Jase enthused.

Quinn shot him a *personal* eye roll, then turned back to his wife. "He left us the house, Ginnie. The one you had your brother steal from Lawrence. It's ours."

A grin stole across Jase's face as he yanked the envelope from Quinn. "And all I ask in return is that you let *me* give the best man speech for your vow renewal. Then maybe Quinn and I can be friends again."

Quinn clapped him on the shoulder. "Sure we can. As soon as you've served your jail time for mail tampering."

Jase's worried eyes sought Ginnie. "He wouldn't really turn me in would he? We're family."

Ginnie smiled sweetly. "It's hard to say, Jase. Quinn is kind of unpredictable. Very little black and white with him. Guess you'd better be on your best behavior."

And Quinn grinned a wide, toothy smile that made Jase jump.

THE END

Made in the USA
Charleston, SC
31 January 2016